VAMPIRE'S KISS

GUARDIANS

VALERIE TWOMBLY

INTRODUCTION

He's no guardian angel.

Being the first vampire Guardian ever created, Seth Ruiz struggles with his identity. While his sanity balances on a razor's edge, it's only a matter of time before he succumbs to the evil inside him. When realization strikes that the fiery Kaitlyn belongs to him, he must not only battle his past demons, but fight his desire to claim her or chance killing them both.

She's a demon slayer.

Handed a dagger as a child, Kaitlyn O'Hara has slaughtered demons her entire life. It should come as no surprise that she is also destined to save a crazy vampire. When fate reveals her true identity, she must search her heart for the courage to move forward.

Katie holds the key to help save humanity. With Seth's dark side edging closer, he prays he can keep it together long enough to protect her through the challenges she must face. However, he could prove to be her biggest threat.

He fights his desire to claim her. She battles to save him. Together they wage war to protect humanity. Survival may come at a price.

This book formerly published as Primal Hunger. Revised 2nd edition.

PROLOGUE

TEMPLE of the Gods
1 BC

SETH KNELT at the feet of the man who towered over him. "How may I serve you?" He dared not look up at the one who called himself Zarek, but the god's heated gaze stared at him with intent. Why glare at him? Did Zarek contemplate a deed he found distasteful? Seth had no idea what the man could be considering or how he ended up with his knees planted in the cold dirt of a land he didn't recognize. His body naked except for the plain linen shendyt he wore. *How do I know the name of this Egyptian garb?* When he searched his memories, he realized he had few.

He scanned the area. To his right blackness filled the sky and fire crawled along the ground in a mad search for something. Perhaps it sought out the screams that filled the acrid air or it was the cause of them. On his other side were green rolling hills bathed in a soft golden light. While nice to look at, he found himself turning his head back toward the blackness, desperate to crawl into its depths. It whispered to him with promises of evil and destruction and caused his pulse to race. Something sharp punctured his lip and he winced. Instinct told him to show no fear. The man who towered over Seth radiated more than enough power to smite any who angered him.

A firm hand touched his shoulder. "Do not fear me, for I am your maker, your god." The man smiled and it was then he noticed the fangs that extended from his mouth. Seth ran his tongue across his own points. The taste of blood caused his stomach to clench.

"It is called hunger. The pain you feel in your gut."

"How do I make it stop?" He clutched his side to keep from doubling over. *Show no weakness.* Droplets formed on his brow and his body trembled. "If you are my creator, why this torture?" Was it a test of his strength? If so then he would endure.

"It is not torture, my son. Only the darkness in you." The man turned his head toward the black void. "It calls to you, doesn't it?"

He was unsure how to answer, so decided on the truth. "Yes, my lord." Even as he spoke the words, he fought with every ounce of his being not to move toward it. Follow the fire. Find the ones who screamed and make them shriek even louder.

"That is because your birth has yet to be completed."

He tipped his head. "I do not understand."

"You will. Soon."

A brilliant flash of light shimmered next to Zarek, and was quickly replaced by a beauty so bright, Seth forgot about the darkness that whispered his name. The woman wore a thin, white gown that showed every curve of her body. His mouth watered to taste the pink areolas that pushed against the fabric. He watched in awe when she moved her dark curly mass of locks away from her neck to reveal the beat of her pulse against creamy flesh.

Seth licked his lips.

"Come to me." The siren's voice beckoned.

He was unable to move, not sure of what to do, but the points in his mouth lengthened. They ached and he dug his nails into the dirt beneath him.

"You must feed. Go to her," Zarek commanded.

Seth crawled to her and gazed up. Her swirling silver eyes met his and she opened her arms in a welcoming gesture. He stood and stepped closer. Instinct kicked in and had him placing a hand on her waist and a palm to the back of her neck. She tipped her head. The pulsing vein sang of life, and death. Something inside him snapped, a primal hunger drove him and he sank his fangs deep into her throat.

He growled.

She moaned.

Sweet, warm nectar filled his mouth and power flowed through his veins. A barrage of visions assaulted his mind, of a child running through a field of flowers. Laughter rang when a dark-haired man scooped the young girl into his arms and swung her in the air.

"Daddy!" she giggled.

The man pulled her to his chest in a tight embrace and turned to face Seth.

Zarek.

The vision faded and Seth was pulled back to the woman he held in his arms. She was so soft he could spend an eternity caressing every inch of her. Their souls touched and emotions bubbled to the surface. He was desperate to keep her with him. Always.

Something was wrong. He pulled himself free from the pleasure and realized her heart slowed. Breaths grew shallow. She was dying. He fought to release her, but his muscles refused to loosen their grip. Panic set in. *No! No, please don't die.* Why did she not push him away? Certainly, her father would stop him. Instead, her warm elixir continued to flow down his throat and caused him to embrace her harder. Her breathing stopped, followed by her heart. His sharp teeth retracted, but he kept his head buried in the soft flesh of her neck.

"No! Please." He lifted his head and gazed at his god through tear-filled eyes. "You are powerful, bring her back." He needed her warmth beside him.

Zarek shook his head. "I cannot. She chose her path."

"She was innocent." He spoke through clenched teeth. "I did not mean to take her life." He cradled her head with care and laid her gently on the ground. He placed a kiss on her lips and let a tear touch her cheek before he turned back to his maker, determined to end his pain. "Slay me."

Zarek crossed his arms over his naked chest. His biceps swelled until Seth thought the gold bands the god wore would snap. "No."

Seth dug his nails into his palms and set his jaw. "You stood by and allowed me to kill your daughter. Why?" *And why allow me to feel. I don't want to feel this pain.*

"You were created from darkness and evil." Zarek waved his hand toward the burning fires. "In order to bring balance to chaos you needed the light. My daughter sacrificed herself to give you what you required."

It was Seth's turn to shake his head. "I do not understand. What am I? Why am I here?" *And why do I have no memory?*

"You have been born this day of dark and light. A guardian, a protector of humanity who will do my bidding."

"How can I protect when I take life? You said I was evil. I do not think one such as I could guard another soul."

"Your dark side will fight against those who intend harm to my children and the light will keep you balanced." Zarek dropped his hands to his side and looked over at his daughter. Seth followed his gaze and had he not known better he would have thought her asleep. If only it were so.

"What was her name?" he whispered.

"Vivian. Among your many gifts, one will be to take the memories of those you feed from. You will see the life they have led and know their most intimate thoughts. You can discard them at will, except for Vivian. You will always remember my daughter and her sacrifice."

Seth dropped to his knees at Zarek's feet. "I will serve you well and honor her always." *I will carry her in my heart as long as I draw breath.*

Zarek brought his own wrist to his mouth and bit. He then

offered his blood to Seth. "Drink." Even though he feared the same outcome as Vivian, he feared the god's wrath even more, so he obeyed. The liquid scalded as it hit the back of his throat and his head began to swim. Knowledge loaded into his memory and became his own. The sudden realization of who and what he was hit him, as did the understanding of the evil he would fight and the people he was sworn to protect. The love of a father for his daughter mixed with Seth's already burning emotions. A searing pain on his left bicep nearly made him release his grip on the god, but he knew he had to drink until commanded to do otherwise.

"Enough."

Seth released his king and looked to his arm where a marking in black ink had appeared. He frowned. A winged lion with a strange head and the outline of an eye above it colored his bicep.

"The sphinx represents the guardian of the king. Above it is the eye of Ra for Vivian."

Seth straightened and shifted his shoulders back. "I am honored, my lord."

Zarek tipped his head. "Good. Today we begin your training and soon your brethren will join you."

He knew he should feel honored, but as he looked at Vivian he considered his birth already cursed. One he would have to fight for eternity.

CHAPTER ONE

SETH STARED into the glass of whiskey and dug his nails into his thigh. Sanity, an old friend that rarely visited anymore, slowly crept back and cleared his mind. It took him a moment to realize he still sat at the bar of the Fire and Ice club next to the beautiful Kaitlyn.

"We need to talk." He turned to stare into her cool blue eyes.

She tipped her chin up. "I couldn't agree more. Follow me to my office." The redhead slipped from her stool and the emerald dress slid down her legs. When she turned, Seth caught a glimpse of creamy thigh through the slit up her gown. The prick of fangs into his bottom lip reminded him he needed to regain control before he threw her to the floor and drank from her slender neck. No, make that her femoral artery. He wanted to taste the strawberry essence straight from her silky thigh.

"Are you coming, Mr. Ruiz?"

Oh, he wanted to be. He grinned. "I wouldn't dream of missing the opportunity to see your office." *Or perhaps drape you across the desk and rip that gown straight down the middle.* He pulled in a deep breath and reminded himself there would be no drinking or fucking this woman. As much as he wanted to, he didn't trust himself. Images of Vivian dead on the ground were replaced with Kaitlyn's. So much time and still the goddess haunted him.

He followed her across plush carpet like a hound after a bitch in heat. Passed several tables and bustling staff that prepared for a busy evening. On the other side of the room was a large stage with a dance pole and three cages hung above it from the ceiling. "What kind of club is this exactly?" Like he needed to ask since the evidence glared at him, but for some reason he wanted confirmation.

She glanced over her shoulder. Ruby lips curled upward and white teeth flashed in contrast. "A gentlemen's club, of course."

"Indeed. Let me guess. Dancing girls?"

Kaitlyn pushed open a six-paneled, oak door and glided through. Seth followed and scanned the room. Black lacquer desk on one side with two leather chairs placed in front of it and across the room a sectional faced a sixty-inch flat screen. She directed him to a chair opposite the desk.

"Why? Would you care to partake of our services?" She handed him a black leather folder, the gold letters on the front read 'Fire and Ice'. He opened it to find a menu of available services.

He scanned over the items. Everything from a standard massage to things much more intimate. While the house specials weren't spelled out, he could only assume what each meant. He tossed the menu to the desk. "How much for an entire evening?"

She rounded the desk and took a seat in a plush high-back chair, placed her elbows on the glossy surface and steepled her fingers under her chin. "So, you want the club's exclusive? Ten thousand, up front, in cash." She leaned back, riffled through a drawer and pulled out a photo album. "Frankly, Mr. Ruiz, I'm surprised."

He raised a questioning brow. "And why is that, Ms. O'Hara?"

"You're a handsome man. I would think you'd have no trouble in the female department."

"Oh, but I don't. I can have any woman I choose." He leaned forward. "What about you? Will I find your photo in that album you hold in your hands?"

Her eyes narrowed. The woman read like a book and irritation was plastered all over her pretty face. "I am not for sale," she spat.

"Really? You seem to have no trouble asking others to sell their bodies."

She slammed the album shut. "Look. I don't need to explain myself to you. The girls I hire only give what they are comfortable with and they are paid very well." She rose. "I think it's time you left."

She walked around and stood in front of him. Waited.

Seth rose from his chair. "Tell me, would you take twenty thou?"

"No." Anger radiated off her and pricked his skin and for some reason it aroused him. He grabbed her arms, pressed her against the desk and stared into her eyes. "Enough of these fucking games. I want the dagger, now be a good little girl and fetch it for me."

"Get off me," she whispered through clenched teeth.

He was taken aback. Why did she not fall under his enthrallment? Humans were so easy to manipulate with a quick stare.

"I'll give you to the count of three, Mr. Ruiz. If you do not take your hands off me, I will knee your man junk so far into your body you'll be eating cock for dinner."

He couldn't help the grin that slipped across his lips. "I'm afraid I'm now wise to your tricks." The memory of her knee planted in his balls when he'd last tried to rescue her still fresh in his mind. He pressed his groin closer, pinned her to the desk and enjoyed watching her eyes widen as his erection pushed into her.

"What are you exactly? It's not every day I encounter a human female slaying demons."

Her gaze narrowed indicating anger, yet the musky scent of her arousal coated the back of his throat as he inhaled. Damn she smelled good.

"I'm none of your business, but I may ask the same of you." She jerked, tried to free herself but he held steadfast. "Why is it you keep showing up and how do you know about the dagger?"

"That blade is dangerous and you need to give it to me," he growled. His patience waned.

She spit in his face. "Go fuck yourself."

He didn't miss a beat. "I'd much rather fuck you and watch you writhe beneath me as you experience the best orgasm of your life."

A delicate red brow shot up. "You think highly of yourself, don't you."

"Was that a question?"

"It was more of a statement."

To hell with the gods and their rules. He'd obeyed them for thousands of years, but not today. He let his fangs elongate and again enjoyed the look of surprise cross her face. "There are so many ways I could pleasure you."

"W-what are you?"

"Your guardian angel, sweetheart."

She tipped her head back and let out a nervous laugh. He was surprised that even after he revealed his pearly whites, she was still aroused. He had to wonder what type of shit she was into.

"Where are your wings then? Oh, and aren't you supposed to have a halo? For some reason I picture horns as being more appropriate for you." She tried again to break free, but he held steady.

"This conversation is getting us nowhere. I want the dagger."

Sapphire eyes glared at him. "Unless you plan to kill me you're not getting it." Plump lips curled into a wicked smile. "Even then you'll never find it."

He'd reached the breaking point. The scent of strawberries mixed with her musky arousal had his mouth watering. If he didn't leave soon he'd either drain her or fuck her. Probably both.

"You win this round, but I'll be watching every move you make." He let his gaze roam to her full breasts and rest there a moment to make his point before moving back to meet her stare. With a snarl, he flashed from the room, saddened he wouldn't be able to see the look on her face.

KATIE'S JAW UNHINGED. Partially due to the fact the sexy man with the fangs had vanished into thin air. The other was from the fire that currently smoldered between her legs. Her arousal had been beyond her control and it annoyed the hell out of her. Granted, the man was sex on a stick. Better than any she'd seen in her club and she had meant it when she'd told him he shouldn't have any trouble getting a woman. Hell, had he pushed, she might have stripped and spread herself across the desk like an offering to the gods.

His eyes had thrown her off though. Almost black, they seemed lifeless. Then there had been something else about him that was dark. She questioned her senses, the ones that told her who was demon. Since she was a child she'd been able to pick up on evil. It had a particular odor. Not sulphur like some would think, but they smelled of death.

The dark-haired stranger had smelled like hot cinnamon candy. Yummy and delicious and she had fought to keep her tongue from flicking out and tracing a line along his darkened jaw. It was only when he'd pinned her that she'd caught a slight whiff of death. The two scents were at odds with each other and indicated an internal battle. When he'd flashed a pair of long, thick fangs, she'd wanted to beg him to bite her. She rubbed her temples and wondered if maybe she needed a vacation.

The phone rang, pulling her back to reality. Her anger fired up again. Clearly Mr. Ruiz had somehow tried to seduce her with some kind of demon magic. He may not have the scent of a full blood, but he was something evil that needed to be put down. If he came near her again, she wouldn't hesitate to plunge the dagger into his black heart.

She grabbed her cell off the desk. "Hello?"

"Ms. O'Hara?"

She didn't recognize the voice. "Yes, this is she."

"Ms. O'Hara, this is Mrs. Hansen, I live next door to your father. He hasn't come out for his paper yet today and he doesn't answer the door. It's so unlike him."

Fear clawed her with its poisonous talons. One thing she could count on was her father liked routine. He always picked up his paper from the front yard at six in the morning. Sharp.

"Mrs. Hansen, I'll be right over and thank you for calling." She pushed the 'end call' button and ran from the office.

"I have an emergency. You'll have to take over for me." She yelled to her assistant manager, Angie, as she rushed out the front door. She hurried to her car that was parked in a private lot next door. Even in her panic, she sensed a pair of eyes on her. Was it Mr. Ruiz? She started the engine and squealed down the street. The only thing that mattered was her father and she prayed he was all right.

SETH STOOD across the street and watched as Kaitlyn ran out the door and climbed into her car. His sixth sense told him something was wrong.

"So, what gives with the sexy firecracker?"

He jerked and found Baal standing next to him. The demon's golden eyes pinned on the redhead.

"Why are you here?" Seth asked.

"Aren't you going to follow her?" Baal leaned against the brick building, arms over his chest, ankles crossed.

Seth sucked on a toothpick. "In due time. I have her scent so I'll be able to find her."

"So, I'm guessing no luck on the dagger then?"

He pulled his coat tight to fight against the chill. Winter in Chicago was having a hard time letting go. The April weather had been hell. "No. Again, why are you here bothering me?" Seth liked the demon, but he wasn't in the mood for company. Not when he had a painful erection that still pressed against his jeans.

"Aidyn sent me to keep your ass out of trouble."

He threw his toothpick to the sidewalk and began walking down the street. "I don't need a babysitter."

Baal tossed his head back in laughter and came up beside him, his expression turned serious. "Look, Aidyn was taken away by Zarek and gods knows when he'll be back. Lucan…"

Seth stopped in his tracks. "Wait. What do you mean taken away?"

The demon's golden eyes darkened. "He's being punished. Was shackled and dragged off by Gabriel and a few of his goons in front of everyone. I think the gods mean to set an example."

His fangs dropped and he fisted his hands. "Why would Zarek punish my leader?"

"Look, you've been off line for a while. Aidyn apparently broke some law and now has to pay. You know how it is with those fuckers. They change the rules like we change underwear."

Seth fought to regain control of his senses. His first reaction was to flash to Zarek and demand answers. However, he knew he was in no position to be demanding anything. Besides, it would only make matters worse. He needed to hold to his promise to Aidyn and get that damn dagger back before the curse pulled him completely into the darkness.

"Where are the others?" Seth asked.

"Lucan has gone into hiding for gods knows whatever reason. Garin, Marcus and Gwen are off fighting demons with the Draki and Cassie has been sent to the Temple of the Gods with the baby for safe keeping." He raked his fingers through his brown hair. "Things are not going well. My people are also in the fray. Lowan's puppets are popping up everywhere."

Seth didn't like the sound of any of it, but he had his own orders and needed to carry them out. He started down the sidewalk again. "I need to get that dagger."

CHAPTER TWO

KATIE WHIPPED into the drive of her father's small bungalow to find Mrs. Hansen on the front porch wringing her hands.

"Oh, I'm so worried."

She cast her own frightened glance at the silver-haired woman as she slipped her key into the lock and pushed open the door. "Dad?" No answer. The house was silent as a morgue. No lights had been turned on yet so she reached for the wall switch and flicked on the corner floor lamp. It took a moment for her eyes to adjust, but when they did, everything looked to be in place. She padded across the living room with the neighbor on her heels.

"Dad?"

A slight tinge of death tickled her nose and caused her heart to pound as the panic rose into her chest. She pushed back tears as she ran down the narrow hall toward the bedroom. "Dad!" She rushed through the doorway and flipped on the light. Her father laid with his back facing her, still snuggled under the covers. Dread filled her as she rounded the other side. His face was pale. She checked for a pulse.

Faint.

"Is he..." Mrs. Hansen's voice drifted off.

"He's still alive. Call an ambulance." Katie pulled the covers back and gave him a shake. "Poppa?" He still didn't respond. She looked for injuries, but saw none. Confusion set in. If demons had been here there would be physical evidence. Had they come searching for the dagger? Maybe while her father had slept and he'd been none the wiser. Still, it didn't explain his current condition. She raced through the conversation they'd had on the phone last night, he hadn't indicated he wasn't feeling well. Then again, he would never tell her he was sick. She reached for his hand and mentally scolded herself for not coming over personally to make sure everything was okay. After all, he was eighty-five, but had always been active and physically fit. His last check-up was only last month and the doctor had given him a clean bill of health. Had said her father was fit for his age.

She kissed his cheek and refused to let her tears escape. "Everything will be fine, Poppa. Please hang on." She gave a mental curse. *Where the hell are the paramedics?*

Sirens blared in the distance and seconds later she saw the flashing lights in the driveway.

"This way," Mrs. Hansen's panicked voice shouted.

Footsteps and the sound of a wheel that needed lubrication filled the deafening silence, yet seemed so far away. Finally, two blue-uniformed men were ushered through the door by the neighbor. For the first time since she arrived, she let out a breath.

"What happened?" the younger one asked.

"I don't know. Mrs. Hansen, the neighbor called me and said my father hadn't left the house to get his paper. He was fine when I spoke to him on the phone last night." Katie reluctantly let go of her father's hand and moved off the bed. She stood in the corner and watched while they checked his vitals and radioed the hospital. An IV was started and tears rolled down her cheeks to see his aged hand, so frail looking, with a tube attached to his splotched skin.

Katie chewed her knuckle and watched as they picked up her father and placed him on the stretcher. She followed down the hall and out the front door. "I'm riding with you." She turned to Mrs. Hansen. "Will you please close up the house?"

The older woman pulled Katie into a hug. "Don't worry about it, dear. You go with your father and I'll see to everything."

"Thank you." She turned to climb into the back of the ambulance and gave one last look out the door. She was being watched. Had Mr. Ruiz followed her? She was beginning to think owning the dagger was nothing but a curse.

SETH STOOD next to Baal and watched the house across the street where Kaitlyn had disappeared into. Paramedics showed up and loaded an elderly man into the back. His fiery redhead climbed into the ambulance behind the stretcher with the help of a young, good-looking EMT and Seth's fangs extended once again. He didn't like the human touching her.

He inhaled.

Strawberries mingled with sadness reached him and he could only assume the man was someone dear to her. The ambulance tore off down the street and the silver-haired woman who'd been watching walked to the house next door.

"Do you sense what I do?" Seth knew Baal would, but he needed the conversation.

"Oh, yes and by the stench I'd say there were two of them. We need to go in and see if they found the dagger. If they beat us to it..."

Seth held up his hand. "I don't need reminding. You go. I need to follow her and find out what's going on." The demon's stare burned a hole into him, but he refused to meet Baal's gaze.

"You have it bad for this one. Is it possible she belongs to you?"

"No." He would have known. Would have felt the need to claim her yet he hadn't. Hope that he would ever find a mate, one who would save him from Drayos's curse had diminished long ago. Now, all he could wish for was to keep his mind in check long enough to finish his job. He pulled up Vivian's image, remembered her dark hair and how she lay dead on the ground all because of him. He ground his teeth. When would he ever find peace?

"I'm going to track her. If you wish to search the house just be sure you leave everything as you found it." He started to walk away, but Baal grabbed his arm.

"I'm supposed to be watching you."

Seth jerked free. "As I said, demon, I don't need a damn babysitter." He didn't wait for a reply before he flashed away. Seconds later he found himself outside a hospital room. Machines beeped and pierced his sensitive hearing, but then another bitter heartbreaking sound reached him. A female's sobs. He scanned the room. It was only Kaitlyn and the patient, so he entered. The elderly man lay in bed with tubes and wires attached to him. Death lurked in the corner, waiting to claim its victim. Kaitlyn sat on the edge of the bed, one hand wrapped around the man's and she stroked his hair with the other. Her tear-streaked face cut through Seth like a hot blade. She sensed his presence and looked up.

"You." Venom dripped from her voice. "Get out."

"Let me help."

She wiped a tissue across her eyes. "How can you help?"

"I did not lie when I told you what I was."

She let out a nervous laugh. "If you were truly my guardian angel, my father wouldn't be here right now."

"I don't control life and death." He cocked his head. "Well at least not humans."

She sneered at him. "Then whose life do you control?"

"I am sworn to protect humanity. Demons, at least the evil ones, are whose destiny I control."

She gave a half-hearted laugh again. "And why should I believe you?"

"You saw me fighting with them not long ago."

"You mean when I saved your ass?"

He shrugged. "Think what you wish," he stated as he moved to the bed and touched her father's other hand. He closed his eyes and through the din of voices that always rang in his head, he reached into the old man's mind. The connection was weak and he was shocked at what he found. Demons had done this to him. Their signature left telltale signs all over his insides. They'd ripped his soul to shreds. Seth opened his eyes and gave a hard stare at Kaitlyn.

"Do you know what happened to him?"

"The doctors said he had a severe heart attack, but I suspect it was something else." She chewed her bottom lip. He hated seeing her so weak.

"To humans it looks like his heart, but the demons got to him."

She swallowed hard. "How do you know?"

"I can see inside him." He looked down at the frail man and wished he could save her father. Instead, he had to tell her there was no hope. "Your father will die, but I can give him enough strength to speak to you one last time."

Her bottom lip quivered and she sniffled. He sensed she fought to keep control, probably didn't want to show too much weakness. "Can you really do that?"

"Yes."

"Tell me, is he suffering? Please, if you are what you say, don't let him suffer."

"I will see to it that he doesn't." He closed his eyes once again and reached for her father's mind.

Are you here to take me to the light?

No, another will escort you. Do you recall how many demons attacked you? Seth asked.

There were two. Nasty-looking creatures.

Seth had no doubt. He needed to hurry, time was running out. *I have one last gift for you. Your daughter is here, speak to her.* Seth poured his energy into the dying man.

KATIE HESITATED and considered calling for security, but then her father's eyes popped open.

"Poppa?" she gasped.

"Katie, me darlin' girl." His voice was so low she had to lean closer to hear over the drone of the monitors.

"Oh, Poppa, you're going to be okay." He looked so weak and frail it pulled at her heartstrings

"No, wee one, tis me time. The angel here is giving me the strength ta say me goodbyes."

She sent a quick glance at Mr. Ruiz who still clutched her father's hand, his eyes closed. A chill crept up her spine. Could he be telling the truth? It would stand to reason if there were demons then there would be angels. She should be angry that she had been left alone to fight evil and even more so that her father was now on his deathbed because of it. She couldn't help feeling she was responsible, but she had to force back all her emotions and concentrate on her father.

"Poppa, you shouldn't talk such nonsense. I need you here." Her father was all the family she had left. The thought of him leaving her was unbearable. She had always been strong and independent thanks to him. It was how he had raised her after her mother died when she was only six. She tried hard not to remember all the strangers gathered around when her mom had gone missing. At the time she had blamed herself. She must have done something wrong and her mother had run away. Weeks later though, they found her mutilated body and it became evident what had happened.

"Katie, ya listen ta me now. I love ya, lass, but I'm old and tired and ready ta see your ma. Those demons though, they be vile creatures. Promise me ya will let the angel here protect ya from harm."

Her tears spilled and she choked back a sob. "I will avenge your death, Poppa. On that I swear. You go and be with Momma now. I'll be fine." No, she wouldn't. She'd never be fine again, but she would hold onto the thought of her parents being together again. Her father had missed her mother terribly, had never remarried, having been so devoted to the woman he loved.

"Course ya will, Katie. You're a special lass and as I've always told ya, destined for greatness. There's a letter tucked deep in me safe that your ma left fer ya. Tis time for ya to read it and learn who you really are. Goodbye, me lass." His lashes fluttered and his eyes closed. His chest rose and a ragged breath escaped. The heart monitor flatlined.

She buried her face into the crook of his neck and sobbed. The last person she loved had left her. Alone.

CHAPTER THREE

SETH HOVERED in the distance and watched the funeral. He shrouded himself in magic so the mourners wouldn't see him. Baal popped in beside him.

"Where the fuck have you been?" His gaze never left Kaitlyn.

Baal snorted. "Miss me, vampire?"

He finally turned to acknowledge the demon next to him. "Not really."

Baal schooled his features. "On a more serious note. I found two demons hanging around the father's house."

Seth straightened. "What kind of demons?"

"Lowan's minions. They were looking for the same thing we are."

"The dagger. Were they the same ones who killed her father?" He glanced back to the funeral and noted people beginning to leave.

"No. They were lowly scouts."

"You're sure of this?"

Baal leaned against a tree. His legs stretched out and crossed at the ankles, arms folded over his chest. "I assure you, my techniques for getting them to talk before I took their heads off are what legends are made of."

Seth cocked a brow. He knew there was a reason his king kept the demon around. "I'm impressed. What else did you discover?"

This time Baal straightened. His body language said this wasn't going to be good. "Lowan is trying to get into Vandeldor."

"Shit. Does Marcus know?" Marcus, second in command, would now be in charge since Aidyn was indisposed. "I thought we took care of that problem when we stopped the demons the last time they snuck in?" They had almost lost Lileta's mate Caleb and some of his brethren. The three dragon shifters had gone deep into the mountain of their home and fought the demons, pushing them back while Aidyn collapsed the mountain on top of them. It had been difficult getting the dragons back before they perished. The guardian's home of Vandeldor had been burned and left in ruins. Aidyn had been forced to find them a new location to hide in while they fought the demons that kept finding ways into the human realm.

"I thought so too, but looks like Lowan refuses to give up. I was hoping you'd locate Marcus for me," Baal responded.

"What about your sister, Lileta? Are you going to tell her what Lowan is up to?" So much fucked-up shit had gone down in the past several months. Caleb had rescued Baal's sister who'd been missing since she was fifteen and if that wasn't enough, the gods deemed they were to be mates. A Draki and a Kothar demon: a match that should have never been, yet it had. Then came the shock that Lowan was Lileta's real father. The demon High Lord had taken possession of her and raised all kinds of hell. In the end he had been shoved back into his hole, but not without a fight. At least now everyone understood why the gods, including Hades himself, refused to become involved and simply destroy Lowan. The fucker was a demigod and the gods had their own rules they abided by. One being they couldn't kill each other. This left the guardians to clean up the mess. Thankfully, the Draki and Baal's own people stepped in to assist.

"I have no plans on telling my sister anything. She's been through enough for now."

Seth scrubbed his palm over his face. "Kaitlyn's father was killed by demons."

"Damn that sucks. She know?"

Seth nodded. "I told her, but I think she suspected anyway."

Baal moved his gaze toward the funeral. "We'll never get that dagger back now unless by force."

"You let me worry about that. In the meantime, I'll locate Marcus." He closed his eyes and tried to sift through the voices in his head and wondered how long before he would no longer even be able to find the telepathic connection to his brethren. His clock was ticking.

Marcus?

Seth. You okay?

Yes. Baal needs to speak with you. There have been some developments you need to be made aware of.

Why do I feel like I'm not going to like his news?

Because you're not. Seth heard the mental sigh.

Send him to me. Any luck with the dagger?

Not yet. That's another story.

Just get the job done and get back here.

The connection snapped shut and Seth turned to Baal. "He's in New York, now go." Baal vanished and Seth was again left alone with the voices in his head.

KATIE SAT on the chair by her father's grave. All the others had left, but she couldn't move. Was afraid to be by herself, which seemed silly. She was used to being on her own, but this was different. There would be no more visits to her father. All that was left for her was his empty house, which she didn't want to go back to. Never in her entire life had she felt so alone. She'd always pushed people away, which left her without friends or lovers. Her father had been the only one to understand and now he was gone and she was left to sit by his grave and grieve.

Some place deep inside she found the strength to stand. She had to go so the workers could clear the area. Plus, it would be dark soon. She turned and found a familiar face staring back at her.

"Mr. Ruiz."

"Call me Seth."

She studied him. Noted the dark navy wool coat with its collar flipped up. His hands were shoved into the pockets. Even out here he was sexy. His blue eyes bore into her and for some reason she found herself sobbing.

"I'm sorry," he whispered.

Strong arms encircled her and pulled her close. She buried her head into his chest and cried. Never before had she let herself fall to pieces and especially in front of a stranger. To allow a man she hardly knew comfort her was foreign, yet it felt completely right. At the moment she didn't want to think about anything else. Only wanted to embrace the feeling of the strength that encircled her. She still sensed darkness in him, but for some reason it didn't matter.

"Can I take you home, Ms. O'Hara?"

"Please, I'd like that," she replied into his coat.

Before she could gather her wits and step away, her body began to tingle. Darkness swirled around her even though she knew the sun hadn't completely set yet. Seconds later, she stood in her father's living room. She pushed Seth away.

"What the hell?" They had been standing in the cemetery not more than seconds ago. "How did you do that?"

He smiled and strode to the sofa placing his large frame at one end. "I flashed us here."

Stunned, she didn't move from her spot. She licked her lips. Her throat so parched it felt like sandpaper every time she swallowed. With slow, careful movements, she headed for her father's liquor cabinet. Pulled out his best bottle of Irish whiskey and poured herself two fingers. After taking the entire contents in one swig she let the warmth flush her body. Now she was ready to talk.

"So, you really are an angel? What did you do to my father in that hospital room?"

He sighed, unbuttoned his coat and stretched his arm across the back of the couch. "I'm not an angel. I'm a guardian. Angels have wings. As you can clearly see, I do not."

She shook her head. It seemed Mr. Ruiz—if that was even his real name—liked to play games. "Let's say we start at the beginning." She poured herself another whiskey then remembered that he had joined her in a drink at the club. A wicked thought ran through her mind. *I wonder if angels or whatever the hell he is can get drunk?* "Mr. Ruiz..."

"Please call me Seth."

"Very well, but only if you call me Katie."

"Katie it shall be."

She had to suck in a breath. The way her name rolled off his tongue, in a slight accent she'd never noticed before was like the sweetest music she'd ever heard. "Agreed. Would you like a whiskey, Seth?"

"I was hoping you'd offer to share."

"You'll have to pardon my manners." She turned and poured a second glass then walked across the room. "It has been a difficult day." She handed him the tumbler then took a seat in the chair to his right.

He tipped back his glass and drank. She nearly moaned out loud when he licked his lips and the memory of his hard body against hers came flooding back, quickly followed by irritation at herself. She didn't like not being in control, and at the moment she felt as if her life was on a downward spiral.

"Let's start from the beginning, shall we? Tell me what a guardian is, exactly."

He leaned forward, set his glass on the coffee table and pushed off his coat, tossing it to the other side of the sofa. Her gaze went immediately to the hard muscles that bunched under the black tee he wore and the urge to crawl back into his arms frightened the hell out of her. It wasn't like her in the least to crave a man. Granted, she liked sex as much as the next gal and certainly had never been above having a good time. With no strings attached, of course. Somehow though, this was different. Primal in a way. Like she needed him the same as she needed to breathe.

"I was the first one of my kind created by Zarek to protect humanity."

"Who is Zarek?"

"King of the gods." His reply was matter of fact.

"Gods?" She raised her brows. "Are you saying there is more than one god?"

"Believe what you want, but yes."

"I see. Well, we can come back to that later." She took another sip and dug for her courage. "I seem to recall you flashing a set of fangs at me back in my office. Care to tell me about those?"

He smiled again, but this time there were definitely fangs. Sharp, pointy and why did she find them sexy? She must remember to have her head examined or perhaps that vacation she'd been thinking about.

"Many immortals have them. However, guardians drink blood. Human blood." He smiled again and she found herself touching the throbbing vein on her neck before she pulled her sweater up higher. She set her glass aside and thought about what she knew so far. It was a good thing she was open-minded. Of course, with her past experience with demons, she wasn't surprised to learn there were others and had actually always wondered about it.

SETH WANTED TO LAUGH. The look on Katie's face when he'd said they drink human blood had been priceless. A combination of desire and fear, both of which sent out bursts of essence mingled with strawberries. He found himself clenching his jaw and fighting the urge to taste her. Instead, he needed to gain her trust so he could get the dagger back.

"You needn't worry, Katie. I have no plans to devour you."

A look of disappointment washed over her before she quickly regained her composure. "I don't understand. If you are to protect humanity, then how can you kill us?"

He reached for his glass and took a long sip and knew she waited with baited breath for his answer. He found making her wait entertaining. "I never said we kill anyone. The gods require a sacrifice for their gift of protection. We drink, but we don't kill." He leaned over the arm of the couch and touched her thigh. "As a matter of fact. My bite would bring you the most intense orgasm of your life."

She gasped, pushed his hand away and leaned farther into the chair.

He gave a chuckle and reclined into the comfort of the couch. "Don't worry, Katie. I've no need to feed therefore I won't make you come. Not today at least."

He watched her swallow then flick her tongue out to lick her lips and wondered what it would be like to have the plump perfections wrapped around his cock.

"What did you do to my father?"

Change of subject and he found himself relieved because he was beginning to sport another painful erection. "I entered his mind and told him he needed to say goodbye. I gave him my strength so that he could do just that." He watched her eyes tear up and it ripped at him. "There was no saving him. I saw what the demons did to his insides. I would have liked to save you from the pain of knowing, but since you have a skill for killing demons I figure you deserve to know."

She wiped away a tear that escaped. "Thank you for that. I do appreciate your honesty and the fact you gave me a moment with him before he left."

Silence fell between them for several minutes. He understood she needed time to regain herself and he obliged.

"Why do you want the dagger?"

He was surprised she asked the question so soon. "It's dangerous in the wrong hands. It doesn't discern between good and evil, it kills all immortals."

She thought for a moment. "How do I know anything you're telling me is true?"

He shrugged. "You don't. But be warned, my patience will run out and I will take it by force if necessary."

She straightened, her blue eyes blazed with fire. "I don't take kindly to threats, Mr. Ruiz."

He tossed back the last of his whiskey then set the glass on the table. "Ms. O'Hara. I don't threaten, I promise. I have a duty to fulfill and do not think for one moment I will let you stand in my way." He rose and towered over her. Uncomfortable with using scare tactics, but he found them necessary. "I have the ability to simply take your memories and procure the dagger. However, I am willing to give you the opportunity to come to your senses and give it to me. You have forty-eight hours before I will be back for it." He flashed from the house and stood on the sidewalk watching as she turned off the lights.

"Did you get it?" Baal asked.

"Not yet, but I will." He turned to face the demon. "Did you meet with Marcus?"

"I did. He is sending Jax and Darius to check things out back home. They are to report back if so much as a speck of dirt stirs."

Seth nodded. Their home of Vandeldor, a realm outside of this one has been vacated some time ago, but it didn't mean it was forgotten. He wouldn't put anything past Lowan and having the Draki on their side was a huge plus. It was literally eyes in the sky.

"So, you banging the firecracker in there?"

"You are crass."

Baal smiled. "It's why you love me."

Seth rolled his eyes. "No. I'm not banging her, as you call it. Why do you ask?" Did the demon want her for himself?

Baal's golden eyes glowed. "I figured since you hadn't simply taken the dagger then maybe you were fucking her. Since you're not, perhaps I can have a go with her. I'm confident I can seduce it away from her."

He snorted. "Demon, do you think with anything but your cock?"

"No, I thought you knew me better than that. Besides, maybe if you thought with your small head more often, the big one would stop torturing you."

He knew what Baal meant, but nothing was going to stop the crazy voices inside his head that had been adding up for centuries. Taking a woman to his bed was risky at best and he only did so when the urges couldn't be sated any other way. He had to admit that Katie stirred a fire deep inside him, but he would fight the urge to have her. He prayed she was smart enough to take his threat seriously because he didn't think he would remain intact if he had to take her blood.

"I gave her forty-eight hours to give me the dagger. If I have to resort to taking her memories to find it you may have to kill me afterward."

"Shit. We'll hope she comes to her senses." Baal slapped Seth on the back. "We'll get that blade one way or another."

The air shifted and prickled his skin. A shadow appeared in front of them and dark wings formed, followed by the body of Gabriel. Zarek's winged warrior propped a sword on his shoulder.

"Angel boy, what's up?" Baal asked.

The angel curled his lip and bared his teeth. "I'm watching you, vampire. One small step out of line and I won't hesitate to take your head. Matter of fact, I'm itching to do so." He flexed his fingers around the handle of his blade.

Seth hissed. "If you think to intimidate me you are sadly mistaken. You should know I do not fear death."

"Your head over my mantel would be a major trophy," Gabriel growled back.

Baal stepped forward. "What the hell is going on here?"

"This doesn't concern you, demon," the angel replied.

"I beg to differ." Baal stiffened.

"He's right, Baal. This is a fight between the angel and I that goes back to...Well the beginning of my existence," Seth responded.

"Yes, it does. Perhaps I should kill you now? I doubt Zarek would miss you. He might even thank me."

Baal produced his own sword. "You'll have to get through me to do it."

The angel laughed. "Vampire hired a demon as his body guard? You should take care, Baal, and remember who you are dealing with."

Baal spat at the ground. "Fuck you. I don't fear you or Zarek. I live by my own rules and I have promised Aidyn I would watch over Seth. If it comes down to it I will be the one to take care of business."

Seth let out a groan and scrubbed a palm down his face. "This would almost be humorous if it weren't for the fact you are arguing over who gets to have my head."

Baal narrowed his golden gaze. "Go home, angel, before I pluck your fucking wings like a damn chicken and stick you on a spit."

Gabriel growled something unintelligible before he vanished. Seth turned to Baal. "Really? I'm an ancient, older than you, and I don't need a babysitter."

"What happened between you two?"

"None of your business." In all this time Gabriel still hadn't gotten over Vivian's death. Qadira had always been a favorite of the angel and the warrior had been livid over the distress caused to the goddess when she'd lost her daughter. Seth couldn't blame him though. Hell, he still wasn't over the trauma he'd caused.

KATIE WATCHED out the window as people—well at least they looked like people—popped in and out. One had wings as black as the night and carried a sword. Another confronted him and the two looked as if they might come to blows all while Seth stood there. Her intuition told her they were arguing about him and she had to wonder what he'd done to upset the winged one.

There was one thing for certain. She wasn't handing the dagger over to anyone. Her mother had left it to her and she refused to part with it. Not to mention the fact she needed it to end the lives of the demons responsible for her father's death. She'd hunt every bloody one of them down and make them all pay. Besides, she didn't trust the one who called himself Seth. Something was off about him. Well, in forty-eight hours she'd be out of town and into hiding if she had to. Lay low for a time and hopefully they'd forget about her.

She slipped into the den with a flashlight in hand, figured if she kept the house dark they'd think she was asleep and leave her in peace. Moving around her father's desk, she went to the wall and took down the oil painting. Turning the safe's dial, right, left, then right again until it clicked. She closed her eyes, took in a deep breath to calm her nerves, then tried the handle. Fear raced through her at what she would find. Poppa had said there was a letter from her mother and she worried why he had never told her about it before. With a shaking hand, she opened the door. The narrow beam of light she shined inside revealed a sealed, white envelope with her name scrawled across the front.

She reached for it then glanced around the room to make sure no one had popped in. Satisfied she was alone, she slid to the floor and crawled under her father's desk. Flashbacks of hiding under the heavy mahogany furniture when she was a little girl came flooding back to her. The fit was tighter than it was as a child, but a sense of comfort still surrounded her. She focused the light onto the front of the envelope and stared at her name. Maybe if she concentrated hard enough, looking at her mother's handwriting would somehow bring her mother back. Bile filled the back of her throat and she swallowed. Opening the envelope, she pointed the light at the paper.

Dearest Kaitlyn,

If you are reading this then that probably means one of two things.

Either your father has passed or you are closing in on your thirtieth birthday.

She wiped away a tear. Her mother was correct on both accounts. Her birthday was next month and the thought of being alone caused an ache deep in her chest.

No matter what the circumstance, it's time for you to be made aware of your heritage. You are the descendant of a god. I'm sure there are many questions that have arisen in your life. Like the dagger your father gave to you and the fact that you have probably taken to killing demons. Most humans can't see them unless a demon chooses to be seen. You, however, are special. Just as I was and the women in our family before us. Unfortunately, our creator, your real father the Phoenix god, has never made himself known to us. The blade that you hold is called the dagger of Embara and it will kill any immortal.

I know your father told you that he adopted you. You were only a baby when we met and he fell instantly in love with you. He also accepted both of us for what we truly are. Special.

Katie looked away from the page and blinked. Her real father was a god? She had always known she was adopted, but this was crazy. "Well it seems you were truthful about the dagger, Mr. Ruiz." A pain started behind her eyes. While being the daughter of a god seemed illogical, so had everything else about the day. She would try and reserve judgment until she finished the letter.

Our race is dying out. I can't even tell you if there are any more like you left in the world. Many have been killed by the demons before they could bear any children.

I need you to read this next part carefully, your life may depend on it.

She pressed the letter to her chest. Her breaths increased until the threat of hyperventilation loomed over her. "Holy fuck. There's more?" How much could she be expected to handle in one day? She steadied her breathing and drew from the strength deep inside her. While afraid to continue reading, the need to have some kind of answers nagged at her, so she brought the flashlight back up and pointed it at the page.

If you do not mate with an immortal before your thirtieth birthday, your powers may overwhelm you and could kill you. What you don't know is before I met your father, I was mated to a Kothar demon. Yes, there are many good demons in the world and he was able to help me complete my transformation. However, he was killed only six months later and I was left alone. Soon after I became pregnant and gave birth to you. Thank goodness my mother had lived long enough to explain our heritage and the fact I may one day mysteriously become pregnant.

After your birth I met your father and, well, you know the rest.

"No, mother. I don't really know and what the hell kind of transformation did you have?" She let out an exasperated sigh and rubbed her temples. In less than five minutes she'd learned about good demons, Immaculate Conception and some kind of transformation, yet she hadn't learned shit. She was almost afraid to read further.

Since I have no idea what kind of power you will have, you need to seek out an immortal. Perhaps the Kothar can help you as well. An ugly war has been foreseen, you may have already noticed an increase in demon activity. It has been told Hell will open up and the vilest creatures will spill out and taint humanity.

Katie pressed her palms into her eyes. "No pressure or anything." So now her mother was telling her to seek out a demon?

The other task you must consider is finding the book of Mitne. It is a long-lost text that is believed to be hidden in the Valley of the Kings. We were always taught that the Phoenix god had a hidden chamber in that sacred region of Egypt and inside would be all the answers we seek. To my knowledge none have been successful in finding it and all who have tried perished. I wish I could tell you more about who you are, but know that you are the descendant of a god. You are capable of many good things.

I love you, Katie, and I know how you must be feeling right now. You have a difficult road ahead of you and unfortunately you will travel it alone.

She snorted. "No, Mom, I don't think you have a clue how I feel right now. I don't even know."

There is a second packet inside the safe. It contains a map of where the tomb is thought to be located. Whatever you decide, I know you will be successful. Please be careful.

With all my love,

Mom

"Be careful?" How could her life have gotten any more messed up? She clicked off the flashlight, wanted to be alone in the dark with her thoughts. Thoughts that were a jumbled mess. She had always been a strong woman. Her father had raised her to stand on her own two feet and when he'd given her the dagger, they had talked about the supernatural. She had to wonder why he didn't tell her who she really was. Had he even known? Katie understood there were creatures in the world that nightmares were made of. Her instinct had always served her well and at the moment it screamed at her to find the tomb.

She rubbed her temples, the pain behind her eyes turned into a full-blown headache. "Damn it, Mom. Your letter only leaves more questions than it answers. Will I really die if I don't mate?" What would she encounter if she went to the Valley of the Kings? More information would have been nice in helping her make a choice.

"Oh, hell!" She crawled out from under the desk and stood. Flicking on the flashlight she again dug through the safe until she found a large manila envelope. Pulling it out she moved back to the desk. This time she opted to flip on the lamp. Rolling her shoulders, she glanced around the room. The sensation someone watched her crawled up her spine, but she was alone, or so she hoped.

Bringing her focus back on the envelope, she grabbed an opener and ran it along the seam. Inside was a yellowed piece of folded paper. With great care, she unfolded it and spread it out across the desk.

"Great. How the hell am I supposed to read this?" It was covered with symbols that appeared more like hieroglyphics than modern writing. Obviously, this was going to take more research and time was not on her side.

"Oh, damn! How could I forget?" She once met a professor who worked for the Field Museum and his specialty was Egyptian artifacts. She'd have to go back to her office and pull up his information. It was time to call in a favor.

CHAPTER FOUR

SETH STARED at the ceiling of his filthy hotel room. The stench of piss and vomit assaulted his senses and the bed under his back was more like a block of wood with worn out springs and tufts of cotton than a mattress. The voices in his head were particularly loud tonight and it was one of the reasons he chose to stay in this hellhole rather than a luxury suite. He was more comfortable with the riff-raff on the streets than polite society anyway. One thing he'd learned, he could make the voices settle down when he got his fix.

It had happened by mistake when he'd drunk from a woman a few months back. He'd smelled the drugs in her blood, but she had been the only source of nourishment at the time. Imagine his surprise when his mind went silent. He had relished every second of it until the dark voice came. It seemed there was a price to pay. Either live with the thousands of voices that filled his head or drink from the heroin addicts and deal with one destructive voice. He had decided the latter was far better and he'd been able to control the one dark echo in his head.

Until now.

He sat up and threw his legs over the edge of the bed. The clock on the nightstand said it was one in the morning. It was time for him to troll the ghetto and get something to eat.

He flashed into the darkness, most of the street lamps either broken or burnt out. Not that he needed the light to see.

With determination in his step and a hunger that burned his belly, he kicked empty beer bottles from his path and walked down the dark alley. Fire burned in barrels scattered along the sidewalk and bums littered the pavement. He raised his nose to the air and sniffed. The smell he searched for tickled the back of his throat and made his mouth water. He narrowed his gaze and marched forward. Passed a demon that was busy sucking the soul from an old man. The beast looked up with fear in its eyes, but Seth snarled and continued onward.

Leave it. You're almost there and soon you will have what you seek.

The voice was correct as always. Around the corner a young man shoved a needle in his vein and the darkness in Seth became giddy. This would be a fresh taste, something he hadn't had in a while. He waited out of sight until the addict had finished and tossed the syringe to the ground. Within seconds, Seth was in front of him.

"How do you feel?" he inquired.

The druggie looked up, his eyes bloodshot and licked his lips repeatedly. "Fucking awesome."

Seth grinned. "Wonderful." Seth grabbed the man by his greasy hair and jerked his head to expose the vein. Debated taking the jugular, but reminded himself it was messy, not to mention against the rules. He still had a conscience. Barely.

His fangs extended and sank deep into the pulsing flesh. The man tasted like he hadn't bathed in weeks, but Seth didn't care once the warm elixir coated his tongue and went down the back of his throat. Heat filled his belly and the voices began to quiet. Except for one.

Mmm, tastes so good. Drink it all!

He wanted to. Didn't want to stop until he had every last drop. The addicts breathing became shallow.

You must stop before you kill him. His conscience warred with the dark voice.

No, take it all!

He took another long pull. Wanted to jerk away yet unable to. Then Vivian's image came into view. Her lifeless body taunted him and he shoved the bum away. The man slipped to the ground while Seth wiped his blood-covered mouth on the sleeve of his shirt. He tipped his head back and closed his eyes letting the rush from the drug course through him. For a brief moment in his pitiful existence he felt normal then reality slapped him across the face. He straightened and knelt to check the man for a pulse. Weak but still there. The guy's body was damaged from drug abuse and the loss of blood wasn't going to help. Seth backed away with the knowledge he'd just shortened the man's life.

He ran his fingers through his hair. "Fuck!" He flashed from the area and stood on the sidewalk in front of the house where he'd left Katie earlier. The neighborhood was silent, a stark contrast to where he'd just left.

Go take her.

"Shut the hell up."

"Your dark side is showing."

He faced Baal. "You can shut the hell up as well."

The demon grabbed him by the collar and shoved him against a tree. "Listen up. I know what you did. You think I can't sense the addiction inside you? You fucking idiot, I'm a demon and I can smell your despair." He released his hold on Seth. "Damn it. Your curse is growing. There isn't much of you left."

The curse of Drayos. The stain that grew inside every guardian and threatened to snuff out their light. Without that side of them they would become bloodthirsty monsters and humanity be damned. It affected each one differently. Seth had always had the ability to retain a person's memory, but with the curse he couldn't let them go.

Thousands of people fought for dominance in his mind. Even he was surprised he had lasted this long. His brethren had no idea how bad off he really was.

He leveled his gaze on Baal. The demon had always been a good friend to the guardians and Aidyn trusted him. Perhaps that was why Aidyn had sent him to guard Seth. "Do me a favor."

"What?"

"If I get to close to her, kill me."

Baal cocked his head to look at the house. "The firecracker?"

He sighed. "Yes."

The demon met his gaze and even in the darkness Seth saw recognition burn in the demon's golden eyes. "You have a thing for her."

He set his jaw, his body stiffened. "More than you know."

"Son of a fucking bitch! This is good news. Maybe she can save your vampire ass like Cassie did Marcus." The tone in the demon's voice was way too damn happy.

"No."

"Why? Am I mistaken in that she is your mate?"

He ground his teeth and fisted his hands. "She is." When the fuck had he realized it? He wasn't even sure. He supposed the night he'd rescued her he had known but blocked it from his mind.

Baal stepped closer until they were almost touching. "Then what seems to be the problem? I figure as far gone as you are, claim her and deal with the fallout later."

"Therein lies the problem, *demon*. I am beyond repair and am just as likely to kill her as to mate her." Even as he spoke the dark voice was busy painting pictures of her naked body tied to the bed. Bite marks. His marks covered her flesh. He swore to Zarek, if he had the means himself he'd take his own head. "You must promise to keep this between us and do as I say." He closed his eyes. "Do not let me touch her." He curled his fingers into his palms. Gods he wanted to touch her.

"Well, isn't this just a bowl of sour grapes," Baal snorted.

The demon had no idea how sour it really was. Finally, he'd been granted a mate, but he was too far-gone to claim her. He fought the urge to rip someone to shreds. He'd spent his entire existence trying to stay as far away from women as possible. Only when his desire for sex and the need for blood had reached a critical point did he seek them out. Always he lived in fear of what he'd done to Vivian becoming another reality. He couldn't risk the life of the woman inside. Heaven, Hell and everything in between be damned if he killed his own mate.

KATIE MANAGED to sneak out of the house and back to her office without a hitch. She had no idea where the guardian, angel, whatever the hell he called himself, had gone but she was thankful he wasn't bothering her. The sun began to peek over the horizon and it was going to be an exceptionally warm day for April. Finally, everyone was sick of the cold weather after a long Chicago winter.

Flipping through her appointment book, she went back to four months ago and ran her finger down the list of clients.

Bingo.

Professor Bradford and there was his cell number. She looked at the clock, far too early to call so she decided to shower and change. As she moved from her desk to the hidden panel at the back of her office, she was grateful once again she'd had the foresight to have a secret room built. Tilting the painting on the wall to one side, the panel opened and she walked through. She shed her jacket, unzipped her jeans and stepped out of them kicking them off to the side. Next came her sweater and it landed beside the bed as she marched for the bathroom. She turned on the shower and finished undressing before she stepped under the hot spray.

Water sluiced down her back and helped to relieve the ache of tired muscles. The past few days had been hell and everything sat heavy between her shoulders. So many things to consider and the letter from her mother had jarred her like nothing else. Reading her words was like losing her all over again.

She rested her forehead against the shower wall and let the tears fall. In seconds, racking sobs escaped. Ones she had kept bottled up for far too long. She was tired. Tired of being the strong one and for once in her life she wished for someone to hold her so she could fall to pieces. The memory of Seth and his strong arms pulling her close had been like home. Comfortable. She ached for it again and found herself wondering what he tasted like. Would his kiss be gentle or demanding like him?

With a shudder, she turned and faced the spray, let the water wash her tears away. It was all the time she had to feel sorry for herself. Weakness would most likely get her killed and love would break her heart.

There was time for neither.

She reached for the bottle of gel and squeezed a generous amount onto the sponge. Glided the foam across her skin then did a quick rinse before she washed her hair. She wanted to look over the letter and map again before calling on the professor.

In minutes, she had exited the shower and dressed in a clean pair of jeans and a lightweight, black, fleece top. A cup of coffee in her hand, she sat at the small desk and read over the letter again. With a sigh, she came to the same conclusion as the night before. If what she read was accurate, she was screwed.

Impending doom loomed over her head if she didn't marry an immortal or so her mother said, but she wasn't really sure what it meant. Maybe this was part of the reason she'd been having trouble sleeping, along with her lack of appetite. Not to mention the damn migraines that continued to plague her. Even a neurologist had found nothing wrong and the prescription he'd given her had done little to touch the pain when it hit.

She took a sip of coffee and laid out the map. "Great, I wouldn't even know where to find the demons you spoke of mother." The dull ache behind her right eye indicated she'd better find them fast.

DAYBREAK CAME and still no movement in the house. Seth had left Baal hours ago. Most likely to get another fix. The guardian teetered on the edge and it would only take a wisp of wind to push him over.

"Fucking vampire." Baal shoved his hands in his jeans pocket.

Baal, any luck?

Aidyn. Baal was surprised to hear from his friend so soon. *That depends on what you mean by luck? Are the two mated yet? No. Have they met? Yes. Talk about giving me a fucked-up job.*

I gave it to you because I knew you could handle it. I have no idea when I will be released.

Baal grunted. He despised the fact his friend was being punished, but knew better than to ask questions about it. Aidyn had contacted him and begged him to take this assignment and keep it quiet. How he'd known Katie and Seth were destined, Baal had no idea and wasn't going to ask. He wondered if Aidyn knew about Seth's little habit, but again he'd keep the vampire's secret. If Baal looked at it logically, Seth was bound to die anyway and at least the drugged-up blood he drank might buy him some time. One thing was certain. Baal couldn't blame Seth for not wanting to mate with the fire-cracker. This late in the game no one knew if she could actually save him and if he did mate her and everything went south she would end up on the losing end.

The fact that Seth still had enough common sense not to drag the woman down with him was the only reason Baal would keep his word and not tell the others. He would also kill the vampire if things got too bad. It was another reason Aidyn had asked him to intervene. The guardian king knew that any tof the vampires would honor the code and take Seth out, Aidyn just didn't want them to have to do it. It would be hard enough to lose one of their own and Baal had already proved he had no issues killing.

I vow I'll do everything possible to get them together, but it's not gonna be easy. He will fight me every step of the way.

I know, but try. His life depends on it. I have to go. Aidyn broke the connection.

Baal looked again at the house. "Something isn't right in there." He decided to flash inside and take a peek. Once in the house he knew immediately Katie had managed to sneak out. "Fuck me." Now he'd have to find Seth and tell Seth he'd lost her. The vampire would be the only one who could track her, but first he opened his senses and searched for any kind of magic. If the dagger was in here he would find it.

Nothing.

Well he didn't figure he'd get so lucky, but he'd hoped. "Shit, now to go piss off an unstable vampire. Just my fucking luck."

CHAPTER FIVE

PROFESSOR BRADFORD HAD AGREED to meet Katie at the local bagel shop over on First Street. With a quick glance at the clock, she realized she'd better hurry and reached for her keys then thought better of it. To take her own car might not be the best idea. Last thing she wanted was to be spotted, so she reached for her papers instead then ran outside and hailed a cab. Glanced around to see if anyone watched her. Like she'd know anyway. She opened the door and slipped into the back seat and gave the driver instructions.

The restaurant was a good twenty-minute ride and she couldn't help the nagging suspicion she was being followed. Even so, she refused to look behind her. It would only cause the cabbie to become suspicious and that was the last thing she wanted. She rubbed the back of her neck to try and relieve some of the tension, hoping another migraine didn't come on.

When they pulled up out front, a mix of relief and anxiety came over her and she handed the man his fare. "Keep the change." She jumped from the back seat and walked to the door. Again, eyes bore into her back and she gave a sideways glance, but with the bustle on the sidewalk there was no way to tell who watched her. She slipped inside and spotted the professor already seated at a booth sipping coffee, a bagel in front of him. With a confident step she walked to him and slid into the seat across from him.

His brown eyes lit up. "Ms. O'Hara, you look lovely this morning."

She offered a warm smile. "Thank you, Professor Bradford, and thank you for agreeing to meet me."

"Please, call me Hank. What can I do for you, Ms. O'Hara?"

"I'll call you Hank if you'll call me Katie."

His smile reached his eyes. "Of course."

"Good." She set her map on the table. "My father passed recently..."

"Oh, I'm so sorry."

"Thank you. Anyway, as I was going through his belongings, I came across this piece of paper and wondered if you could make any sense of it?"

He reached for his glasses and perched them on the end of his nose. Pushed his coffee and bagel aside then unfolded the paper, spreading it across the table. He was silent for several minutes before he peered over the tops of his glasses.

"Very interesting. It looks like a map, but this is inaccurate."

She narrowed her gaze on the paper. "How so?"

"Well, this indicates there is a hidden tunnel in Seti the second's tomb, but that area has been gone over with a fine-tooth comb. It also says something about a book called Mitne and again that's impossible. There have never been any books of any kind found anywhere in the Valley of the Kings."

"Hmm, I see." She leaned back and tried to feign boredom. "I wonder why my father had this."

The professor shrugged. "Perhaps he purchased it thinking it was a legit map. I'm sorry."

"No, don't be. At least now I know it's basically garbage. I'm sorry to have wasted your time." She reached out and grabbed the paper and folded it. "I'll tell you what. Let me give you a free night on the house. Whatever you want. You just stop in anytime and I'll make sure my assistant knows."

The flush started at his neck and raced up to his forehead. "Why thank you, Katie."

"You're welcome. I hate to run, but I still have a lot of things to take care of."

"Of course."

She slid from the booth and walked out the door. Hailing a cab, she headed back to her office. Little did the professor know he'd given her a place to start and an object to search for. It was best he thought the paper a fake anyway. Last thing she wanted was anyone else involved. Now, she just had to figure out how to find the hidden chamber, not to mention how the hell she was going to get into the Valley of the Kings and snoop. The place must have top-notch security. She rubbed her temples and tried to think if there was anyone she could hire to help her get inside.

SETH OCCUPIED a corner of the darkened room. The blade embedded deep into the muscle of his thigh. He winced, but continued to push the point further until it hit bone and a sigh of pleasure escaped his lips.

You need to find the girl. Must have her!

"You need to shut the fuck up," he replied through gritted teeth and gave the knife a twist. The visions had grown worse and the only thing that helped was pain. The sharp, mind-numbing kind he received when he sliced into his own flesh. It also delighted the dark voice and since he refused to give it the girl, it seemed to settle for the pain. Seth wondered who he had drunk from in his life that had been more fucked up in the head than him.

He pulled out the dagger and watched the blood trickle down his leg. If only he could bleed to death, but his wound knitted together within seconds. How the hell had his life brought him to the point of being alone in a seedy hotel room with a knife stuck in his thigh? He'd once been a guardian, a warrior who fought evil in the world so humanity could sleep in peace. Now, he was the evil. More messed up than the addicts on the street corner. He eyed the syringe next to him on the floor. He'd already prepped it for injection. Would a direct hit be the same or better than drinking from an addict?

He looked back to the healed wound on his leg, then back to the needle and he thought of Vivian. He could almost see the disappointment on her face at what he'd become. He ran his fingers through his hair and ripped chunks from his scalp. *Gods just fucking let me die!*

"What the hell?"

Seth used his legs to push his way up the wall and winced. He was not in the mood for company.

"You stupid motherfucker," Baal growled.

"Demon." Seth laughed and noticed how his voice reverberated around the room. He watched the demon's gaze fall to the blood on his thigh.

"What happened to your leg?"

He flashed the blade that still dripped his blood. "The voice enjoys my pain."

Baal scraped his fingers through his hair. "Dear gods. I should really call Marcus, you have fucking lost it." Then his gaze darted to the syringe on the floor.

Seth lunged, but found himself blocked in a cocoon of magic that held him in place. "I'll kill you. You vowed to tell no one." He twisted and snarled, but remained contained. Baal stepped closer until he was within inches of Seth. Seth swore if he could free himself he would roll the demon's head across the floor.

"Listen up, dick wad. I'll take you out like yesterday's trash and not blink a fucking eye." He narrowed his gaze. "However, I need you to find that damn mate of yours. So, straighten your vampire ass up so we can get the dagger back." He stepped back. "After that I couldn't give a rat's ass what happens to you." He reached for Seth's blade and in the process of taking it slapped a band of silver on Seth's wrist.

"Sorry, but this seems the only way to control you."

The barrier broke away and Seth crumpled to the floor. The band riddled in Kothar magic meant he was now as weak as a human.

"Once you come back to your senses, we will find your mate."

Seth snorted. "I have no sense, demon, but how the hell did you lose her?"

"Too busy worrying about your ass."

The voices crept back into his head. A din in the recess of his mind. "I didn't know you cared."

"I don't, but we need that blade back." Baal eyed the syringe again. "Please tell me that's not what I think it is?"

Seth gave his head a shake. "I'm a mess." If he was capable of having a panic attack there was no doubt he'd be having one now. It was getting more difficult to discern reality from the fiction in his mind. He was about to do the one thing he'd never done in his entire life. "Help me."

Baal growled and pointed a finger at the syringe zapping it to dust. "You're done with the drugs." His features softened. "If you need to hurt yourself physically, I get it. I'll even look the other way, but this other shit? I'll make what Aidyn would do to you look like a fucking stroll in the park."

Seth breathed a sigh of relief and hated to admit that was exactly what he needed. He would never tell his brethren he had a problem. Couldn't stand to see the look of disappointment on their faces, especially Garin. He was closer to the guardian than any other and the thought of what it would do to his friend ate at him. With Baal things were different. The demon wouldn't take his shit.

"I owe you."

Baal snorted. "I'll collect later. In the meantime, can you pull your shit together long enough to track your mate?"

"Release me." He held out his wrist so the demon could remove the silver band.

Baal complied, but kept a wary eye on him. "How do you feel?"

Seth assessed himself. His powers returned now that the silver was removed. "The voices are back but I'll manage."

"Good. Now, find your mate."

KATIE DUG her passport from the desk drawer then opened up her laptop. She needed to find a flight to Egypt and the sooner the better before that crazy man came back looking for her. She dabbed at the bead of sweat on her upper lip. Another hot flash engulfed her and she reached for the hem of her top and whipped it off. Had she been older, she could attribute them to menopause, but she was too young for that. Doctors had run tests and found her hormones to be in perfect working order. They concluded it was all in her head.

She grabbed an ice cube from her glass and ran it across her chest and between her breasts.

"What a stunning sight."

"Shit!" She jumped and looked across the room. Seth, and this time he had company. A rather delicious man with raven hair and golden eyes. "Don't you ever knock?" She held up her hand. "Actually, don't answer that and no I'm still not giving you the dagger."

The other man stepped forward. "What are you?"

She arched a brow. "What do you mean, dumb-ass, haven't you seen a woman before?" She thought about grabbing her shirt, but couldn't stand the thought of the fleece next to her skin. She'd rather sit there in her bra and let them stare than burn herself alive.

He crossed his arms over an expansive chest and stared. "I've seen plenty of women, though usually they're writhing beneath me naked."

This exchange wasn't helping her body temperature in the least and neither was staring at him. "Mr. Ruiz, you can take your pet and leave now."

The delicious eye-candy tossed his head back and laughed. "I do really like her, Seth. She has spunk and would be a great match for you."

Seth stepped forward. "Zip it, demon."

Katie jumped from her chair. "Demon? You bring a demon into my club? I knew you were crazy, but..." She tilted her head. She couldn't sense this one. There was no smell of death.

"Relax. He's a Kothar, on our side."

"Kothar?" She recalled the name from her mother's letter. So, this was who she was supposed to seek out? Interesting.

He stepped closer. "My name is Baal and I don't believe in beating around the bush. We need that dagger back and I would be grateful if you'd hand it over."

"Why? Give me one good reason to give it to you."

"I can think of several, but mostly it is far too dangerous in the hands of a human," Seth replied.

"Umm, fang face. Your mate here isn't exactly one-hundred percent grade A human."

"What?" Seth and Katie yelled in unison.

Katie narrowed her gaze on Seth. "What do you mean mate?" *There is that word mother referred to.*

Seth waved his hand and dismissed her. "What do you mean not human?" Then he turned back to Katie. "Why do you not seem surprised by the fact you're not human?"

"Didn't you notice her body temperature is much too high?" Baal circled her like a tiger ready to pounce. "There is something else, but I can't place it."

"You're right. Now that you mention it, she is off."

"Okay, I hope you both know that you're not scoring any brownie points here. In case you were never taught, compliments, flowers, candy and jewelry are how you win a woman."

The two men looked at each other then back to her.

"Fine, how much do you want for the dagger? Cash or jewels? You name your price," Seth said.

"I..." She gripped the edge of her desk for balance. *Oh god, not now!* Another attack was imminent and she was helpless to stop it. The vision flashed in her head of her lying on a cold, stone slab like some kind of sacrifice, except she was certain she was dead. It wasn't the first time this particular vision had hit her. It always happened right before she blacked out.

She swayed, the voices of the two men in the room with her became an echo as everything dimmed. She had a moment to wonder if they were the ones who would be taking her life.

CHAPTER SIX

SETH SENSED Katie falling before she ever hit the floor and wrapped his arms around her, carrying her limp body to the sofa where he laid her down.

"Something is very wrong with her," Baal stated.

"Obviously." Seth allowed his annoyance to seep through. He touched her temple and searched her mind. "She's worried about an impending trip to Egypt, a map of some sorts and a letter from her mother."

"Why don't you just drink from her then obtain all her memories? We'd know where the dagger was."

He glanced at Baal. "I'm not tasting her blood. To do so would start the bonding." He already held guilt for invading her mind even though it was necessary. "You're right though, she isn't fully human and something is going on inside her."

Katie stirred with a moan. Her thick lashes fluttered before blue eyes filled with fear stared back at him. Was she afraid of him? It would be best if she were, yet he wanted her to look at him with desire instead. It was a foolish thought.

"You blacked out. Does this happen often?" he asked.

Baal handed him a glass of water and Seth helped her sit up before pressing it to her lips. Katie knocked it away and pinned him with a death glare.

"Stay the hell out of my head."

With those words her mind slammed shut and Seth was tossed out. He turned to Baal. "She just blocked me."

The demon's brows shot up. "No shit?"

Katie swung her legs and sat up. "Stop talking about me as if I weren't here."

"Very well." Seth moved out of the way and took a seat in the chair across from her. "I think it's time we were all truthful since it seems we need each other." He couldn't stop looking at her breasts as they rose and fell with each heavy breath she took.

"Hey, asshat. My eyes are up here." She pointed.

Seth scowled. "Then put some fucking clothes on." He leaned forward as if that would push home his point. "After all, you sell sex so you should know better than to put the girls on display if you don't want to be ogled."

A whistle came from across the room. "Way to earn brownie points, vampire."

Seth glared at the demon from the corner of his eye. "I'll endeavor to do better." He put on his best smile. "My apologies. Now, as I said, it seems we need each other."

"Ha! Why would you think I need you? It seems I have something you want, not the other way around," Katie replied.

Baal took a seat in the other chair. "Oh, I'd kill for some popcorn right now. This oughta be most entertaining."

Seth ignored him. "I beg to differ. I had enough time to see the map and know you need us to decipher it. Besides, there are changes occurring inside you that maybe we can help you with."

She stared at both of them for a long while and after several minutes her shoulders dropped in defeat. "Fine, I'll tell you all I know."

Relief came over Seth, at least it was a start. "How about we start at the beginning. How did you end up with the dagger?"

"My father gave it to me. Said it was a gift from my mother."

The two men looked at each other before Seth replied, "Who was your mother?"

Katie rose and walked to the desk where she grabbed an envelope then handed it to Seth. "Until last night I didn't really know. She died when I was a child."

He pulled the paper from the envelope and unfolded it. Baal came up behind him and read over his shoulder.

The demon whistled. "I never expected that."

"Neither did I," Seth responded. Now he understood her fear. She had no idea what was happening or if she would even survive. He knew what it was like to feel helpless when it came to your destiny. He fought with it every second of every day.

Katie planted herself back on the couch. "Do you know what she means?" She rubbed her temples. "The episodes are becoming more frequent."

Concern ate at him. He may have decided to not mate with her, but she still belonged to him. "What happens, tell me everything."

"Headaches, followed by intense heat. Recently I've started having visions of my death then I blackout shortly afterward." Her eyes widened. "Do you know of this god? Maybe he has the answers."

"'Fraid not, doll. That god has been dead for centuries."

Seth nodded. "Baal's right. The dagger went missing and when I discovered you had it, well you can imagine my surprise." He frowned. "It ended up in the wrong hands once and killed some of our friends. It's why we want it back."

"I can see why you have been so adamant about it. Still, my mother wanted me to have it, I can't just hand it over to you." She sighed. "Is there anyone who knows something about this Phoenix god?"

Baal spoke up. "Oh sure, there are several gods who would know.

Trouble is no one can summon one now that the guardians' home is off limits. We can't make them come to us."

Seth jumped from his seat and began to pace. "We could try, who would be most likely to heed my call for help?"

Katie watched him walk back and forth. "How many are there?"

He didn't miss a step. "More than you care to know. Zarek, the king, is busy torturing my leader so I dare not summon him." He didn't miss her cringe at the mention of torture. "His wife is most likely to ignore us as well since she despises me."

Baal scratched his chin. "Argathos is usually pretty reasonable."

Seth stopped. "True. It's worth a try." He looked over at Katie and noticed she chewed her bottom lip. The pink flesh beckoned him and he forced himself to turn away. He closed his eyes and searched for the telepathic thread. His was a bit different than the others. Being ancient gave him more of a direct line.

Argathos?

No reply.

Argathos, you are needed here. There is a situation that requires the attention of a god.

Bingo. He felt a stir in his mind.

KATIE WATCHED the two men banter back and forth, her mind in a daze. She could scarcely believe she'd actually showed them the letter. However, the last episode had scared the shit out of her and that was no easy task. Her mother's warning also in the forefront of her mind and the fact she had a real live Kothar demon sitting in the chair across from her. There was one thing her father had taught her and that was to never be afraid of asking for help. She always believed what goes around comes around and if you did the right thing, karma would be kind to you in return. Trouble was, was she doing the right thing by trusting them? Seth had given her the chance to talk to her father before he died. Then there was this stupid attraction she had to him though she'd never admit it.

Would she give them the dagger? Not a chance in hell, but maybe they could work together. Something told her all the answers she would need were buried in the Valley of the Kings.

Dots of bright white light danced in the center of the room. Swirled into a mini tornado and reached for the ceiling. As the light dissipated, a tall man wearing jeans and a tight-fitting black tee replaced it. His chestnut hair fell to his shoulders and the darkest brown eyes she'd ever seen stared at her.

"Argathos." The two men knelt at his feet and she wondered if she was supposed to do the same.

"Is she why you summoned me?"

He glided closer to her and she held her breath. "Umm." She fidgeted with the fringe on a throw pillow and suddenly realized she was still only wearing her bra and jeans. Her face heated and she wanted to crawl under the couch, but his eyes never left hers. Perhaps he could teach the other one a thing about manners.

"Remarkable," he whispered.

She swallowed. Wanted to speak, but couldn't find her voice. Katie had no idea for sure who he was, but assumed from the conversation previously he was a god. Even if she hadn't overheard, there was a power that emanated off him. The kind that told her he was more than anyone else in the room.

"You are the daughter of Pyros."

Seth moved next to him. "She holds his dagger."

The man smiled. "That is a good thing then. At least it's in capable hands."

Relief flooded her. Hopefully now they'd all stop trying to take it away from her. She cleared her throat. "Did you know my father?"

He nodded, his features appeared thoughtful. "I did indeed. He was a brave warrior and a good man, if not a bit stubborn."

Baal snorted. "Well at least we know where she gets it from."

"My lord. She appears to be going through some sort of change. Can you help her?" Seth asked.

Argathos' stare was intent. It was as if he looked into her soul and for all she knew he did. "She must complete his quest. That is if she is worthy."

"Quest? Do I need to go to Egypt?" Katie managed to squeak out.

He shrugged. "Yes. I'm sorry I can't help you further. I can only tell you that your time is limited. Death will take you if you don't hurry. Of course, death will take you if you fail as well." He shimmered and was gone.

Katie stood, mouth agape. "Was he really a god?"

"Yep," Baal replied.

She shoved her fists on her hips. "Well, he was no help at all."

Baal laughed. "Welcome to the club, sweet cheeks. Welcome to the fucking club."

A headache began behind her eyes again and she went to the desk and plopped in the chair, resting her head in her hands. "Baal. You saw my mother's letter. She mentioned your race and said you could help me." Bile rose, but she willed it down. "Can you help me?"

"You should be asking your mate for help, not my people."

She looked up. "What?"

"You should learn to keep your mouth shut," Seth spoke through a clenched jaw.

She glared at the sexy man across the room. "What the hell is he talking about?"

"Nothing. We don't have time for this nonsense. Show us the map so we can begin this journey, and put your fucking shirt on," Seth growled.

SETH GRITTED his teeth and tried to ignore the scent of strawberries that wrapped around him and tempted his resolve. Already the points of his fangs scraped against his tongue and he had to force them to retreat. Being in close proximity to Katie was Hell on earth and when he briefly entertained the thought of claiming her, the dark voice returned to taunt him.

Yes, she would look tasty chained to the bed with our bite marks covering her creamy skin. I bet she tastes better than anything you've ever had.

The visions slammed into him so hard he had to take a step back.

Dude, you okay? Baal had managed to find a way into his head.

It's back, the dark voice telling me to do unspeakable things to Katie.

Damn it.

I'll manage, just stay between her and me.

Baal scowled. *Just where I want to be. Between a vampire and his mate.*

Seth ignored his last comment and focused on the map Katie had spread out on the desk. She looked at him.

"I need to book my flight while you figure this out."

"You don't need a plane. I have a much faster way to get us there," Seth replied as he studied the symbols. He tipped his head and turned the map around, gazing at it from all angles.

"By the way, when do you turn thirty?" he inquired.

"Next month."

He looked up. "How long do you have exactly?" His heart began to pound.

"Three weeks."

Baal shifted beside him. "Holy hell. Well that may explain why your symptoms have increased in frequency."

"Now do you understand why I need your help?"

"Oh, fuck this shit. Seth, if you're not going to tell her then I will. She deserves to know her options."

Seth stared at the map, could feel their eyes burning a hole into him and wouldn't be surprised to smell smoke at any second. Baal was right and maybe if he were truthful with her she would agree that he was too unstable to mate with anyway. He straightened.

"Fine. It seems lately the gods have been intervening and giving us a mate. It looks like they have declared you mine."

At first her laughter started as a snicker then turned into a full-blown snort fest. "Well, first off how do you know this and second, what exactly is a mate? I mean I know my mother mentioned it in her letter, but it sounds so archaic."

"I know this because I am drawn to you like a moth to a flame. The only reason we were able to find you is because I can track you. There is no place you can hide now." He ran his fingers through his hair. "A mate is basically a wife, except we marry for eternity."

Both brows on her delicate face shot up. "I don't think I like the sound of any of that." Then she wrinkled her forehead. "Why do I get the feeling you don't want a mate?"

"Because I'm loco. You're better off with one of Baal's people."

She edged her chair further away from him. "Well, thank you. Yes, I have no desire to have a crazy husband. Actually, I have no desire for any of this and I sure as hell don't want to mate, as you call it, with someone I don't love." She frowned. "Do people like you love?"

Baal crossed his arms over his chest. "What he has neglected to tell you is you may be the only one who can save his life."

In that moment he wanted to kill the demon. "I am beyond saving and yes we love. The connection between mates is deeper than anything a human will ever experience."

"You don't know that." Baal turned to Katie changing the subject back to his sanity. "Marcus, who is also a guardian found his mate who happened to be a human. Her blood and their bond reversed the curse a demon put on them centuries ago. Long story short. Seth has to drink blood to keep up his power. Every time he does he shares the memories of the person he drinks from. With the curse he can't purge them, so basically, he has thousands of people living in his head. If he doesn't find a cure soon, he will succumb to the darkness and turn into an evil that gives even me the shivers."

Seth rolled his eyes. "You would make such a fantastic match-maker. Perhaps you should consider starting your own web page. Now, can we end this discussion?"

"Um, will we have any warning before you turn into Vlad the Impaler?" Katie wrung her hands. He hated seeing her so nervous because of him.

"Oh, believe me. Even Vlad will be small-time compared to a guardian gone rogue," Seth replied. "I have power he didn't. I can hide under the radar." He reminded himself that scaring her was a good thing. "But yes, Baal will know when to kill me." He hoped.

CHAPTER SEVEN

IF KATIE HAD THOUGHT her headache bad before, trying to comprehend everything that had been thrown at her in the last twenty-four hours gave her a migraine. There was simply too much information being hurled at her and she felt as if she would snap at any moment.

"I can't deal with this mate stuff and all. Can we just concentrate on the map and form a plan?"

Seth nodded. "Finally, we agree on something." He ran his index finger across the map. "This indicates there is a hidden tunnel in Seti's tomb. And I'll be damned. The Book of Mitne is said to be there."

"What is this book? The professor said there were no books in the Valley of the Kings."

Seth grunted. "Your human professor would have no clue on these matters. The book is the Book of Light. Mitne, is an old language humans have no idea even exists. It's the one common language between immortals and is older than time itself."

"Really? So, what's it called, this language?"

"Draconic," Baal replied not missing a beat. "It's the language of the dragons or Draki as they are called."

"Oh, for the love of god. Dragons? They are a myth." Though she couldn't help the slight chill that ran up her spine. Demons, gods, why not dragons?

Both men pinned her with narrowed eyes.

"What?"

"Well, don't be surprised when you see a large flying lizard above our heads in the desert." Baal looked to Seth. "We should really have another escort for this trip."

"Yes, I agree."

Katie dropped her lower jaw. "You two are serious?"

They ignored her.

"Who should we ask?" Seth questioned.

Baal scratched his chin. "I'll ask Caleb who he can spare. Be right back. Oh, and behave yourself while I'm gone." He vanished into thin air.

She shook her head. "I'm not sure I'll ever get used to all this nonsense." The other thing that plagued her was the attraction she had toward the crazy vampire. "Remind me when this is over, should I survive, to get my head examined."

She went to the wet bar and poured herself a whiskey. "How long will the demon be gone?"

"Why?"

She nearly jumped out of her skin. Seth had come up behind her and stood so close she could feel his hot breath on the back of her neck.

"Do you fear me, Katie? Before you answer that you should know I can smell your emotions."

She spun to face him, ready for a standoff. "Well then, if that's the case then you should already have your answer."

He bared his fangs. "The demon was foolish to leave you here alone with me. You should know that the urges I have to mate with you could be both of our undoing. Take heed to keep your distance."

She pursed her lips into a thin line. "You're the ass that came over here and bothered me. I was simply pouring myself a drink." She shoved past him, her patience worn thin when suddenly the room filled with light and the demon, along with another man appeared.

"That really has got to be the best way to travel."

The stranger, with his hazel eyes and cropped brown hair smiled. "Actually, flying is far more fun."

"Well, I don't know about that. I've flown plenty and I just can't see how it could compare to...well to the vanishing act you all seem capable of." She took a sip of whiskey.

The handsome stranger looked from Seth to Baal. "She has no idea, huh?"

Seth folded the map and looked as if he were bored. "Katie, this is Diego. He is a dragon."

Laughter erupted and it was so fierce she began to choke. "Really? Well, you are nothing like mythology has led us to believe. And to think, I thought dragons had wings and scales. Baal, didn't you call them a flying lizard?"

The demon's face paled and it was Seth's turn to break into laughter. "I think you have finally met your match. Katie, you have a wicked tongue. I can't say I've ever seen the demon turn ten shades of pale."

The man they called Diego scowled, his gaze bore into Baal. "A lizard? I should char your ass right here. You should be thankful I love my sister in-law and know she'd never forgive me for turning you into ash."

Baal shrugged. "It was a joke."

"Okay, enough of this. Diego, would you be so kind as to escort Katie home?" Seth grabbed a pen and paper from her desk and began jotting a list. "Pack these things and wear comfortable clothes. Come back here when you're done."

She scanned the items. Backpack, jeans, boots, jacket, flashlight, the dagger. She looked up and raised a brow.

"We have no idea what we'll encounter. I've seen you use the blade and you're quite good with it."

"I'll take that as a compliment. Thank you." She set down her glass. "Let me grab my purse then we can hail a cab."

"Uh, I think it best to travel my way," Diego replied.

"Oh, how does this work again?"

He opened his arms. "Step closer."

She obeyed and walked right into his open arms. The last thing she heard was an animal growling before she was sucked into a vortex.

"FANG FACE, get a damn grip. You know the dragon has no desire for your mate," Baal's voice penetrated the hundreds of others screaming at him.

Seth clenched his fists then relaxed. "I'm never going to make it through this. I need an out." He produced his blade and sliced it across his palm. Sweet relief filled him as he watched the blood well up in his hand. He curled his fingers and headed for the bathroom, realizing he couldn't leave any trace of himself for Katie to find. She must never discover what he had done to himself. Another reason he could never mate with her. He was beyond repair.

"Broken," he muttered as he stuck his hand under the faucet and watched his blood mix with the water then swirl down the drain. He splashed water on his face and looked at his reflection in the mirror. Dark eyes stared back at him and he wondered who he really was. He looked the same, but he'd been empty for so long he couldn't even remember what it was like to be whole. He knew the stain now covered over eighty-five percent of his soul. Time was running out and in the last several weeks the growth had sped up. He wasn't even sure if he would make it out of the Valley of the Kings alive. One thing was certain, he needed to make sure Katie got mated. He may not be able to claim his mate, but he could damn sure be certain she was safe and cared for after he was dead. The need to protect her was a primal instinct and he vowed to hold on at least long enough to know that was accomplished.

He stepped from the bathroom. "They are not back yet?"

Baal faced him. "No, but it hasn't been that long."

Seth nodded. "Tell me. Are there any of your men that you'd recommend as a mate for Katie?"

"You serious about this?"

"I've never been more serious about anything."

"We aren't even sure it will work. I mean it's apparent she has been destined for you." Baal shook his head. "What makes you think she can take another?"

Shit, he hadn't thought of that. "I guess I just assumed she could mate with any immortal. After all, her mother did."

"You know how the gods are. If they deemed the two of you to be together then I see no alternative. Besides, my gut tells me her mother didn't have a destined mate."

"Maybe if I had found her a year ago. Hell, even a couple of months ago, but my rate of deterioration has increased. I'm hanging on by a frayed thread." He leveled his gaze on the demon. "I don't have months, I have weeks at best."

"Damn, I hadn't realized you were that far."

"And we come back to the problem of even if I wanted to claim her, I have no way to convert her. Vandeldor is off limits."

Baal paced and Seth wondered if the demon's concern was for him or more for his brethren that would mourn him when he was gone.

"What if you tried taking some of her blood? Maybe it would be enough to slow the darkness."

"We don't know that it would work and it would only place her in danger."

Baal stopped in front of him. "Look, it seems to me you both need each other in order to survive. Neither of you have anything to lose at this point by trying. I think you need to come clean with her and at least give her a chance to turn you down. Both Diego and I will be there to protect her and I'll take your fucking head if you can't contain yourself."

Seth absorbed every word and the demon had several valid points that he hadn't contemplated. "I'll speak to her when she returns." *And what will I say exactly?* What could he offer her? As far as he could see nothing at all other than he was a threat to her safety. He rubbed his temples. What he wouldn't give for a moment of peace and quiet.

"THAT WAS unbelievable and a little less frightening this time since I knew what to expect." Katie had held on for dear life to Diego when they'd been sucked into a void. Seconds later they stood in the middle of her kitchen. "I am forever spoiled on how to travel."

Diego chuckled. "You still haven't experienced the sensation of flight. While you can't shift into a dragon, you can fly with one."

She walked to her hall closet and rummaged for a backpack. "I still can't believe it. If it's true, then how is it there have been no sightings?"

"We can remain cloaked from the human eye and your radar. We used to live in another realm called Vandeldor, but since its demise, we have other areas where we hide."

She pulled out a black canvas pack. "Amazing. Can I watch you shift?"

He looked around. "Not enough room here, but when we reach Egypt then yes. I'd offer you a ride, but I don't want to start a war with Seth."

She looked up from her pack. "Why would that start a war?"

Diego snorted. "You're his mate. He's probably freaking out as we speak because we're alone."

"I don't understand the whole mate thing. Then again no one has really explained it to me." She pulled out the list and went back to the kitchen to grab the flashlight. "What is it exactly?"

"Destiny really. It's different for each species, but in a nutshell? Fate dictates who you will spend eternity with. There is no rhyme or reason that we've been able to figure out and lately it's been even crazier. We all think the gods are up to something with the advent of evil." He laughed. "Hell, they mated my brother to a demon. In all of history that's never happened."

She wrinkled her nose and shoved the next item on the list into the bag. "What about love? I know Seth said there was love, but it all sounds too much like pre-arranged weddings."

"Oh, don't be mistaken. There is love." He shrugged. "Since I'm not mated I can't tell you how it really feels. My sister in-law would be able to. They say it's a deeper connection than any human could ever have. More like soul to soul. I know my brother and his mate would die for each other and not think twice about it."

"Interesting." Maybe she was wrong about this mating thing. Perhaps it needed further investigation if not for herself then to appease her curious nature.

"I just need to change and grab some extra clothes. I'll be right back." He nodded and she marched to her room.

"So why are you doing this? The trip thing?" Diego yelled out.

She shoved a pair of jeans, underwear and a couple of tees into the pack. Then headed for the bathroom. If nothing else a toothbrush and paste was all she needed from there, oh, and a hair brush.

"Didn't they tell you?" she hollered before going back to the bedroom to grab the dagger from its hiding place. She did a quick sweep of the room to make double sure no one was watching and reached behind her dresser to pull the blade from a secret drawer in the back. She strapped the dagger to her hip and pulled on a jacket before she grabbed the pack and headed back to the living room.

"Oh, they told me, I just wondered why *you* are doing it. You seem to be taking things pretty well, for a human." He held up his hand. "No offense." He gave her a funny look. "I thought you were changing?"

"I changed my mind, and if my mother is correct I'm not all human." She stopped beside him. "Truth be told? I will do anything that will aid me in avenging my father's death. If it means traveling with a band of immortals or marrying a crazy vampire, then so be it. I'll deal with the aftermath later."

It wasn't until the words had left her mouth that she realized she would marry, or mate as they called it, the half-baked guardian. It didn't mean she had to stay with him, but if it gained her an extension to her life so she could hunt the demons? Then pity the person who stood in her way.

KATIE AND DIEGO entered her office and she dropped the pack in a chair.

"We need to talk, alone." Seth gave the evil eye to the other two men.

Baal cleared his throat. "Come on Diego, let's go find the bar." The two scurried out and closed the door.

"Sit." Seth directed to the sofa.

"Bossy much?"

"Always. Look. I'm going to be straight with you and tell you everything I know. It seems like the right thing to do."

She put on a fake smile. "Thank you. I think."

"Some of this you have already heard. Yes, I am on the verge of going crazy. The voices in my head are not my own. Hell, I'm not sure I can even tell the difference anymore."

"I can't even begin to imagine what it's like."

"When the curse finally consumes me, they will have to kill me. It's why Baal is here. My glorified babysitter."

"Why do they have to kill you?"

"Because I will no longer have control. We feed from humans.

Blood gives us power, but it is done in such a way as to bring no harm. If the curse takes control, I will forget that I was created to protect. Instead I will become a savage and the havoc even one of my kind can bring on humanity before he can be stopped is something I never wish to bear witness too again. Factor in that I am an ancient, the first guardian created and that makes me more cunning than my brethren. I could take out entire cities before anyone could stop me."

A chill crawled up her spine. It was hard to imagine the handsome, soft-spoken man in front of her was capable of such acts. Then again, he almost seemed to have a split personality. One moment kind and the next he was barking orders and issuing threats. She had to remind herself of what she was dealing with, but it didn't sway her decision.

"You should also know that the voices tell me to do unspeakable things to you. It's also why I have directed Baal to stay between us."

"What kind of things?" she whispered almost disgusted with herself for wanting to know.

"It's best you didn't know. Anyway, Marcus, who is one of my brethren, found his mate and she was the cure to his curse. Baal thinks you may be my cure, but we don't know if Marcus and Cassie were a fluke. I'm also so far gone I'm not sure our mating would work and then..." He shook his head.

"What? Please finish."

"So many factors. If we were able to complete the mating which I'm not even sure how to do since you're not totally human. Well, if my curse wasn't cured then my death would be painful for you in more ways than you could imagine."

"I get the feeling this mating is more than walking down the aisle in a white gown."

"With Cassie, she was transformed into one of us. That act took her mate drinking her blood until she was near death then placing her in stasis. I don't have the option of placing you in stasis nor do we even know what that would do to you." He jumped up and began pacing. "Fuck, you're the daughter of a god which makes you a demigod. That alone makes no sense why they would choose a mate below your station." He stopped suddenly. "I am so stupid."

"What?"

He ran to the door and flung it open. "Baal! Get in here."

The other two men came rushing in. "What's wrong?" Baal asked, looked over Katie as if to assess her condition.

"Lileta," Seth said.

Baal pinned him with golden eyes. "What about her?"

"She's the daughter of a demigod, hence one herself. Maybe she could shed some light on this?" Seth questioned.

Baal scratched his chin and Diego's eyes lit up.

"We can go to her. I'm not sure how much help she could be, but maybe she could help Katie in some way," Diego said.

Katie had no idea who this Lileta was, but if there was even a slim chance Lileta could help she wanted to take it. After the conversation she'd just had with Seth, it had caused her to sway for a moment. However, she had promised retribution for her father and nothing would stop her. Even placing herself in harm's way. "Yes, I like this plan. Can I see her before our trip?"

Diego nodded. "Let me connect with her and ask. I'm sure she'll agree."

While the dragon appeared to be having some sort of mental conversation with his sister-in-law, Baal stepped in beside them.

"You should know that Lileta and I do not share the same father. It was only recently that we found out her father is Lowan."

Katie was sure she had a puzzled look on her face. As she started to open her mouth to speak, Baal held up a hand.

"Lowan is the ass who is unleashing all the demons. He is the grandson of Hades himself."

She felt her jaw drop several inches. "Hades? Your sister is related to Hades?" Could things really get much worse?

"Actually, he's not altogether a bad god. His grandson on the other hand is the product of a guardian and another demon High Lord that just happened to be Hades' son, Drayos."

"Well, if he isn't so bad, then why doesn't he stop the madness?"

"Because Lowan is blood. Imagine killing your own grandson? The other gods can't interfere because Lowan is a demigod. That leaves the rest of us to take care of shit," Baal stated.

She felt another headache coming on.

"Lileta says she would love to meet you."

Good. The more she learned, the more she wanted to be part of this fight they kept referring to. It also sounded like getting rid of Lowan might stop the rest of the demons. There had to be a way to locate this demigod. She retrieved her pack. "Let's go."

IT ONLY TOOK seconds for the group to appear in the entry to the Draki king's home and Lileta was there waiting to greet them. She hugged both her brother and Diego before she moved to Katie. Seth watched with a wary eye. His distrust of everything and everyone no doubt brought on by the darkness. He knew there was nothing to fear from the female demon.

"You must be Katie. I'm Lileta." She extended her hand. "It's nice to meet you."

"I'm pleased to meet you as well. I'm told maybe you can help."

Lileta's golden eyes closed as she continued to hold onto Katie's hand. Several seconds passed before she opened them again. She smiled. "You have the mark of a goddess."

"W-what?" Katie stammered.

Seth was beside her in a heartbeat. "What do you mean a goddess?"

Lileta nodded. "She has the mark to become a goddess. At the moment, her transformation hasn't occurred." She looked back at Katie. "I'm not sure how though. I mean how you transform. I can see your body is in turmoil and wants to shift. Probably into the Phoenix." She shook her head, a frown on her face. "I'm not sure what it means, but I can see your time is limited. If we don't figure it out you'll burn up alive."

"Son of a bitch. I've never known a demigod to become more than what they were. This is interesting." Katie had been out of his league as a demigod, but as a goddess? She was untouchable. What the hell were the gods thinking?

Lileta looked at him. "I understand your hesitancy to mate, but have you thought about exchanging a small amount of blood?"

Katie wrinkled her nose and cringed. Apparently, blood exchange wasn't going to be an option. Lileta touched her arm.

"I know it sounds...well, gross. Maybe it will help to slow down the process for both of you. If you are really meant to be together it can't hurt. Perhaps you can find a more tasteful way."

Katie looked from Lileta to Seth. He was unable to read her eyes.

"I'll think about it. That's all I can promise."

Lileta smiled. "It's all anyone can ask." She pulled Katie into a hug. "I wish you the best." She stepped back. "Will you be leaving soon?"

"I think we should wait until nightfall," Diego replied.

Seth nodded in agreement. There was no sense in making the trip during the daylight. Too many people would be around to ask far too many questions.

"Good. You can stay for dinner then. Caleb will be home soon and I'd love to show Katie around."

He watched Lileta drag his mate away.

"What next?" Baal slid in next to him.

"She will have my blood, like it or not." If there was even the slightest chance he could save her, then he would make it so. He only had to devise a plan.

LILETA LED Katie across golden marble floors and through an over-sized room that held several statues. They ranged in size from as tall as her to nearly three times her height. The colors were all different. From solid black, to red, to bronze. The only thing they held in common was, they were dragons. She wanted to stop and inspect each one, enjoy their beauty but Lileta continued at a clipped pace to an arched opening on the other side.

When she stepped through, she found herself on a large balcony that overlooked a valley of green grasses, and a multitude of wild flowers. Mountains capped with white peaks loomed in the distance. The picture was breathtaking.

"Where are we?"

The woman next to her smiled. "Deep in the Carpathian Mountains. No man steps foot here and even if they did this place would be hidden from their eyes."

"Romania?"

"Yes," the demon replied.

"I've never seen anything so spectacular." Katie could stare at it all day. For the first time in forever she had a sense of peace, but doubted it would last long. This moment in time was the calm before a storm that she had no idea if she'd survive. To find out that she was a demigod was shock enough, but a goddess? She wasn't even sure she comprehended. It was all surreal.

She strained to see something in the distance. A bird flitted—no it was bigger than a bird. It flew closer and flashes of gold nearly blinded her. She put her hand up to help cover the glare of the sun. "What is that?"

Lileta laughed. "That would be our ward, Leria. Her father was Odage and his mind was taken over by Lowan. He was put to death by the guardian king for his crimes against humanity. Caleb and I consider her our daughter now."

The creature drew closer and Katie could see just how spectacular it was. "A dragon! A real live..." She slapped her palm over her mouth and watched in awe as the beast the size of a small private jet hovered in front of them. Bright golden eyes stared back at her from a giant head with two beautiful horns. Lileta grabbed her hand.

"Come on." She led her across the balcony to a set of steps where they descended to a large rocky outcrop.

The dragon landed with more grace than she would have ever expected. Lileta dragged her closer, but Katie hesitated.

"Don't be afraid," Lileta whispered.

The creature lowered its head level with hers. Warm eyes gazed at her and she was compelled to extend her hand. The beast nuzzled its nose into her palm and Katie sucked in a breath.

"I don't know why I was expecting a cold nose."

Lileta chuckled beside her. "Dragons are anything but cold."

"You're beautiful." She would have never imagined the creatures of lore would first off really exist and second be so majestic. "Do they all look like you?"

Wind and flashes of color swirled around the dragon, its imposing body began to shrink and before she could blink a beautiful young woman stood in front of her. Her jet-black hair flowed down her shoulders and her blue eyes sparkled.

"No, we all look a little different," the girl replied.

Lileta stepped next to the girl and placed an arm around her shoulder. "Leria, this is Katie. She is a friend of Seth's."

The girl extended her hand. "I'm pleased to meet you."

"And I you."

"Sweetie, how were your lessons?" Lileta asked.

"Jax says I'm going to be a force to be reckoned with and I'm a natural with a blade." She kissed Lileta on the cheek. "Caleb had some things to do, but said he'd be home soon. I'm going to shower." She looked back to Katie. "Nice to meet you." Then scurried off.

"She is beautiful in both forms. How old is she?"

"Thank you, she just celebrated her eighteenth birthday. She has had to grow up fast and already she has broken the hearts of many Draki. Several had hoped she would be their mate, but so far it doesn't seem to be in her future."

Katie liked this demon and what a surprise since she'd been killing them for years. It pleased her that not all of them were the evil spawn of Hell. "I know I don't have a clue about how the other half lives, but isn't she rather young to be thinking about such things?"

Lileta stared out over the valley. "Things are different in our world. At eighteen her mate can claim her and I fear that will start a war of its own."

"I don't understand."

Lileta let out a laugh. "None of us do really. I can only say that the man who is her destiny will likely meet the sharp end of Leria's blade and gods help us all if he can't convince her not to kill him."

"Oh." What the hell else was there to say? Katie had no right to question their ways. They fought their own demons except in their case they knew more about the evil of the world than she could ever imagine. Hell, she couldn't even understand what was happening to her own body and how she fit into the scheme of things.

"We should head back. Help me in the kitchen?"

"I'd love to." Finally, something to keep her busy. "Can I ask you something?"

Lileta offered a warm smile. "Of course. I'm sure you have tons of questions and I'll help any way I can."

"That's an understatement. What can you tell me about this mating thing?"

Her companion stopped and faced her. "It is a love and a bond like you will never experience with a human male. I don't mean to belittle what humans have, but the connection Caleb and I have...Well you know when you get those butterflies and you can't stand to be apart?"

Katie nodded.

"It's like that but ten times more intense and it never fades. I carry part of his soul and he mine. There is never any guessing what the other is feeling because you will experience their emotions." She laughed. "They will know when they've pissed you off and work even harder to try and fix it."

It sounded blissful, but there had to be problems. "If you always know what the other is feeling how do you ever have any privacy?" That was one thing she would never give up.

"For us it's simple, we just throw up a block. You can opt to let people in or not and you'll learn. As a goddess you will become very powerful."

"I don't know what to think of all this." Though she had already tossed Seth out of her head.

Lileta looped her arm around Katie's. "Come on, let's go fix dinner and we can chat. I can't wait for you to meet Caleb."

CHAPTER NINE

AFTER AN EARLY DINNER, Katie had gone to one of the guest rooms for some much needed rest before they departed later in the evening. Seth tossed idea after idea out the window on how he was going to convince Katie to take his blood. He'd thought about sneaking some into her wine, but then worried diluting it might change the affect. *Why does the damn woman have to be so stubborn?*

Finally, he decided to try speaking with her again. If that failed he wasn't above resorting to force. She may end up hating him, hell he was pretty sure she did already so no loss there. His fate was already sealed, but hers didn't have to be. Hopefully, once he was gone she could then choose who she wanted to be with. Fall in love with another god perhaps?

The thought caused him to snarl.

"I'm going to Katie's room," he announced to Baal.

"You sure that be wise?"

"Probably not," Seth replied.

"You got twenty minutes then I'm coming in."

Seth eyed the demon. He was really beginning to like the man and had no doubt Baal would indeed be barging in at twenty minutes on the dot. "Noted." He stormed off down the corridor and toward the guest wing of the Draki leader's home. He stopped at the door and stretched out his senses. She was awake. Good. He was going to just barge in, but thought a more civil approach might be best. Raising his hand, he knocked.

"Come in," Katie called from the other side.

He turned the handle and pushed open the door. "I sensed you were awake."

She sat propped up in bed and flipped through a magazine. "Yes. I find sleep hard to come by these days."

He stepped inside and closed the door behind him. If Katie was uncomfortable, she never showed it. She was a strong woman and it was one thing among many he liked about her.

"I came to speak to you about taking my blood."

She set down her magazine and crossed her arms over her breasts. "I'm not drinking blood. You may be a vampire, but I am not." Her blue eyes challenged him.

"I will not disagree. However, you are meant for great things, Katie O'Hara and if you're dead they will never come to pass."

Her eyes softened. "I don't know what I'm supposed to do or become. But you, you're a guardian and your life is much more valuable than mine." She tilted her head. "Why is it you aren't asking to take my blood? What if I'm the answer to keeping you sane?"

He smiled. "You are my mate, therefore your happiness, your health and your life will always come before mine or anyone else. I am beyond help, but perhaps when I'm gone you can live a happy life." He wanted to choke on those words, but his happiness was never meant to be. "Besides, you can't kill any demons if you're six feet under."

She raised a questioning brow.

"I know you want to avenge your father's death. Let me help you."

KATIE WAS certain she had a blank stare as she looked at Seth. Other than her father, there had been nobody to give a shit about her or her welfare. Then again, she was a loner. Didn't make close friends because she was always afraid they would somehow be used against her. Who knew what the demons she had been fighting these past few years were capable of? They had killed both of her parents after all.

"What do you want in return?" There had to be a catch, always was. She tried to study him for a reaction, but he remained stoic. Did the man ever show emotions? She found herself wondering if he was capable of any then remembered what he had done for her father. That was definitely not the act of a man without feelings.

"Nothing. As I said, I only want you to live."

"That's very admirable of you. I just don't think I could bring myself to drink blood." The thought made her stomach roll, but he was correct in that she both wanted revenge and therefore needed to live.

"I understand. It won't take much, a few drops perhaps and I think I can help you with it."

"Can you do some kind of compulsion on me?" She pulled her bottom lip through her teeth.

"No, I tried that already and you are immune. However, I might be able to help you relax, make it more pleasurable. Besides, I don't see any alternatives at this point."

She tried to relax, but her body kept tensing at the thought of drinking blood and her stomach lurched. "No, I suppose there's not." She let out an exasperated sigh. "All right, if you can keep me from gagging or tossing my cookies then I guess we can try it." *I can't believe I just agreed to this.*

He slid in next to her on the bed. "You are feverish. How do you feel right now?"

"Like my head is going to explode."

"The timing is good then." He stretched out and spread his legs.

"Come sit here and lean your back against my chest." He patted the spot on the bed.

She swallowed. Memories of how her body had reacted to him earlier came flooding back and she wasn't sure she liked the idea of being so close to him. "How do I know you won't go bonkers on me and do something stupid?"

"I can only ask you to trust me. My honor is all I have to offer." He smiled. "Plus, there are several who would flash in here in seconds should you scream."

Something told her his honor meant a great deal to him, plus the thought of the others close by offered comfort, so she complied and moved to the spot he had indicated. Stretched her legs out and leaned into his chest. As she feared, her body immediately recognized the hard muscles she'd felt before. Every inch of him was like steel and she bit her lip and wondered if the erection between his legs would be the same. Her answer came as his thickness pressed into her lower back.

Her pulse increased and heat flooded her core. *Damn it!* Now was not the time for her libido to kick in.

"I'm going to bite my wrist, bleed a little then heal it. You'll only have to lick up what is there. I'll connect to your mind and give you something else to think about."

"O-okay." She was beginning to think perhaps it was better to simply drink the damn blood since it might take her mind off the lust that coursed through her.

Katie.

"Oh shit, that's weird." She wondered how he did that? Speak in her mind.

I'm going to send you mental images then press my wrist to your lips. When I do...

"I got it." *Hurry up before I change my mind.*

In seconds pictures of rolling green hills and stone fences appeared. Sheep dotted the landscape and grazed leisurely. In the distance she could see the ocean as it crashed against jagged cliffs.

The images so real it was like she was really there. Something was pressed against her mouth and she parted her lips to accept the sweet taste of chocolate.

Umm, tastes so good. She swore she heard Seth moan and his erection grew more rigid. His wrist was gone and she was disappointed because she wanted more of the sweet elixir. The pictures faded too and when she blinked she was back in the guest bedroom of the Draki's home. Strong arms were circled around her waist and with them came a safety she had never known before. Not even her father had been able to give her this level of comfort.

"Are you all right?"

She searched for her voice. Never before had a man rattled her to such an extreme and she had to fight the urge to turn to him and find out if his lips tasted the same as his blood. Her pulse raced and butterflies did acrobatics in her gut. Holy hell, if a few drops of blood did this to her, what would more do? Or for that matter, what would sex with him be like? Her body begged her to find out, but with the intake of a sharp breath, she finally managed to find semi-calm and turned her head to meet Seth's blue stare. "How did you know?"

"I know many things about you, Katie O'Hara."

She bit back a tear. He had given her a glimpse of her homeland, Ireland. A place she had always wanted to see, but had not had the opportunity. "Thank you." She licked her lips as she stared at his. He leaned closer and looked as if he might kiss her and she desperately wanted him to.

The door swung open with a great force and a man cleared his throat. Katie jumped and scooted away, back to the other side of the king-size bed. Baal stood in the doorway with a sly grin on his face.

"Twenty minutes," he exclaimed, pointing to a non-existent watch on his wrist.

"Your timing is impeccable," Seth growled.

"Great. Well glad to see you both in one piece. I'll just be out here." He jabbed his thumb toward the corridor. "Carry on." He closed the door behind him.

"Now what?" Katie asked. The magical moment lost and probably for the best.

"Now we wait and see what happens. The answer should come quickly."

"Will you wait here with me?" She would never admit she was scared. "I don't want to turn into something that will endanger anyone here. If that should happen, please kill me."

TIME STOOD STILL and a calm like he'd not experienced in decades washed over Seth when he'd held Katie in his arms and gave her his lifeblood. He'd worried the dark one—as he'd not so fondly nicknamed the bastard in his head—would make an appearance, but he'd remained silent. It had been a long time since he'd felt like he had done something worthy and feeding his mate had been satisfying. Having her so close was like heaven. A place he wished he could spend eternity, but he would not be claiming her. She deserved better than him and she needed stability, something he lacked. Still, it didn't stop him from wanting her. Needing her.

Katie sat on the other side of the bed and chewed her bottom lip. He desired nothing more than to nibble on the swollen flesh himself and perhaps make her forget her troubles. Having had her so close to him caused an erection so hard he dared not move, knowing how painful it would be. Instead he placed a pillow over his lap to hide his arousal. Part of him wanted to throttle Baal for interrupting. He'd been desperate to taste her mouth, still was. The other half was grateful the demon had kept his word. He was positive had he kissed her it would not have stopped there.

"How do you feel?"

"Actually, my headache is lessening a bit."

"That's good. Let's wait a while longer and see if anything else changes."

She nodded and picked up the magazine she'd been looking

though when he came in. He had to stifle a groan when she flicked out her tongue to lick her fingertips and turned the page.

"What's wrong?"

He wrinkled his brow. "Nothing, why you ask?"

"I thought I heard you moan. You in pain?" She held a look of concern.

"No." *Yes.*

"There, your mouth said no, but your... Oh hell, you're still in my head."

He blinked. "No, I swear I disconnected from you."

Her eyes widened. "Then why can I still hear you?"

"Maybe it's my blood?" No way had such a small amount started a bond.

She pursed her lips. "Do you know what I'm thinking?"

He cocked his head. "I'd say from the look on your face you'd like to throttle me?"

"Good guess. Are you saying you aren't in my head?"

"I'm saying exactly that. Unless you'd like me to go there, I have no idea what is in that pretty little head of yours."

"Stay out!"

He couldn't help but chuckle. "Yes, ma'am."

She narrowed her gaze. "Are you patronizing me?"

"Not at all. How do you feel now?"

Katie closed her beautiful blue eyes for a moment then opened them. "Much better."

He nodded. "I sense your temperature has returned to normal as well. You should try and get some rest. We'll leave in a couple of hours." He swung his feet over the edge of the bed and stood. "I'll leave you now." His feet felt like they were encased in concrete as he walked to the door. He exited the room and passed Baal in the corridor.

"Sorry dude, but we agreed."

Seth held up a hand. "No, I'm glad you're a man of your word. I need to be alone."

The dark one had returned and Seth needed to find some place private. He closed his eyes and flashed outside. The rocky outcrop gave him an exceptional view of the moon as it danced across the valley. At least he could enjoy it while he inflicted his pain. It seemed such a contradiction and almost wrong that he be in such beautiful surroundings while his mind was in the darkest of places. He pulled the dagger from its sheath, rolled up his sleeve, twisted his arm palm up and made one long slice from his wrist up to his elbow. Blood welled and the voice in his head laughed. Sweat beaded at his temples. What he really wanted was a fix, but he had promised and knew it was for the best. Katie needed him to get her through this journey.

"I make an oath to the gods, I swear I will see you to Egypt and back, Katie. After that, I can't vow anything."

He shoved the blade through his palm until it came out the other side. He gritted his teeth and the dark one quieted, left him with only the thousands of other voices. At least those he could deal with. As he pulled the knife back out of his hand, a tear slid down his cheek. The only other time in his entire existence he had ever shed one was for Vivian. Now he cried for Katie. His beautiful mate that he could never claim.

CHAPTER TEN

IT WAS the middle of the night when they finally arrived at the desert location where the Valley of the Kings loomed in the distance. It was decided they would 'pop in' as Katie liked to call it on the outskirts then approach by foot so they—or in this case—her companions could detect any disturbance. She may have been loath to admit it earlier, but now that they stood in the middle of an expanse of sand with only stars to light the way, Katie was glad to have the other immortals help. To think she had originally planned to come here alone, now looked like a ridiculous idea.

Diego flew high overhead and searched for danger. He also planned to land completely cloaked and do a ground sweep in case he missed anything from the air. In the meantime, she, Seth, and Baal trudged through the sand only a short distance away. They hadn't gotten far when Diego landed in front of them and shifted.

"I detected demons. I'm guessing they are Lowan's goons since they're Wendigo," Diego stated.

"Ahh, son of a bitch! I hate those fuckers," Baal groaned.

"How many?" Seth questioned.

"At least four." Diego shifted his weight. It was evident the dragon was itching to fight.

"Oh, one for each of us. Let's go." Katie felt pretty damn good since she'd had a taste of Seth's blood and was ready to take on the world. She pulled her blade from its sheath.

Seth touched her arm. "While I've seen you fight and you are remarkable with that dagger, you have no idea what you're up against. These creatures are the foulest."

"Right, not even I like them and I'm a demon." Baal gave a visible shiver.

"Well we can't stand out here forever. I'm going to make a guess and say that whatever lies inside those tombs is real, else why would the demons be hanging around?" Katie wanted to get this over with. Her clock was ticking and getting louder every second.

"I don't disagree, but we need to form a solid plan before we go storming in there," Seth said.

"I second that. I've no desire to be tortured by one of those beasts. Again. Ever." Baal put emphasis on the last part of his statement and Katie wondered what they had done to him. Probably best to never find out.

"I can try and go in cloaked, but I'm not sure how far I'll get without getting stuck. Those passages can be pretty narrow."

"No, Diego, we don't need you trashing the place. We're going to have to try and draw them out to us. Best if they didn't know we have a Draki in our midst." Seth grinned. "You can be our secret weapon."

Diego slapped his hands together and rubbed. "You get them out into the open and I'll toast 'em."

"I have a plan," Seth declared.

Several minutes later, Katie had sheathed her weapon in exchange for her hands being bound behind her back. The plan involved the demons thinking she was a captive and of course, they'd want to steal her for themselves. Seeing how they would be able to detect their approach, it was the only plan they could come up with. Diego would take to the sky and cloak himself. He only needed enough room between them and the demons to make his attack. Fine with her. After hearing how these men were actually afraid of the Wendigo, Katie wasn't sure she wanted to meet up with them either.

"Stop looking at me with drool on your lip," she snapped at Seth.

"Sorry. My dark side has itched to see you tied up. Though the circumstances are different, this is still pretty damn sexy."

Baal chuckled to her left. She shifted in his direction. "I thought you were supposed to protect me from him?"

His golden eyes flashed at her. "I am. Has he harmed you?"

Katie stumbled through the sand, her temper about to detonate like a stack of TNT. She wasn't sure who she was more pissed at, them for coming up with the idea or herself for going along with it. Either way she hated being helpless.

"You are anything but helpless. The rope is loose enough you can pull your wrists free," Seth replied.

She pinned him with a glare. "Get out of my fucking head!" One of these times she was going to kick the shit out of him. Maybe as soon as this upcoming fight was over.

"I sense them stirring." Seth held up a hand for them to halt.

"Demons! Show yourselves," Baal yelled.

A dark figure loomed in the doorway. There wasn't enough light for Katie to get a good look, but she could tell the demon was as tall and wide as the opening in which it stood. "Holy shit. I've never seen one so big."

"Wait til you see the ugly fuck up close," Baal whispered.

She wasn't sure she wanted to. The scent of death hung heavy in the air and she had to swallow hard to keep from vomiting. Seth leaned into her.

"You okay?"

"Fine," she managed through gritted teeth. The fact that he could sense her distress only fueled her anger even more.

"You have something we want," came a raspy voice from the darkness.

"And what would that be?" Seth asked

"The dagger, but we will take the girl too," came back the reply.

Seth took two steps forward. "She is my prisoner, come out and we can barter."

The Wendigo made a noise that sounded like a cross between a laugh and a growl. Katie wasn't sure what to make of it.

"We don't barter, we simply take."

"Well, either way you ugly fuckers are going to have to come out here and take her," Seth interjected.

Baal glared at the guardian. "Way to piss him off more, vampire."

The demon proceeded down the small ramp followed by three more large figures. If Diego's count was correct, all of them were coming out into the open.

Katie, get ready to run. Seth's voice slammed into her head. She loosened her restraints and fondled the handle of her dagger. Ready to break free at a moment's notice.

I still don't get why we can't do the flashy thing you do? To run seemed absurd.

Because we need them out in the open and away from the tombs. Chasing us will do that. Besides, they will anticipate us flashing and running will surprise the hell out of them and cause them to hesitate.

She still thought it was a stupid idea and her heart beat erratically in her chest as the demons drew closer. It was still too dark to see clearly. However, what she could tell was they towered at least seven feet tall, had a massive head with lots of sharp teeth and damn if they weren't the most frightening things she'd ever encountered.

"It looks like we outnumber you. If you surrender, perhaps we will go easy on you." The one who had spoken to them before bared his fangs while the others proceeded to try and circle around them.

Run.

She didn't have to be told twice. Matter of fact she was more than happy to bow out of the fight. She dropped the rope that bound her, freed her dagger and turned to flee. Her senses said the other two were right behind her, but she dared not look back to make sure. Running in sand was difficult enough. Add to it their lives were on the line and yeah, she needed to concentrate on how fast she could escape.

Explosions rocked the ground and someone tackled her. Katie started to fight back when she recognized the hard body that pinned her to the ground. She was able to peek around Seth just in time to catch Baal lob a ball of flames at the demons right before Diego swooped low and shot out one long stream of fire. First one demon became engulfed then the rest went into a blazing inferno. The creatures screeched before they turned to ash.

Diego landed and shifted while Seth helped her to her feet. She brushed sand from her jeans. "That was incredible, but remind me to never piss him off." She referred to Diego.

"Indeed. It pays to have a Draki as a friend." Seth brushed sand from her hair. "Are you all right?"

His constant concern for her welfare warmed her insides. "I'm fine. What about you?"

"I'll survive."

They approached Diego while she still tried to get the sand off her. When they were close enough, she ran to the dragon and threw her arms around him.

"That was awesome! Thank you." There was a low growl behind her. And Diego grabbed her arms and untangled himself.

"Katie, unless you want a fight between your mate and I, you should refrain from touching me."

She pulled back and looked at Seth. His eyes glowed and his lip curled into a snarl. A hint of fang showed. She stepped away from Diego. Would have chided the guardian with the fact that she could touch any man she chose, but thought better of it. She didn't really want to see the two of them fight. Besides, it wasn't fair to Diego to put him in the middle.

HE TRIED NOT to show emotion when she'd run into the arms of another man, but there was no stopping it even though he knew it was nothing and the young shifter wasn't a threat. Instinct had no reasoning.

"I don't sense any other demons, but we need to remain on high alert. That was too easy and could have been a trap," Seth said.

"Agreed," the other two men stated in unison.

"Katie, you will stay between Baal and myself."

She moved in next to him as they headed for the entrance to the tombs. "You don't own me, you know."

"I'm well aware," he growled, not meaning to, then stopped to face her. "Just do me and everyone else a favor. Stay out of other men's arms. At least until I'm dead. I can only control myself for so long and I really don't want to fight over you." He watched her features go from hurt to schooled in a matter of seconds. Had he really meant to scold her like that? Under normal circumstances he would have had more patience. However, the voices were beating against his brain and he only wanted to put this mission behind them. Without another word, he headed to the entrance then stopped at the locked barrier.

"Um, won't they have some kind of security?" Katie asked.

Baal stepped forward and touched the door. A loud clank indicated it was unlocked. "Don't worry, my magic will fool any security they have in place. It will look like any boring night with the dead." He pushed the heavy door and walked through.

Seth waved Katie in and followed behind her, Diego took up the rear. There were dim lights along the corridor, most likely so the people who monitored the cameras could get a good look around.

"According to the map, we need to head this way," Baal stated and led them through the entryway. They walked by several displays. Most showcased ancient artifacts, some real and some replicas.

Seth watched Katie move in front of him, her head turned back and forth as she tried to take in her surroundings. He wished they had more time, he could show her so many things and tell her about the secrets the tombs held. After all, he had been alive when it was first constructed. Hell, he'd actually lived through every king that graced these tombs. However, even he was surprised by the map and had to admit he was a bit skeptical that they would turn up with anything.

When the foursome finally reached the tomb the map had indicated, Katie faltered. He reached for her, grabbed her arm and spun her to face him. Pain filled her eyes.

"What's happening?" He tried to enter her mind, but he was blocked.

Her lip trembled. "V-voices. So many." She cradled her head in her palms. "Oh, god, it hurts."

"Give her your blood."

Thank gods for Baal and his voice of reason.

Seth cradled her to his chest and slid down the wall to rest on the floor. "Give us some privacy."

Diego nodded. "We've gotcha covered." Then he and the demon slipped into the darkness.

Seth bit his wrist then pressed it to Katie's lips. "You have to drink. I'm sorry I can't get in your head to help you." She latched on without hesitation and he worried how bad it must be that she wouldn't even resist. After a minute and at least one mouthful of blood she pulled back and licked her lips.

"You made it taste like chocolate again." Her eyes told him how grateful she was.

"I didn't do anything. You had a barrier up that I was unable to breach."

She blinked her beautiful blue eyes that were clearer than only moments ago. "I'm not sure how I would do that. All I know is it felt like my head was going to explode."

"Can you tell me about it?"

Her gaze dropped to her lap. "Dark evil voices. So many it was hard to make out what they were saying. There was one however, it stood out among the others and..."

She'd fallen silent so he tipped her chin up then cupped her cheek. "I can't help you unless I know. What did it say?"

She swallowed. "It showed me visions of you cutting yourself."

He schooled his features. What the fuck had happened that she had seen such a thing. Was it possible? No.

Katie? He tried to reach for her mind again.

"What?"

"I just wanted to see if the barrier was still there. Are you all right now?"

"Yes. Much better. Is this part of the whole mating thingie?"

"I'm not sure what's happening."

Her eyes narrowed and she studied him like a virus under a microscope. "You're not telling me everything. Earlier, when you came to my room you opened up and I felt like you trusted me enough to tell me the truth and let me make up my own mind. Don't stop now."

He could deny her nothing. "I'm not a hundred percent certain, but I think somehow you were hearing the voices inside my head."

"Dear god. That's what you have to listen to all the time?"

"Yes."

"What about the visions? Why did I see you shoving a dagger into your thigh?"

Hell if he wanted to tell her the truth. For some reason he cared what she thought of him and that wasn't a side of him he wanted her to see. Then again, maybe it would disgust her enough she'd understand why he chose not to mate with her.

"Those visions you saw were real."

Her jaw dropped. "You cut yourself? Why?"

He released her from his embrace and helped her to her feet. "The pain calms the voices."

She gave him a skeptical look. "I still feel like you're not telling me everything."

There was no need for her to know all of his dark past. It was bad enough she'd not only heard the voices in his head, but also seen him doing unspeakable acts to himself. There was no way he was telling her the man he'd drunk from to find her had planned to kidnap her and do horrible things to her. He was confident that was who the dark one was.

"We need to get going." He helped her through the dim corridor.

CHAPTER ELEVEN

KATIE LET Seth lead her back to the others, but had decided their previous conversation wasn't over. He was keeping something from her and she didn't understand why, but it bothered her. Immensely. Maybe it was the fact she now had a much better understanding and appreciation for what he went through. She was also grateful beyond words for his help, because she was pretty sure if the voices had not shut up she would have found her way to the highest point and jumped.

She made a mental note to get the demon, Baal, off to the side and interrogate him. Something told her he would be much more cooperative in answering her questions.

When they finally approached Seti's tomb, Seth moved to the back wall. "The hidden corridor should be here." He ran his hands over the stone surface.

Baal stepped beside him. "I suspect there will be a trap of some sort."

Seth nodded. "I think if we're smart about this... Katie, can you come here?"

Katie broke away from looking at the scenes depicted on the walls, wishing she had more time to study them and sidled up on Seth's other side. "Do you know how to get in?"

"You're the daughter, therefore I believe you are the key to unlock the door. The map indicated a symbol of the Phoenix on the floor. Everyone start searching."

They all spread out, flashlights in hand, starting in the center of the room and worked their way outward. It was tedious and Katie's back ached from being bent over, but they needed to find it. Time was not on their side and soon the workers would show up to begin their day.

"Over here." Diego waved.

Everyone scurried to the corner where the Draki stood. He pointed. "Down there, it's faint." He stepped back and let Seth in to take a look.

"Yes, it's very faint but I think that's it." He grabbed Katie's arm. "Sorry, but you're going to have to bleed."

"What?" Panic raced through her.

"You're going to have to bleed on the symbol to open the door. It's the only way to prove who you are."

"Oh, right. I got this." She pulled her dagger out and made a slice across her finger, wincing against the pain. The blood pooled and one, then two drops hit their mark and hissed like acid on steel.

"Something's happening," Baal said. "Keep at it."

Katie lifted her head to stare at the demon. "Shall I just gash my wrist?"

He shrugged. "Whatever suits you."

She rolled her eyes and held back a giggle. The demon had a smarter mouth than she did and that she could respect. She glanced at Seth and noticed he stared at her bloody finger. The look in his eyes one of hunger, then he flicked out his tongue and licked his lips before he tore his gaze away. A few more splats of her precious life force and a rumble started to shake the ground.

"Look, the wall is moving." Diego pointed at the opposite corner where the wall had slid back several feet. She brought her finger to her mouth and sucked on the wound.

"I'd kill for a band-aid about now."

"With my blood in your veins, you shouldn't need one." Seth whispered in her ear as he passed by. She shined the flashlight on her finger and gasped.

"It's healed."

"Let's move out of here. This place will be swarming with humans soon," Diego called out as he disappeared through the opening.

"Stupid dragon," Baal yelled. "You want to get your head cut off? What if there is a trap on the other side." The demon went next, shaking his head.

Seth looked at Katie. "This is it. We have no idea what awaits us on the other side. Extreme caution needs to be used. Are you ready?"

Katie noticed his fangs had made a special appearance. "My blood do that to you?" She indicated toward his mouth.

He swallowed. "You are mine, therefore the scent of your blood is hard to resist."

"Why don't you taste? I mean maybe it will help you." She surprised herself, but meant every word.

He shook his head and took a step back. Fear flashed in his eyes. "I can't trust myself to stop. Now the others wait. Are you ready?"

"Not really, but what choice do I have. It seems my fate lies on the other side of that stone wall." Whatever it may be. Good, bad, ugly or indifferent, she had to take a leap of faith and pray it was the right choice. She pulled her shoulders back, lifted her chin and walked through the opening. Seth was on her heels when the wall moved back into position leaving them in total darkness. Someone produced a torch and she almost laughed at how archaic it was yet it fit the situation. Diego went first, followed by Baal, herself and Seth right behind her. The passage was narrow, hot and lacked fresh air.

She shined her flashlight on the floor so she wouldn't trip on some-thing she probably didn't want to see anyway. Sweat trickled down the back of her neck and she wished she'd had the foresight to tie her hair up. Her tee clung to her and all she could think of was a shower.

They walked until her legs ached from a steady decline and she had to wonder how far into the center of the earth they had descended.

"Can you see any end to this sardine box ahead?" she groaned.

"Not yet, but I can feel fresh air," Diego replied

The dragon was right. She inhaled and brought the coolness into her lungs and prayed for something other than the tight squeeze they had passed through. Seconds later she received her wish as the passage widened into a small room. In the center stood a stone pedestal and on top of it lay a book.

"Serious? It can't be that easy," Baal said.

"Do you think that's the book we're looking for?" Katie had to agree. This seemed much easier than expected. Where were the falling rocks and shooting arrows? Maybe she'd watched too many movies.

Seth moved closer to the pedestal, yet held back and circled. Studied it with great intent. "I have to agree with Baal. I can't believe we could just waltz in here."

The demon strode up next to him. "I sense some heavy magic surrounding it."

Seth nodded. "So do I." He moved around it again then stopped suddenly. "Here is where the weave of magic starts." He pointed, but Katie saw nothing except air.

"I can't see it, but I know it's there," Baal stated.

Diego came up closer. "It looks like one big ball of energy all entwined together."

"There is an inscription." Seth pointed. "It says '*ergriff wer chosen hianag shilta unravel wer vers*'."

"Ah, English version please." Katie didn't hide her sarcasm.

Diego piped up. "Only the chosen daughter can unravel the power."

"Does it mean me?"

Seth's gaze met hers. "I would guess, but who knows for sure. We don't even know what will happen if the wrong person tries to take the book."

She shuddered. "Well either way I'm screwed so what do I do?"

He looked back at the pedestal. "There's more. It says the rightful owner will be able to reach in and remove the book. Anyone else who tries will be burned to death."

She took a step back. "I guess we know what happens to the wrong person." Why did everything have to end in someone burning? "Why can you see all of that and no one else can?"

Seth stepped back beside her. "I'm not sure. Maybe it has something to do with my origins."

She pinched the bridge of her nose. "You mean being a guardian?"

"No, more like I was the first. I wasn't born, but created. The others who were created after me have perished."

"So where did the guardians I met come from?" She had a feeling the answer was a bit more complicated than her mind could handle at the moment.

"They were born of parents. Ancestors of the originals created." Seth was matter of fact.

For some reason the thought of him with another woman ticked her off. "You mean you fathered children?"

"I indirectly fathered all the guardians. After I was made, Zarek created two males and two females from my DNA. They went on to bear the first children, not me."

"So, the gods raised you?" She couldn't wrap her mind around it.

"Why are we discussing this now?" Irritation evident in his voice.

She shoved her fists onto her hips. "Do you need to be some place? I got all day and since I'm the one who has to stick my hand into whatever—" She waved toward the book. "I'd like to learn all I can about who the hell you are."

He let out an exasperated sigh. "Very well. No one raised me, as I was never a child. I was created as you see me now."

"Well that kinda sucks." Katie was gaining a whole new respect for the man. He'd never known the love of a parent or bedtime stories. So many things he had missed out on. She found herself wondering if he knew how to love at all. Had he ever been in love? How many women had he slept with in his life? Being so old, he had to be great in bed. *Where the hell did that come from?* She was starting to think she was going off the deep end as well.

Seth turned to the other two men. "Leave us."

"Seth?" Baal stepped closer to him. "What are you planning?"

"I wish to speak to my mate. Alone."

Baal must have been satisfied with the answer since he and Diego vanished. Katie however... Her nerves began to fray.

"What exactly are you planning?"

"Your pretty head is swimming with questions." He stepped closer. She backed away. He pressed forward until her back hit the stone wall. "Do you fear me now?"

"No."

"You lie. I can smell your fear. Do you think I will harm you?"

She refused to answer, mostly because she didn't have one.

He placed his palms on either side of her head and caged her in. There was no place to go and his erection pressed into her. Common sense said she should have cringed, instead heat flooded to her core. Why the hell was she aroused?

"You are aroused because I am your mate. It is the way of things and there is no stopping what the gods deem as fate." He ran his nose along her neck and she shivered. The thought that he might bite her brought both excitement and desire.

"I won't be taking your blood, because once I do I will not have the willpower to stay away." He ran his fingers through her hair. "I am not a man you wish to be tied to, but there is one thing I will ask of you."

She licked her lips, and stared into his eyes. "What?"

"I'm a sucker for pain. I need to know what I'm missing. What I will never have. I need your lips pressed against mine. I want to know the taste of you on my tongue."

He was a sucker? Maybe she was as well. She cupped his cheeks and pulled him closer. Her mouth locked onto his. The hard muscle that pressed against her body was a stark contrast to the softness of his lips. She opened and allowed his tongue to sweep in. He tasted of hot cinnamon candy, her favorite and she kissed him harder. His hands moved down her arms and came to rest on her hips. Her nipples tightened and pressed against her bra and she wondered if his erection was as painful.

Katie swore the world stopped and there was nothing but them and the stolen moment they shared. Her body burned, but in a different way than she was used to. It ached for him, all of him and she had to fight to keep from ripping their clothes off and begging him to take her.

Seth broke away and left her gasping for air, her pulse raced and her skin grew hypersensitive. What had he done to her? She studied him and took pleasure in noting his eyes gave everything away. He desired her as much as she did him.

"That was a mistake," he declared.

"Was it?" She didn't think so. Matter of fact, nothing in her life had ever felt more right. She fisted the front of his shirt and ached to tear it to shreds. "We may both die tomorrow. Hell, could be five minutes from now. Why can't we simply enjoy each other?"

Seth grabbed her hands and pushed them away, taking three steps back. "We cannot consummate this relationship. To do so will bring us even closer together."

He was going to leave her hot and bothered. *Bastard!* She pushed off the wall, her Irish temper flared. "You're right, of course. We'll get the book and move on." She couldn't help but look at him and grin. "Perhaps that sexy demon will cool my lust." *Take that, you ass!*

He showed no emotion, which pissed her off even more. She stormed to the pedestal. "May we both be damned." Reached for the book and removed it from its resting place.

Nothing. All remained quiet and the world hadn't stopped, at least as far as she knew.

CHAPTER TWELVE

LOWAN SIPPED his goblet of blood wine and tapped his fingers on his chair. The excitement that zinged through his body had him feeling like a small child with a new toy.

"My lord, you summoned me?"

His gaze moved to Chaval, the Sumari warrior. He smiled at the fact he owned such a prize possession as a Sumari. They were rare. Chaval's father was a demon and his mother fae. The combination of magic and demon warrior brought him incredible strength. Not to mention what his dark magic could do.

"Chaval, are we ready to open the barrier?"

The man tipped his head, his blue gaze a stark contrast to the white hair that fell to his shoulders. "My lord, we are ready."

"Excellent!" Lowan rose and gave Chaval a hard slap on the back. "You are sure this will work?"

Chaval curled his lip. "Certain."

"I hope for the sake of your pretty little sister it does." He grabbed the warrior's chin in his vice-like grip and forced their gazes to meet. "I must say though, there is almost a part of me that wishes you to fail. Your sister would make a suitable mistress. Her beauty is beyond words." He licked his lips. "I can picture her naked and tied to my bed."

The demon inside Chaval surfaced. His eyes flashed red and he snarled.

"That's it, let your anger rise. Your hatred will serve me well in the coming war." He removed his hand from the warrior's chin and placed it on Chaval's shoulder. "Kneel before your king."

Lowan forced Chaval to his knees.

"Revere me as your leader and I will bestow you with a place of honor by my side. Cross me and those you love will feel my wrath." Lowan knew he could never torture Chaval into submission so he used the only weapon available to him. The threat against those the warrior loved. He'd nearly turned the Sumari's mind to mush trying to extract the information, but in the end, he had been successful and now used it to control one of the most lethal men alive.

"Acknowledge me as your god and king," Lowan snarled.

Chaval curled his lower lip inward, his eyes darkened even more. "I forsake all others, my lord. I pledge my loyalty to only you." He reached out and took Lowan's left hand into his and pressed his lips to Lowan's knuckles.

"Good. Rise up and let us make our way back to Vandeldor. We have some guardians to kill." Lowan could scarcely believe he was finally going to be free of his confinement. His freedom also meant he could avenge both his mother's and father's death. Yes, all involved would pay and dearly. Eventually he'd even seek out the gods. They had allowed his family to perish and aided in his imprisonment, including his grandfather, Hades. Yes, he too would fall under Lowan's sword.

SETH CHOKED ON HIS ANGER. *How dare she threaten to sleep with the demon!* The fact he had just told her they could never be together was irrelevant. Then she marched over and grabbed the book. Consequences be damned.

"Woman, I swear to the gods…"

The ground rumbled and the wall to his right moved to reveal another doorway. He turned toward the other side from where they had come and noted something was off. He swung his head to study the room from one corner to the other.

"Son of a bitch. We need to leave. Now!" He grabbed her arm and jerked her, maybe a little too hard toward the new opening.

"What the hell?" She clawed at him, but he held fast.

"Gods damn it, woman! Can't you see the fucking room is shrinking?"

She stopped fighting to turn her gaze to the room he was trying to drag her from. Her eyes widened and a gasp escaped before she began to push him.

"Hurry up! What are you waiting for? We need to get out of here."

He rolled his eyes at her sudden change of attitude and proceeded through the opening. Another tight fit, but at least there was light coming from somewhere up ahead.

"Oh, for cripes sake. Why do all these passages have to be so damn narrow?" Katie bit out.

Seth narrowed his gaze. "Why the hell did you have to just march right over and grab the book?"

"Well, pardon me. For some stupid ass reason, I thought that was why I was here."

"Vexing woman," he hissed under his breath.

"What?"

"Nothing. Not a gods damn fucking thing."

"Yeah, I thought so."

He swore the woman would be his undoing and at the moment he wanted to both throttle her and fuck her. Luckily for her, he managed to curb both desires and instead concentrate on getting them out of immediate danger. Afterward…well, he made no guarantees.

"Can you just do that thingie you do?" Katie asked.

"Thingie? What precisely is a thingie?" Everything grated on his nerves and he didn't bother to hide his irritation.

She let out an audible sigh. "You know. Just flash us from here." She snorted. "Dumb ass."

Oh, that took the cake. He stopped so fast she walked right into him. He turned and glared, even let his fangs descend and hoped he looked a menace.

"Don't you think I have tried that already? Something is blocking my ability."

She opened her mouth, but he raised his hand to silence her.

"Before you open that flap of yours. Yes, I have also tried calling the others and that too appears to be blocked. So, for the moment we seem to be stuck here. Together."

She crossed her arms over her breasts, book in one hand. "Well then what damn good are you?"

Dear gods, grant me patience. "Let me see the book. Perhaps it will tell us something."

She handed it over without hesitation. "Now that's the best idea you've had."

He snatched it and opened it to the first page. She leaned into him to get a better view and he tried not to notice her soft curves.

"Ack. I hope you can read that, 'cause I sure as hell can't."

"It's written in Draconic, of course, I can read it. It says, 'There will come a time when the balance of good and evil will shift. Humanity will suffer a great loss before the tables can be righted. Only when the fire child has completed her mission will the Phoenix rise again'."

She chewed her bottom lip. "I don't like the sound of that."

"Neither do I."

"So, who is the fire child and what's the mission?"

He continued to scan the page. "It says, 'When the bearer of the dagger of Embara transforms, only then will the god awaken and begin his rebirth'."

"Sounds like a damn riddle."

He nodded. "The gods are known for them. Let's see what else it says." He flipped the page and continued reading to himself before he closed the book.

"Well?"

"It would seem that the Phoenix god has been reincarnated yet has no idea who he is. Once the bearer of the dagger transforms, into what I have no fucking clue, then the god will awaken." He shoved the book back at her. "Of course, it's not that simple."

She shook her head. "Of course not."

"It would also seem in order to save humanity, someone close to the god will have to make the ultimate sacrifice. Only then will the evil be pushed back from where it came."

She clutched the book to her chest. "And that would be?"

He snorted. "Well now you have a lot to learn. Gods don't give you step-by-step instructions. They're fickle that way."

"So, let me see if I have this straight. The person who has the dagger has to transform into something. This will awaken the god from whatever body he possesses. At some point, someone close to him will have to make a sacrifice and then shit will hit the fan?"

"You summed it up beautifully."

"Well, it sounds like a piece of cake. Now what?"

"Now we figure out how to get out of here. The others need to see this and maybe someone will have suggestions." He started to walk.

"Why do I not feel confident? You are an ancient, if you don't understand it then who the hell will?"

"The Draki as a race are older than I. They were the first living creatures created, besides the gods. Maybe, Caleb will be able to provide some answers."

"So, we head back to their place? It sounds like a solid plan."

"Well, I'm glad you approve." He could feel her eyes boring holes into his back.

"Why do I feel like you're being a smart ass?"

"Because I am."

KATIE FOLLOWED behind Seth and clutched the wretched book to her chest. She was beginning to hate the damn thing and if not for the fact they needed it, she would smack him upside the head with it. It had only caused more confusion than it had alleviated. To top it off, she was getting another hot flash and Seth's voices were mumbling in the back on her mind again. How he ever managed to get a coherent thought in edgewise was beyond her. She had to give him credit. Even though he irritated the hell out of her, she really did like him. Another hadn't challenged her mentally in a long time.

"It feels like we have been walking forever." Her legs were tired and she felt like a rat in a maze. Every turn they took led them to another. "Be honest. Do you know where we are?"

Seth stopped and leaned against the wall. "I've no idea nor can I sense anything but rock." He pulled her to him. "You need more blood. Your temperature is rising again. Can you hear the voices?"

"Yes, but they're not as bad as before."

"Good, then we have gotten to it in time." He bit his wrist. "Do you need my help?"

She stared at the blood pooling on his arm. "No, I can do this on my own." She closed her eyes. As long as she didn't have to see it then it wouldn't be a problem. She sucked up the chocolaty goodness and was thankful the taste hadn't changed. After a few laps Seth pulled away and the voices quieted.

"Better?"

"Yes. Tell me something. If I have to have your blood then what happens to me if you're not around?" She dreaded even thinking about it, but it needed to be asked.

"I'm sure once you have a mate you'll be fine."

"So, you're willing to bet my life on it?" She wasn't sure how to feel about that. One part of her didn't want to be tied to a man. The other was pissed that he would simply assume mating with another would be her cure.

"We should continue on."

She pushed herself off the wall. "Right. Lead on then." *Mental note, he ignored my question. Prick.*

Seth continued along the endless corridor. And she followed like an obedient puppy. When they came to yet another junction it was either go forward or take a left. He led them left. She was only three steps behind him when the floor beneath her gave way and she fell.

CHAPTER THIRTEEN

KATIE SCREAMED as the floor beneath her gave way. Her ass hit hard and she slid, reminding her of one of those damn tubes at the water park, except there was no light at the end. Only darkness. She clutched the book tight to her chest, fearing she'd lose it and prepared herself for the inevitable painful exit.

She didn't have to wait long.

In seconds she shot out of the tube, flew through the air and landed on her side. The breath that had been in her lungs made an excruciating escape and she gasped, unable to pull in another. Somehow, she managed to will her body to relax and as the pain subsided her breathing returned to normal. She had no idea where she was and to top it off, it was pitch black. She couldn't even see her hand in front of her nose.

"Seth," she whispered.

Silence greeted her.

She pushed herself into a sitting position and did a quick assessment. As luck would have it there didn't appear to be any broken bones and she wondered if she had Seth's blood to thank for that. She put her hands at her side and felt around the floor. Her fingers dipped into small cracks and the texture was rough. If she had to venture a guess, she'd say it was some kind of stone.

"Seth."

Again, no answer so she was pretty certain he hadn't taken the plunge with her.

"Well this is a fine mess." She remembered having a flashlight in her backpack and prayed it was still there. Slipping the pack from her shoulders, she was relieved to have the weight off even though it wasn't that heavy. She felt around for the pocket and unsnapped the flap. Reached inside and was relieved when her hand made contact with the light. She pulled it out and clicked it on, shining it around the room. The walls had ancient murals, at least she assumed they were ancient since they looked much like the ones she'd seen earlier. As she shined the light around it reflected off of...

She let out a blood-curdling scream and dropped the light.

"Oh, hell no!" Her hands shook. "Deep breath, Katie. It's only your imagination."

She willed herself to pick up the light, which shined in the corner and swallow down her fear. With shaking hands, she pointed the flashlight across the room. Her bottom lip trembled.

"Dear god." The memory of her mother's letter flashed into her mind. *All who have tried have perished.* She couldn't help but think the skeletons which stared back at her were the ones who had failed. She wondered how the poor souls met their demise, and then realized she was better off being clueless.

"Well this tells me there's no way out." Just to be certain she reluctantly shined the light around the rest of the room and found no visible exit. She flipped off the flashlight to save batteries. For what reason she was unsure.

Resting her head back on the wall she closed her eyes and fought tears. This was not how she wanted her life to end. Going up in a ball of flames would be better than slowly starving. There was no stopping the tears as they streamed down her cheeks. Memories of all the things she had wanted to do in life danced before her closed eyes.

Falling in love, having children and leading a normal life. She also wondered if Seth would miss her. Would her death cause him to plummet over the edge? He liked to pretend he didn't want her, but her gut told her it was all a ruse. If everything she'd learned thus far about mates was true, then she was afraid for him as well.

She laughed out loud. Should have known her destiny would never travel a *normal* path.

Katie let herself cry for several more minutes before she wiped her palms over her eyes and sniffed. "I'm an O'Hara and we are not quitters." Her mother would not have let a little detour like this stop her and neither would she. She needed a plan. Even if she were doomed to fail at least she would die fighting to live. Taking a deep breath, she coughed from the stale air. Once her lungs recovered she took a mental stock of her supplies. A couple bottles of water and a few power bars, enough if she rationed she'd be good for a while. Maybe Seth would be able to find her.

Speaking of the vampire, an idea hit her. She closed her eyes again.

Seth?

Hell, anything was worth a try. Maybe he could hear her, or even the others if they were still close by.

She waited.

Seth? Can you hear me? Please tell me you can. I'm in a small room with a few dead people and I need rescuing. Yes, you can rub it in my face later, but first come get me out of here!

She pulled her knees up to her chest and wrapped her arms around them. She'd give him a few minutes. Maybe he heard her but couldn't respond. Perhaps she should hum or something so he could key in on her location. After all, he was an ancient with powers she would never understand. He would find her.

Not knowing what else to do, she began to sing. "Soft kitty, warm kitty, little ball of fur." She rolled her eyes. *God I'm lame.* It was the only song she could come up with. Then her mind started to wander and suddenly...

"Oh, hell no." She rubbed her arms as she realized that these places had all kinds of creepy crawlies. Snakes, scorpions, spiders. She curled into a tighter ball, her pulse raced.

"Why the hell did I have to start thinking about that?" Her mind imagined big, ugly, hairy creatures with poisonous sharp teeth or stingers. The skin on her arms prickled and she rubbed, frantic to get the creepy crawlies off her. Her breathing increased until she was near hyperventilation. She grabbed the flashlight and flicked it on. Shined it on herself and realized she had managed to work herself into a frenzy. There were no bugs, no snakes or any such creatures anywhere in sight and certainly not on her.

"I have to stop freaking myself out," she gasped and tried to steady her breathing. Slow breath in the nose and exhale out the mouth.

Repeat.

Finally, her heart didn't feel like it was about to punch a hole into her chest and make an escape. Her lungs stopped burning and the pins and needles feeling in her limbs dissipated. She licked her lips; her mouth so dry she could hardly swallow. Grabbing a bottle of water from her pack she took a sip. The water would have been much better ice cold, but at the moment she'd take wet over dry. A few more sips then she capped the bottle and placed it back in the pack.

"Okay. I need to think. There has to be a way out of here."

She grabbed the book and shined the light on it. It was nothing but gibberish to her, but she flipped through it anyway. Prayed there would be something she might recognize. With every turn of the page she found some new pictures. When she brought the book closer, she noticed a woman dressed in a white gown. Dark hair flowed along her shoulders and a wide gold band decorated one arm. The woman was beautiful and Katie couldn't help wonder if she was a goddess. She ran her fingers over the image, the need to touch it called to her.

"Who are you?"

A breeze blew across her skin and a soft white light glowed on the other side of the small room. She raised her gaze from the book and swallowed intense fear. In front of her stood the woman from the page.

"W-who are you?"

The woman opened her mouth to speak but only gibberish came out. Katie shook her head. "I don't understand you." Her comment didn't seem to help. The woman held up her right hand, palm faced toward Katie and glided closer, her voice grew louder and the words poured out faster. Katie would have backed up but was already with her back against the wall so she stood to face whatever it was head-on. The only weapon she had was the dagger so she pulled it free and waved it about. The blade flashed in the woman's light.

"Stay back." Katie tried to hide the fear in her voice, but failed miserably. The woman continued her advance. The crazy lady's gaze went to the dagger and the handle began to vibrate. The words rolled off her tongue and Katie started to overheat.

Dear god, she is going to burn me alive.

Sweat slicked her skin and in seconds her shirt was soaked. Her knees buckled and she could no longer stand. Instead, she let her body slide down the stone wall until her ass hit the floor. The air around her heated until her lungs burned.

"P-please, make it quick." She thought of her mother and the letter. *I'm so sorry. I'm a failure.* It didn't appear she was going to uncover any secrets either. Instead she would meet her demise the same as all the others before her. Her mind went to Seth. How would he take her death?

The woman was upon her and Katie met the woman's stare, refused to close her eyes. She would not die a coward. Everything went quiet. The woman had stopped her chattering. Brought her hands together in front of her and a ball of fire formed. Katie held her breath as the woman launched it at her chest.

SETH HEARD KATIE SCREAM, but when he turned around she

was gone. The only thing left was a hole in the floor and it was quickly closing. He leapt for it, but was too late.

"Katie!" He clawed at the ground until his fingers bled, but to no avail. There wasn't even a crevice that indicated a trap door. It was like the floor had opened up and swallowed her.

He stopped for a moment and calmed himself. Tried to reach for a mental link to her. To anyone, but the only answer he received was the dark one's sinister laugh. He tried to flash, but again nothing. It was as if his power had been short-circuited somehow. There was no choice but to move forward and try to find her.

Seth ran down the corridor until he came to a juncture where he stopped and turned to the right. Pushing out his senses, he detected nothing ahead. He made a left but still found nothing. At this point he wasn't sure if it was because there wasn't anything or if his senses had failed as well.

He raked his fingers through his hair and snarled. The need to find his mate and protect her tightened every muscle in his body. His jaw locked and he gained an understanding of how Marcus and Caleb felt. The only reason the structure around him stood was because blowing it to smithereens would only endanger Katie more. Forget the fact he had no power to do so anyway. It looked like the only avenue open to him was to do things the old-fashioned way.

"I'll dismantle this place with my bear hands if I must." He chose the path to the left and ran. The voices in his head screamed. Half shouted left, the others right, but one laughed hysterically.

You should have listened to me. Had you chained the bitch down, you'd have her right now. Pity it is that she has to die like this. Would have been more fun to make her bleed. You could have drained her just like you did the other.

"Shut up!"

He ran into a dead end. "Fuck."

The voices laughed. He turned to go the other way then stopped dead in his tracks. The wall had moved. Hadn't it? He shook his head and turned around from where he had been. A long corridor lit with torches on either side stretched out in front of him. He scrubbed his palm over his face and strode forward. "Who's there?" He knew damn well it hadn't been there before.

Are you sure? The dark one asked and then they all began chanting in their singsong voices. *Are you sure, are you sure, are you sure...* Pain shot through his head and blood dripped from his nose, yet he pressed forward. His lip curled and he snarled. He was so close to the edge a small wisp of wind would send him over into the darkness. In a state of near panic, he tried once again to reach anyone, but his telepathy remained uncooperative.

"No," he cried out gripping his head. It couldn't end this way. He had to at least save his mate then his brethren could send a cold blade through his neck. Worry pulsed through his veins. What if he couldn't find her? What if he did but had already turned? There was no doubt whatever he did to her wouldn't be pretty. He shook his head. Blood splattered the walls, but he didn't give a shit. He wiped his face and walked down the lit path, ever alert to any danger. He gripped his dagger in his right hand for added support.

Like a panther on the prowl for its prey, he lifted his nose. Inhaled until his lungs couldn't expand any further. A trickle of saliva ran down the corner of his mouth and his fangs ached.

Strawberries.

CHAPTER FOURTEEN

LOWAN STOOD with Chaval at his side and watched as his minions readied their supplies. In a matter of minutes, he and his army would take over the guardian's realm. After that came the human world and once he was there all would bow to him. There would be nothing to stop his terror.

"How soon before you are ready?" he asked Chaval.

"I am ready now, my lord."

Lowan clapped his hands together and rubbed. Excitement zinged through him at the thought of killing the guardians. "Fucking menaces." He looked to Chaval. "Proceed."

The Sumari warrior stepped forward and placed his hands on the stone wall. Lowan knew better, it was no ordinary obstacle. Had it been, he would have smashed it down decades ago. This was a force field that blocked his entry into the next realm. The guardian king was powerful, but he was more so. Chaval held the knowledge of the dark fae and the ability to use it.

Chaval chanted under his breath in a language even Lowan didn't understand. *The bastard better not think to try and deceive me.*

The earth groaned in protest as rocks slid against each other.

Explosions were both felt and heard and then the barrier began to crack. At first, small hairline fractures, then they grew into large veins that snapped and popped until the wall started to toss debris into the air. Lowan's pulse raced with each small opening until at last the entire barricade exploded into dust. Once the dust had settled, he sent his army through first to make sure the realm was clear. He knew the guardians could have a trap on the other side just in case he breached their magic. He began to pace, his patience worn thin. He was ready for war and could almost taste his own victory.

A scout came running back. "All clear, my lord."

"Excellent. Come Chaval, we have a war to start." Lowan entered the opening with his warrior on his heels. In seconds, he flashed himself to Vandeldor and stood on a rocky ledge of the Vutha Mountains. The terrain below was burnt and covered in rubble from the homes that once stood there. The dragons had done a good job of destroying everything. Too bad they had become traitors and taken sides with the guardians. However, he had come to the conclusion that having his daughter mate with their leader and live among them was the best thing that could have happened. He hadn't been happy about losing her, but soon realized she was in the perfect position to infiltrate the Draki. One day soon, he would take advantage of that fact and make her betray her mate and his people. He fisted his hands. No one betrayed him. Ever. His daughter would rue the day she had ever decided to do so.

He watched with excitement as his army dotted the landscape below. A wicked laugh escaped him. "Chaval, we need to find the perfect location for my throne."

The warrior tipped his head. "May I suggest the highest point of the mountains? It will provide the best advantage and you will be able to see everyone below you."

Lowan raised a brow. It seemed the warrior was smarter than he'd first anticipated. "You will do well, Chaval. See to the preparations then."

The demon bowed. "As you wish, my lord." He turned and moved out of sight.

Lowan looked to the demon on his left. "Bring me a sacrifice and be quick about it."

The Wendigo bowed. "Does my lord have a preference?"

He rubbed his chin. "Yes. Make her young and beautiful." He felt like fucking before he fed. Perhaps he might even keep this one for a few days before he drank her dry.

"As you wish." The Wendigo removed himself from Lowan's side and he was finally alone to bask in his achievement. Pleasure rushed through him, he was finally in his mother's homeland and it caused him to smile. He only wished she could have been here to witness his success. The one thing he desperately missed was her. She had loved him with every ounce of her being and had forsaken her people for him. Her death angered him again and he began to plot the destruction of the vampires.

KATIE EXPECTED pain to rip into her when the fireball smacked her chest. Instead, there was a rush of coolness that bathed her skin before it dissipated. The woman stared at her with a smile on her face.

"What the fuck did you just do to me?"

"I balanced your powers, but it is only temporary."

She blinked. "You speak English now?"

The goddess shook her head. "No, but you can now understand me. You must hurry though. Time is running out."

Katie pushed herself up the wall until she was standing. She hadn't realized until that moment how tall the other woman was. "Time for what? Are you going to help me out of here?"

"I have done all I can. The rest is up to you, but you must save the guardian. Complete your transformation and the rest will fall into place."

She rubbed her temple. Now she understood what the others had meant by riddles. "I don't know what it is I'm supposed to do. A little, oh I don't know...instructions perhaps?"

The woman leveled her gaze. "I am Vivian. I sacrificed myself so the guardian could live. He belongs to you now and it is your turn to sacrifice for all humanity." She started to back away. "If you don't save him, the Phoenix god will never remember who he is and humanity will suffer. All will be forced to bow to the demon king."

Her heart skipped several beats. "Nothing like laying a huge guilt trip on my ass."

The woman pointed. "It is in the book. Read it and you will know the way."

Katie looked at the book that now lay at her feet. "But I tried."

"Try again." She began to fade.

"Wait! How am I the daughter of the god when he died before I was born?" That question had been haunting her since she'd learned he was dead.

The woman smiled. "Never take for granted the power the gods hold. He put into place a way for his DNA to be passed to each female in your ancestry. They have all failed to complete the transformation. You are the last one who still carries a part of him. Succeed and you will be born again." She vanished.

"I really hate this shit," she growled. "I never asked for any of it." She bent over and retrieved the book. Opened it to the first page and let her eyes adjust. "Oh my." She could read it. She scanned the page and flipped to the next. Read up to where the book had ended previously then something strange happened. Words began to form on the next page and then the next until she had read to the end. Those pages had been blank when she and Seth had looked at them, now she wondered if they had been meant for her eyes only. Closing it she swallowed down bile.

"I don't want to be the daughter of a god. What a mess." She grabbed her backpack and shoved the book inside for safekeeping. Pushed her arms through the straps and thought of her father. Not the god she didn't know, but the man who'd raised her as his own. He'd always taught her to put others needs before her own and it was how he'd lived his life. Her mother had lost hers by doing the same thing. Katie had no one left. She thought about her staff at the club. Many of them had families, children they needed to support. What would happen to those children if the world changed?

She shuddered.

Katie had always thought she was fairly smart. Had gone to college and kept up with current events. Her business was successful and she hadn't wanted for much except a man to love her. In reality her giving up her mortal life could potentially save millions. It was surreal to think her tiny existence would mean so much. Half of her wanted to curl up into a ball in the corner and cower like a scared child. The other said she couldn't fight destiny and if she tried the consequences for humanity would be dire. The price she had to pay was small. It didn't require her death, on the contrary if she walked away from the task handed her then she would die for certain. However, if she chose to follow the path in front of her then she would live. Most likely for a very long time and she would give her heart to a crazy man. No wait...a crazy vampire.

She stretched her neck and rolled her shoulders. "I've never walked away from a challenge. Not about to start now. Besides, I think that damn vampire already has a piece of my heart."

Time to see if Vivian and the book spoke the truth. With her arm extended and palm facing the wall, she closed her eyes and concentrated. At first it started as a small sizzle from her fingertips. Then it turned to blue sparks that arched out and snapped in the air causing her to jump back.

"Holy shit!"

She tried again. This time she held her hand, palm facing upward, and imagined a small ball of light. It started as a tiny dot no bigger than a dime. She concentrated harder and the ball grew in dimension until it was as big as a grapefruit.

Will this be big enough?

There was only one way to find out. She wound back and launched it at the wall. It hit with a loud whack and when the small puff of smoke cleared the only damage was a chunk missing. Not enough to get her out.

"Okay, bigger is better then."

She repeated the process. Staring at her palm she imagined a ball the size of a small melon. She feared going too big since she had no idea what would happen. For all she knew, she'd bring the whole room down on top of her head.

Once she had the desired size, she tossed it. This time there was a louder explosion and debris spewed into the air. When the smoke cleared it revealed a crater, but still no opening. With a sigh she decided the best thing to do would be to continue drilling at the divot already there. She launched another ball of light. Finally, it was enough to make a small opening. She ran to the wall and peeked through the hole and saw a dim light to her right.

Stepping back to the other side of the room she threw another ball and it was successful in making the opening bigger. Hopefully a few more and she'd be able to crawl out. She needed to find Seth, both of their lives depended on it.

EXPLOSIONS CAME from the other direction so Seth turned and ran toward the sound. Smoke and strawberries hit his senses.

"What the fuck?" Worry coursed through him as he stared at the rubble, quickly followed by relief when Katie strolled out of the smoke. She faced him.

"There you are." She looked at him like he was some lost child then moved in front of him. Tipped her chin up and stared into his eyes. "I thought you'd abandoned me."

"What the hell happened here?" He tipped his head to the hole in the wall and the smoke that still bellowed out.

She turned to glance behind her. "Oh that? It's nothing."

He pursed his lips and folded his arms over his chest. "That is most certainly not nothing. I wasn't born yesterday."

She shrugged. "I kinda found a little power of my own, but I must warn you. It's pretty unstable."

He dropped his arms to his side. "Power? What kind of power and where is the book?"

She jabbed her fists on her hips, her blue eyes glared. "Not even a little concern over my welfare?"

"I sense you're fine." He would be damned if he would tell her he'd nearly lost his mind with worry. She was better off thinking he didn't give a shit, but it was all he could do to keep from pulling her close to him.

She scoffed. "Well, I'm fine thank you very much and so is the damn book. As far as my power..." She held out her hand and blue sparks arched from her fingertips. "I managed to blast a hole in the wall and set myself free. Thanks for the help."

He had a momentary lapse of speech before he found his tongue again. "Your transformation has begun then?"

"So, it would seem." She began to walk away then stopped and came back to him. Placed her palms on his chest and leaned into him. Her lips found his and her tongue swept his mouth and left a burst of strawberries before she broke off. She stepped back and looked at him for a moment.

"I'm happy to see you." She turned and walked away.

Seth savored the taste of her and fought the urge that ripped through him to pin her to the ground and have all of her. *Fuck it.* His desires were too deep and after the scare he'd just had at losing her...he was on her in seconds. Pushed her against the wall with her back to his chest and made sure his erection pressed into the crack of her ass. He bent and placed his lips against her ear.

"You play with fire, *torke.*" He watched her lips curl into a smile and he wanted to nibble the plump perfections.

"Angel? Believe me, *itov.* I am anything but an angel," she whispered.

He ran his nose along her neck and his fangs ached. "You learned Draconic while away as well? You should take care in calling me your love."

"I learned many things and I thought you were my destined. Doesn't that make you my love?"

"I am your destined." He suckled her earlobe. "I would gladly give you my love if I were sane enough to have you as my own, but we both know I am not. Now, you really must tell me what happened." He kissed her neck and she tipped her head further to the side allowing him better access and moaned.

"Seth?" Her breathing had become labored and he could feel her pulse beat beneath his lips.

His fangs extended. He was on the edge and wondered what the hell he was doing. He could not take her. "Yes?"

"You should really consider either kissing me or fucking me and be quick about it."

His reserves teetered. "Careful what you ask for. I may very well do both and I will not be gentle." He couldn't. At the moment he wouldn't be able to give her anything but his raw desire and even that would have to be tempered or he would hurt her. She may be part goddess, but her body was still human. He reminded himself that he had vowed to never have her, but she wanted him and he hated the thought of dying and never knowing what she felt like. For once in his sorry ass existence, he wanted to be selfish. He deserved it and so the gods must have agreed since they gave him Katie. He still couldn't mate with her or taste her essence, but he would enjoy her body.

CHAPTER FIFTEEN

KATIE MANAGED to free herself enough to spin and face Seth. She placed her palms on his chest. Her mouth watered at the thought of kissing him again and her body throbbed. Yes, it seemed it was her destiny to save him and that would require giving him her body and as she understood it, her blood. Her worry though was would he take all of her heart as well? What would he do with it? Crush it like a grape or would he give his in return?

She knew it was stupid to even think about it, but how the hell was she supposed to simply give all of herself to a man she hardly knew yet every part of her body craved? Her heart would have to be damned, the world was counting on her to set events in motion and at the moment she needed him probably more than he did her. Something told her that neither of them would leave this place the same person as when they'd arrived.

"Who said anything about gentle? I believe the terms fucking and quick say everything that needs to be said." She pulled on his shirt freeing it from his jeans. He gave her a lust-filled yet suspicious look.

"What is this really about?"

She managed to push the shirt up his chest and run her hands along his naked skin. *Damn that feels good.* Never had she experienced muscles so firm and hard under her fingers. "We may both die yet in this shit hole. You want me and I want you, what else is there?"

Without wasting any time, she jerked the tee over his head and tossed it, then pulled him to her. His mouth covered hers and his tongue speared past her lips. She opened to him and tasted every inch of his mouth. Hot cinnamon coated her tongue and musk mingled with madness assaulted her senses.

The fire in her grew hotter. Was it her power or her desire? She had no idea, but if she was going to go up in flames then there was no other way she wanted it. No other place she wanted to be, but in his arms. Never in her entire life had she felt so safe or so sure of anything.

She gripped his erection through his jeans and his mouth left hers. He hissed and had her shirt removed in seconds. He kissed the swell of her breasts then shoved her bra aside and took her nipple into his mouth. It was her turn to hiss. She sank her fingers into his thick, dark hair and pressed her back into the wall. Her knees were too weak to hold her up.

He pulled the bra past her other nipple and scraped his fangs along the protrusion. God, she had never needed a man more in her life. Knew she should be mortified at the surroundings and circumstances of their little tryst, but it felt raw and dirty and heated her blood even more. Somehow, she managed to unbuckle his belt and pull down the zipper. She reached her fingers through the opening in his jeans and freed his cock. Thick, hot and harder than steel. She wrapped her hand around it and stroked. His entire body quivered and she circled her thumb, spreading his pre-cum over the tip of his shaft.

He released her nipple and raised his head to look at her. Desire burned in his blue eyes turning them black. His fangs glistened in the light and she found herself wanting him to sink them deep and drink her essence.

He snarled and reached for her jeans. Unfastened them and

pushed them down her thighs until they were at her ankles. She toed off her shoes and managed to finish getting her pants off. He wasted no time in shoving her panties aside and dipped a finger into her depths.

She nearly came.

His mouth bruised hers. Their teeth scraped and a fang pricked her tongue. Blood mingled with their kiss, but before she could react he pulled free. Spun her to face the wall and shoved his knee between her legs to force her wider. Not bothering to remove his jeans, he pressed the tip of his cock to her entrance.

She whimpered and tried to push into him.

He dug his fingers into her hips and planted himself to the hilt. Rough denim brushed her ass and her nails scraped the wall. She chewed her bottom lip. His thickness stretched her wide, but god did it hurt so damn good.

Before she could even catch her breath, he pulled out and thrust back in. His hips rocked faster and he pounded into her from behind. There was nothing sweet or romantic about it. It was animalistic and raw and he showed her no mercy, not that she would have asked for it anyway.

"Don't take this for anything other than what it is, Katie. A good fuck," he growled.

"Stop talking." She'd worry about the rest later. Somehow, she would reach him and save his sorry ass.

The friction created by his shaft as he thrust into her had her on the brink. Pressure built and wrapped around her womb. "God don't stop."

He replied with a grunt. Her limbs trembled and a wall of pleasure slammed into her with such force had Seth not had a hold on her she would have slid to the floor. She screamed as the orgasm consumed her and turned her muscles into a quivering mass of gel. She barely heard him roar his own release behind her as he shoved deep and touched her soul.

He pulled her to his chest, still hard inside her and nuzzled her neck. She held her breath and waited for the pain of his fangs in her vein, but it never came.

"Did I hurt you?"

She smiled. "No. I'm not that fragile, but something tells me you held back anyway."

He grinned and nipped her chin. "As much as I could."

She took in a long slow breath. "Are you going to bite me?"

His features hardened and he pulled free. "No."

Now she was offended, plus in order to tie them together he had to have her blood. Vivian had implanted the knowledge in her memories. The transformation Katie needed to make was becoming Seth's mate. Not only would it save him, but it would finish awakening her goddess power thus waking her father. The easy route would have been to simply tell him, but she couldn't. He had to be willing and come to her on his own accord. Christ she was going to have to either seduce him into it or trick him. She was quick to learn that the gods played by fucked-up rules.

IT HAD ONLY TAKEN his men hours to carve out Lowan's temple high on the cliff of the Vutha Mountains using their demon magic. He stared out of the wall of glass, his hands clasped behind his back.

"Chaval, what is the word?"

"My lord, your wench is waiting in your quarters."

Lowan smiled. "Perfect. What of the guardians?" He turned to face Chaval.

"I have done the recon myself. The king is with the gods apparently being punished for some crime he committed. The others are fighting the many demons you have invading the cities."

Lowan brought his fingers together and touched his lips. "This is excellent news. How long before we can expect their company?"

"I have ordered all the troops to retreat. I'm positive the guardians will follow. I expect our men to begin showing up here within the hour."

Lowan stepped closer and clasped his shoulders. "If your plan succeeds in bringing the guardians here you will be rewarded handsomely."

Chaval bowed his head. "Thank you, my lord."

Lowan skirted around him and headed toward his rooms. Anxious to release some pent-up energy before the fight ensued. He flung open the door and was greeted by huge doe eyes, shiny raven locks and plump red lips. He'd not seen such beauty in a long time and was momentarily stunned.

"What is your name?"

The girl moved from the window and stood in front of him before she dropped to her knees. "My lord, my name is Raven."

"Raven. What a lovely name for a pretty girl."

She flashed a smile. "Thank you, my lord. How may I serve you?"

He was a bit perplexed and wondered if Chaval had placed some kind of spell on her. She appeared absolutely infatuated with him. Most females brought to his quarters quaked in their shoes. He walked to the side bar and poured himself a glass of wine. Swirled the dark liquid in the glass before turning back to his whore. "Rise up, Raven, come here."

She jumped to her feet and practically ran to him.

"Would you like a glass of wine?"

Her eyes widened. "If it pleases you, my lord."

He poured another glass and handed it to her. "It pleases me. Tell me, where did my men find you?"

She accepted the glass, careful not to let her fingers touch his. "Why your temple, of course."

He arched a brow. Hadn't realized he had a temple in the human realm. He narrowed his gaze, which caused her to tremble.

"My lord, have I said something to upset you?"

"No, but I don't have a temple. Not yet at any rate." He sipped his wine. "Perhaps you should explain in further detail."

She nodded. "Of course. I assumed that your grandfather's temple would also be yours. I was in a private place where we worship Satan."

He tossed his head back and laughed until tears pricked his eyes. They worshipped the devil that was in reality Hades and he was far from what humans assumed him to be. "My dear. Hades is my grandfather and while he does have an evil streak, he is not what you think."

A puzzled look crossed her face so he placed his hand to the small of her back and led her to a chair by the window. She was in definite need of a lesson before he fucked her. Hell, if she was good he may even let her live for a few days.

"Sit," he commanded. She didn't hesitate and plopped in the chair. He took a seat across from her. "So, you came here willingly?"

"Yes, my lord. I was told I was chosen to be the mistress of Satan's grandson. I am very honored."

He ran a finger around the rim of his glass. *Interesting*. "I see. So how many of you worship my grandfather?"

She blinked and he found her brown eyes endearing. "I'm not sure. Thousands maybe?"

He would have to remember to question Chaval about this further. "And what do you do when you worship?"

She fidgeted with tie on her robe. "We offer a sacrifice. Usually a live animal." She averted her gaze. "I hear that some offer humans, but I have never done that."

He leaned forward in his seat. "Raven, I demand you look at me."

She met his gaze.

"If I asked it of you, would you kill for me?"

"Yes."

He relaxed. This girl was going to be his ticket into the human world. *So, there are those who worship granddad. Well, I will be their savior instead.* "Raven, I will not ask that of you. Not yet anyway. I will, however, ask you to take me to your temple and introduce me to its other members. Can you do that for me?"

She straightened, pride had her shifting her shoulders back. "Oh, yes, my lord."

He sipped. "Good. There is one more thing you can do for me right now."

"Anything," she whispered.

He let his fangs extend. "I find myself hungry."

Raven set her glass on the side table and rose from her seat. Untied the black, silk robe she wore and let it fall to the floor. Pert breasts and rounded hips caused him to stifle a moan. She pulled her long tresses to one side to expose her neck and slipped into his lap. He cupped her firm ass with one hand and ran his tongue along her soft skin.

"My lord, there is something you should know."

"Hmm, what is that my dear?" He could hardly wait to taste her. It had been awhile since he'd had human blood.

"I was chosen by the other members to come to you. I am a virgin."

Fucking perfect. He couldn't have asked for better timing. To have the humans offer him a virgin female as sacrifice just opened the portal to their world. He sank his fangs into her vein and drank. Power filled him. Nothing would stop him now.

CHAPTER SIXTEEN

SETH DRESSED in record time then turned his back on Katie while he waited for her to finish. He couldn't stand to look at her. Between his lust and guilt, he was ripped in two. Lust wanted to fuck her over and over and damn the repercussions. Guilt wrenched his gut. He'd used her like a common whore. Instinct reminded him she was his mate and therefore belonged to him. He had every right to her body and her blood. Gods how he wanted to drink from her and when he'd accidentally pricked her tongue and tasted her...He still couldn't believe he'd been able to refrain. Allowing what just happened between them had been the biggest mistake of his life. His heart felt like someone had placed a vice on it and slowly turned the screw.

I cannot fall in love with her. However, he knew it was too late, he'd already started down that path.

"Are you done yet?" he growled a little louder than he had meant to.

"You know for a man who just got his rocks off, you sure are pissy."

"Sorry, but we need to hurry and get out of here."

She slipped in beside him, her skin still flush from the sex they'd had. Damn he wanted to take her again. He fisted his hands at his side to keep from touching her. *Do it! Throw her to the floor and bind her wrists. Have your way.* He closed his eyes. Damn the fucking voices. He tried to remember when they had actually taken on a life of their own. Used to be they were only memories of those he'd drunk from. At some point the tides had changed and they started speaking directly to him.

"Seth?"

Another voice. A soft feminine siren called to him. She alone rose above all the others. He shook the rest free and realized Katie was talking to him.

"Seth?"

"What?"

"Are you okay?" Her hand was on his arm and concern on her face.

"Fine." He started to turn, but she grabbed a handful of his shirt. "You tempt fate, woman."

"You're lying to me. You don't look fine. How can I help?"

After he'd used her, growled at her, and even threatened her, she still wanted to help him. He didn't deserve a woman like her. "You can't help me. The only thing that can is cold steel biting through my neck. Soon, I'll be a menace."

"I don't believe that. Look, I don't pretend to understand any of this, but if you were a lost cause why would the gods have chosen us to be together?"

He sighed. Really didn't want to go into it, but he owed her. "We may be mates, but fate was cruel. If I had found you maybe even a year ago things would be different. It's too late now."

"How do you know?"

"Because I know if I feed again it will be the last time. Ever. The last shred of sanity I have will cease to exist. I can't chance drinking from anyone, not even you."

Pain filled her eyes. "What happens if you don't feed?"

"I become weak, lose my powers, but I'll still be immortal. I have already bargained with someone to end my life when that happens. I will not be a burden to my brethren."

Her face paled. "Bargained? So, you are paying someone to off you?"

"In a sense. I can't count on those close to me to do it. So, I have taken out insurance so to speak. My time is running out. I need to find you a suitable mate and know you're safe. You need an immortal to help you."

She pursed her lips then slapped him across the cheek. "Fuck you! This isn't the dark ages and you can't just marry me off." She grabbed her pack and stomped away.

The sting on his cheek was nothing compared to the ache in his heart. "I'd be honored to have you, Katie, but I'm not fit," he whispered.

KATIE STORMED down the corridor with no clue where she was going or if Seth followed. *How the hell am I supposed to save him?* Where was Vivian now because she sure as hell could use some guidance. It would be so much easier to simply share with him what the plan was. Everything she'd learned, and believe her, the goddess had dumped a shit-load of info into her brain. Yeah, she could read and speak a language so ancient it wasn't even in the history books. It amazed her how she knew these things.

She stopped and took in a deep breath. Had to find a way to make this work. Somewhere, in her mind the answers were there. She turned to look behind her. Seth followed yet kept a safe distance. He stopped several feet back and stared at her. The man's face didn't give much away. He rarely showed emotion, and was more complex than anyone she'd ever met. At first glance, he was a warrior. A fighter who would never hesitate to step into a battle and protect those who were unable to protect themselves. She'd gotten a glimpse at the inside though. Heard the voices in his head and realized the nightmare he lived with every second of his life. He fought his own internal battle and the fact he had survived this long and not gone over the edge yet was a testament to his integrity. His determination. His will to live. So, how could she give up on him?

As she stood there and stared into his eyes, she saw something that she'd never noticed before. Sadness. There was sadness in his eyes and it ripped her in half. She walked back to where he stood and looked up at him.

"You can't simply marry me off. I'm not a child."

"I need to know that you are safe before I leave this world." He sighed. *Don't kiss her.*

She tipped her head. *Can you hear my thoughts?* She waited but he never answered. Was it possible she now heard more than the voices in his head? She searched her memories and came back with something about the blood tie. She'd drank from him, but he hadn't from her. That could mean she was connected yet he wasn't.

"Are you okay?"

She blinked. "Yes, I was just wondering something. If we were chosen to be together, then how will it work if I take a different mate? I thought mates were destined?"

"I honestly don't know."

"So, I could actually be worse off then, if I bond with another?"

Shit. I never want you hurt. "We will figure out something. There has to be a way. Perhaps once I am gone you will be able to choose your own."

She did hear his thoughts. This could work to her advantage big time. "You think I will be given another chance?"

"You are the daughter of the Phoenix. I think you can do whatever you wish. We need to hurry so I can leave. The sooner the better for you." *Fucking Zarek! Why can't I have happiness once in my life?*

Another piece of her heart was chipped away. She entwined her arm in his and bit her lip to keep the tears at bay. "Let's find a way out of here."

Together they walked the corridor. Sunlight shined at the end and fresh air whisked past them. There was an opening and they picked up the pace until they were both at a dead run. Neither of them wanted to be stuck in this place any longer. As they stepped outside into the sunlight they were transported to the middle of the Egyptian desert. To Katie's surprise Baal rose from behind a sand dune and a large shadow blocked out the sun. She looked up to see a beautiful dragon circling.

"Well it's about fucking time you two showed up," Baal growled.

"Believe me. We are happy to be free of that place," she replied.

Baal placed a hand on each of their shoulders and they were sucked into a black void. When next Katie saw light, she stood inside a room.

"Damn. I wish you would warn me first." She glanced around and found herself in a windowless room. A large conference table sat on one side with a wall of monitors. On the other were several leather chairs and a matching black leather sofa. "Where are we?"

"Our headquarters," Seth replied.

She cocked her head to the side. "And exactly where would that be?"

"Sorry, I can't tell you." He ran his fingers through his hair. "I need to go check on things. Stay here with Baal and I'll be back soon."

He flashed from the room and in seconds Baal stood in front of her. Golden eyes pinned her.

"Did you get the book?"

She moved away and pulled her pack off her shoulders and tossed it on the sofa. "I did."

He glanced around the room as if he was looking for someone hidden in the corner. "Look, I don't know when he's coming back so I'm going to hurry. I was sent on this mission to make sure you two got together. So, did you?"

She felt her jaw drop. "Are you asking me if we had sex?" She thrust her hands to her hips. "And who sent you?"

He narrowed his gaze. "Yes, I am asking if you two fucked and his leader sent me. I don't know the entire story, but I trust Aidyn with my life. When he told me to put you two together I didn't hesitate."

He held nothing back, she liked this demon. "Yes, but he still has it in his head that he will not bond with me. He said he can't feed anymore." She cast her gaze around then lowered her voice. "Did you know he has a contract to have himself killed?"

Baal tossed his head back and laughed. "Sugar, of course, I do. I'm it."

"You?"

He held his hand up. "Now don't go getting your thong in a twist. I have no intention of doing the job." Sadness came over his face. "Unless I'm forced. You need to get him to take your blood, even if you have to resort to trickery."

She sighed. "I tried seduction and the man has a will of steel. He still refused to bite." She touched her forehead. "I honestly don't know how he is still functioning. I've heard the voices he deals with. It's downright frightening."

"He has resorted to pain management."

"What does that mean?"

"It means he's addicted to the blade. He cuts himself to keep the dark one appeased. My concern is when that stops working then what will he resort to?"

She shivered and again another piece of her heart was chipped away as she remembered he had told her that. Somehow, coming from another made it even more real. She began to pace.

"Other than chaining him down and force feeding him, I've run out of ideas."

The demon lifted a brow. "That can be accomplished if need be."

Katie stopped in her tracks and rubbed her arms. "Let's save that for a final resort." She feared that even if they were successful in saving him, Seth would never forgive her for taking away the last of his dignity.

LOWAN WAS drunk on the power that filled him. A virgin...given willingly. Stupid humans, but all the better for him. He'd left Raven in his room with a guard outside the door and planned to keep her until she wore out her usefulness.

"My lord, you summoned me?"

He looked up from the map he'd been studying. Chaval wore the battle gear of a Sumari and even Lowan had to admit he made an impressive appearance. Leather sleeves were strapped to his arms and gold cuffs lined with spikes circled his wrist. A shield of gold and silver was laced to his abdomen. Leather leggings met black boots and the traditional dark leather loin flowed in a strip down the front. But what really caught his eye were several small skulls strung at his waist. Reminders of what happened to an enemy of a Sumari warrior.

"Yes. Have the demons started to arrive yet?"

"They have and word is that the guardians are not far behind."

"Then we prepare for an ambush." He rose and went to the sideboard and retrieved his sword. "I wish to be on the battlefield." He ran his finger along the edge of his blade, blood dripped to the floor. "I'm in the mood to kill a guardian." Lowan flashed to the valley below and Chaval came up beside him.

"Is everyone in position?"

"Yes, my lord," Chaval replied.

The air sizzled and snapped. They were coming and he would welcome them all home with a greeting they would never forget.

CHAPTER SEVENTEEN

"WE HAVE BEEN SUMMONED. The demons have retreated to our home world," Seth said coming through the door.

"Shit," Baal replied.

"What do we do?" Katie asked.

"You will stay here under guard. Baal and I need to leave immediately."

She shook her head. "But I can fight demons. You need me."

Seth moved to her, but he dared not touch her. This could well be the last time he ever saw her again. The desire to pull her to him and never let go warred with his common sense that said he was already tortured enough.

"I'll leave you two." Baal exited the room.

"Katie, I've seen you fight and I know you can. However, you have other things to worry about. Stay here and study the book. I need to know you're safe." He fisted his hands at his side. "I'm leaving two very capable Draki here with you. Should anything go wrong they have orders to take you to Lileta and Caleb."

She nodded. "Okay, but don't you dare die." She cupped his face and pulled him in for a kiss. He tasted the desperation in every tongue swipe and he longed to stay in the comfort of her arms, but it was not to be.

He broke free on a moan. "I have to go. It is my duty." He flashed from the room and could swear unshed tears filled her eyes. He had to have imagined them, why would she cry for him?

Seth took the already opened portal behind Garin, placing them on the beach of Vandeldor.

"Watch for an ambush," Seth lowered his voice.

Garin tipped his head. "I'm ready to torch some demons."

Seth laughed. "I'm not sure my senses can take all that stench, brother."

"Ha. Let's go kick some ass. I'll see you when this is over and we'll have a drink. Catch up on life." Garin moved up a sand dune so he could scout out what was on the other side of the bluff. Seth took a quick glance around. Memories of all the brethren they had laid to rest here overwhelmed him. Not long ago it had been Queen Daria, Aidyn's mother. He quickly tossed aside his thoughts and joined Garin.

"It's quiet. Too quiet," Garin commented.

Several shadows passed overhead, but Seth didn't need to look up to know the Draki had arrived. "It's time to flush them out." Both he and Garin flashed into the forest and met up with Lucan, Gwen, Marcus and several of their brethren. The Kothar had an extensive army as well. He looked to Marcus.

"Do we know how they got in here?" Seth asked.

Marcus's gazed pinched down to slits. "Chaval."

Garin whistled. "Shit."

Seth couldn't agree more. The Sumari warrior was lethal and to have him on the opposite side didn't bode well for anyone. He wondered what had happened to send the man's loyalty into Lowan's clutches.

"Does Gwen know?" Seth asked.

"Dear gods no." Marcus gave a visible shudder. Gwen and Chaval had been friends as children up until the demon had gone to train with his father at the age of fifteen. No one had seen him since, but Seth knew it would break her heart to learn he was on the wrong side of the fight.

"They're coming," Marcus shouted. "May the gods be with us."

In seconds, hundreds of demons descended upon them. Some had come from the treetops, others flashed in. Already the ground was ablaze from the dragons above sending their fire into the mix. Seth ran out of the way. While he wouldn't die from a Draki blast, it hurt like a bitch to heal from the burns.

A demon jumped in front of him and narrowly missed slicing Seth's chest open. He met the beast blow for blow until the demon made a critical mistake and Seth sent his head flying. There was no time to catch a breath. Several trees caught fire and threatened to topple in his path.

Two more demons charged at him and he had to exchange his large sword for two shorter ones. He lunged at the one to his right, while he swiped at the one on his left. Growing tired of their little games, he flashed behind one of them and quickly took its head. The other came at him with a banshee scream and Seth jabbed his right hand, impaling the blade into the demon's gut. As he thrust it upward, he swung the other knife across the demon's neck removing its head.

Blood dripped off him and the ground was coated with the sticky substance, but it only spurred him on. An attack came from behind and one demon managed to come in low and make a deep cut across his thigh.

Seth hissed as pain sliced through nerve endings. Sweet pain that only served to give him the high he sought. If he thought he could get away with it, he'd stand there and let them carve him up like a holiday ham. He could even let one take his head and end his misery, but then he thought of sweet Katie and never seeing her again. He had to be certain of her safety first.

Seth ran at the next demon that tried to attack and lopped off his head. The stench of burning flesh met his nose and sent a bitter taste to the back of his throat. He was surrounded by fighting, but even with being outnumbered, they appeared to be winning and the demons were forced back into hiding.

He spotted Lowan and Chaval in the thick of a battle.

His fangs elongated.

"Dear gods, please tell me that's not Chaval." Gwen's voice gave away her heartache.

Seth dared not take his eyes off Lowan. "I'm afraid so. Perhaps you should leave this place."

"Fuck you, Seth. You know I can still fight."

"I never doubted your abilities. I only question if you could kill a childhood friend?" Her pain radiated off her and thickened the air. Gwen was a born warrior and her brother Marcus had taught her how to fight. Seth would trust her at his back any day, but this one.

"I refuse to believe that he has turned to evil."

"Well, I'm not sure how much more proof you need." Before he could say another word, they were rushed by several demons. Both of them hacked and sliced their way across the battlefield. From the corner of his eye, Seth caught Garin heading to battle with Lowan. He hoped his brethren fried the bastard's ass. Garin had a unique gift and could conjure a fireball that put even Baal to shame.

Seth had no more than dispatched the demons in front of him, than Chaval flashed into the fight. The warrior's eyes fell onto Gwen.

"You shouldn't be here," Chaval whispered.

"I might say the same of you. How could you?" Gwen's voice cracked.

Chaval ground his jaw. "Leave here, before someone hurts you." Then he did the one thing that surprised Seth. He flashed away.

Seth turned to see how the others fared. The demons were getting thinned out and he spotted Garin and Lowan. Sparks flew as their blades scraped against each other. Seth started to head in their direction when Lowan blasted Garin with his power knocking Garin to the ground. Events slowed and Seth yelled as Lowan's blade swung through the air and made contact with his brethren's neck.

Seth's feet locked to the ground and he watched in horror as his best friend's head was detached. A female screamed into his ear.

THERE WAS a ruckus in the corridor and Katie, along with her guards, Diego and Jax rushed out to see what all the commotion was. Several men and one woman all covered in blood scurried by and they had a snarling, cursing Seth in their grip. He was bound and being dragged by two large men while the rest kept a tight circle around them.

"Oh, my god. What happened?" She tried to push her way in, but was grabbed by Diego and pulled back. She dug her nails into his arm, he hissed but held firm. "Let go of me," she demanded.

"I'm sorry. Give them some time to get things settled." He spun her to face him. "Someone will come for you, that I promise."

No sooner had the words left his mouth than Baal approached, his glum expression told her things were not well. His clothes, like all the others was covered in blood and she worried if any was his own. Diego released her and she ran to him.

"What happened?"

The demon put his hand to the small of her back. "Let's go sit." Then escorted her back into the room to the couch where they both took a seat. Katie held her breath. This wasn't going to be good news.

"We were outnumbered, but we managed to push them back. However, one of the guardians lost his life. He and Seth were close and I'm afraid..."

She brought her hand to her mouth, knowing that Seth had been sent over the edge. "We lost him, didn't we?"

Baal nodded. "I'm sorry."

Before her mind could begin to comprehend the news, the door burst open. Her gaze fell on a tall man. Dressed in jeans and a black tee he appeared to be no more than in his late twenties. She couldn't help notice the pain on his handsome face.

"Where have they taken him?" the man growled.

"Lower level," Baal replied.

The man vanished.

"Who was that?" Katie found it odd he was the only one besides her guards that didn't have a speck of blood on him.

"That was the guardian king. What a fucked-up homecoming."

She shook her head. "What do you mean?"

The demon's eyes narrowed and his lip curled in disgust. "He was being held by the gods. Punished for who the fuck knows what crime."

Kate shivered at the venomous tone. It was apparent there was no love lost between the demon and the gods.

"So, the king, can he save Seth?"

Baal pursed his lips. "I doubt it. Had the gods let him join us…well things might have turned out different."

A woman flashed into the room. "Please tell me we didn't lose Garin."

"I wish I could, doll," Baal replied.

She brought her hand to her mouth and Katie saw tears fill her eyes. "I can't believe it. How is Seth?"

Baal looked between both women. "This is poor timing, but Cassie this is Katie, Seth's mate. Katie, Cassie is mated to Marcus."

Cassie rushed to Katie and pulled her into a quick embrace before stepping back. "I didn't know Seth had a mate. Why did I hear that he's been confined to a cell?"

Katie was unsure how much to tell, but then again if this woman had once been human she might be a great ally. "He refuses to accept my blood and I have no idea what's happened to him. Maybe you can find out?"

Cassie sighed. "Stupid, stubborn men." She laid a hand on Katie's arm. "Don't you worry, I'll take care of this." She flashed from the room.

"I'm pretty sure I'm going to like her."

SETH TUGGED ON HIS RESTRAINTS, but was too weak to break them. The voices cried out to seek revenge on those who had bound and caged him like a wild animal. They would pay and he would happily drink every last one until they shriveled into nothingness.

Images of his friend's head rolling across their homeland replayed in his mind. He tried to shake the memory and hoped it was only a figment of his fucked-up imagination, but deep in his heart he knew it wasn't. The link the guardians all held to each other told him that one of their own had been lost to them.

A shadow approached the bars. He growled as his fangs sank into his lower lip.

"You," he spat at his jailer. "You dare show your face here?" He pulled on the restraints that held him to the wall. The cuffs chafed his wrists until they bled. The pain sliced through him and became an aphrodisiac. "Step in. Unless you're afraid."

The man flashed into the cell and knelt to the floor so he was eye-level. "I am so sorry."

Seth spit again, this time making contact with the man's face. "Fuck you, my lord."

Aidyn wiped his face. "I deserve that and more."

"You deserve to die, same as the rest and you will too. I'll make sure of it." He jerked forward and dislocated his shoulder. Pain settled through him like an old friend. "Free me and I may let you live."

"You know I can't do that, but I'll figure out a way to fix this. I promise."

Seth sneered. "If you want to do me any favors, toss me a human. I'm famished."

Aidyn rose and walked away, leaving Seth with only the voices, his hatred and a hunger that burned his gut like a cauldron of acid.

He had to find a way out of here so he could feed. He sensed the presence of another guardian whom he knew very well.

"Why are you hiding in the shadows? Come closer."

"I'm not hiding." Cassie stepped forward and placed her hands on the bars.

"Then you're observing me like a speck under a microscope," he snarled. She flashed inside and his heart nearly stopped. "Get out. You are not welcome here."

Her gaze bore into him. Damn her, was she searching for the stain on his soul? If she carried the same ability as her mate she would see for herself how far gone he was. Knowing Cassie, she would want to try and save him and he didn't want to be saved.

"What are you fucking staring at? Get out, I said." He flashed his fangs.

Sympathy swirled in her eyes. "I know you're still in there, Seth. I refuse to give up on you."

Great. The last thing he wanted to do was hurt her. She had become a little sister to him and if he were capable of loving anyone it would be Cassie. "Don't pity me and don't think for a second if I could free myself I'd spare your life." He liked to think he might, but the reality was even he didn't trust himself. He may very well kill her if given the chance.

She tried to get in his head, but he blocked her.

"Please, let me help you," she begged.

"No. You don't belong here. Leave and forget I ever existed." He turned away and refused to meet her gaze. She hesitated a second before she finally vanished.

He stared at the wall and tried to shove down the voices that kept chanting in his head. They wanted blood and so did he. He'd like to start with Lowan, but unless he was freed that would never happen and a tiny part of him really didn't want out. Watching the death of his friend and brethren, Garin, had given the darkness on his soul something to feed on and it had grown. He only prayed Marcus wouldn't come see him until after Garin's funeral. By then, Seth's hope was the curse would have full control over him. It was already so close he could taste it and the little stunt he had pulled to get himself locked up in here hadn't been far off the mark. He was gone, but if his brethren thought for a moment there was even a glimmer of himself still there they would try to save him. He didn't want saving. Didn't want them to hang on to a dream and he was tired, but he couldn't tell them he was ready to give up the fight. They wouldn't understand even though they said they did. How could they? No one could ever understand what it was like to live with what he had done to Vivian and the voices that were his constant companion. It ate at him like a maggot and fuck Zarek for making him live like this.

When he'd found out about Drayos's curse he'd had to hide his joy. Finally, he could be free, he only had to bide his time. His only other regret?

Katie.

He wished he'd never met her and he sure as hell wished he'd never had a taste of her, because he wanted more. It was another reason the almighty Zarek could go straight to Hell. Seth might have welcomed a mate a couple of years ago, but it was too late now. He worried for her, but knew now that Aidyn was back he would help Katie and figure out what needed to be done. Especially when he found out she belonged to Seth. Aidyn would mate with her himself if he had to and though the thought of her with another man should cause fury, his king was the only one he trusted to set aside his own life for another. It was the only good thing Zarek had done in choosing Aidyn as their leader. To have treated him with such malice when he'd shown up had ripped Seth in two, but it had been the one guarantee Seth needed. His king would have never expected that kind of behavior from him had he been completely sane.

CHAPTER EIGHTEEN

KATIE PACED the room until she thought she'd wear a groove in the carpet. No word had arrived yet on Seth's condition and it was starting to piss her off. She turned to Baal and the two dragon shifters that stared at her.

"If I don't get some answers in the next five minutes, I'm going to fry someone's ass."

"You can fry mine."

Katie jumped at the rich voice that spoke and turned to face him with a glare. "Don't tempt me."

He gave her a forced smile. "You're feisty. I like that."

She was on his heels as he went to the bar and poured himself something from a crystal decanter. "Care for whiskey?"

"No. I care for answers."

He nodded and looked beyond her. "Gentlemen, would you excuse us please?"

The other three fled the room without a second glance, probably thankful to be free of her fury. He waited for them to close the door before speaking again. "I'm Aidyn." He held out his hand.

She accepted. "I'm Katie. You'll pardon me if I'm not sure how to address you. I've never been in the same room as royalty."

He snorted. "There's nothing royal about me. I'm only chosen to lead and make sure the laws are followed."

She narrowed her gaze. "And to take Seth's head."

He swirled the liquid in his glass before downing the entire contents and setting the tumbler on the table. "Right, about that. I went and spoke with him. While he thinks he can fool me, I see through his charade."

"What do you mean?"

He motioned for her to have a seat at the conference table. "He thinks Marcus, our healer is the only one who can see the stain on his soul, but I can see it as well. Also, Cassie paid him a visit and confirmed my belief in that he's somewhat faking it." He scrubbed his hand along his jaw. "He has given up hope and wishes to die."

"Why?" she gasped.

"To be honest, there really isn't much of him left. Only a shred of his soul still holds the light and he knows that. It was why I sent Baal to try and get you two together."

"How did you know?"

"Let's just say I have my ways and I can't divulge all of my secrets."

She wasn't sure... no she was positive she didn't like that answer, but wouldn't press it at the moment. "So, what do we do?"

He flashed a sinister grin. "We trick him at his own game."

She sighed. "Maybe if this is what he really wants you should let him go."

Aidyn leaned in closer. "Have you any idea how old I am?"

She stared at him. Hard to tell, but she knew Seth was an ancient. Still, she hated to way over guess. Would he be offended? "You look twenty-five." It was a safe reply.

He laughed. "I'm five hundred. Young compared to some, but my point is I have known Seth my entire life. If he could only feel worthy of you he wouldn't hesitate to claim you. You have to make him feel worthy and no pressure, but time is ticking for both of you."

"Right. No pressure." Already her body was reverting back to the migraines and hot flashes. "Do you have a plan?"

"Tomorrow, I'll take you to see him. Tonight, I have to say goodbye to a friend."

"I'm so very sorry."

Sadness shadowed his brown eyes. "So am I."

KATIE HAD NEVER SEEN SO many people gathered together. Baal had flashed her out of the compound and to a large valley. Still having no idea where she was, she only knew she was surrounded by mountains and it was lonely despite the hundreds of people. Draki, Kothar and guardians filled the landscape.

Aidyn had said a few words, but she'd not really heard them. Seth's voices were back in her head and she feared for him. She joined in as everyone dropped to one knee and the tower was lit where Garin's body was laid to rest. Sorrow thickened the air and the need to go to Seth wrenched her heart. She knew he was hurting for his friend's death just like everyone else here and while she understood the reason why he was locked away, she hated that he was alone.

Her body began to cramp. She wasn't used to kneeling on the hard ground for such an extended period, but she dared not move. Didn't wish to disrespect these people or their fallen comrade. After several minutes everyone rose and began to mingle. Stories were shared of the warrior and his life along with tears. Talk reached her about how many had been lost. While the demons had faced more losses, the Kothar had a dozen men killed. The only ones who had been unharmed were the Draki.

The stories retold about the battle all had fought on their home ground led her to believe it had been fierce which was another excellent reason for her to push forward. She needed to mate with Seth come hell or high water in order to set things in motion. Hopefully, things that would stop this madness. The thought of it spilling into her world caused her gut to roll. She laughed at herself.

"What do you find so funny?" Cassie slipped in beside her.

"Only my thoughts. I suddenly realized I'm no longer part of the human world nor am I part of this one."

The other woman gave a sympathetic look. "I know exactly what you mean, but we're both part of something so much bigger."

She nodded. "I guess you're right. How did you cope with the changes?"

Cassie smiled and led her away from the crowd. "I fought it at first. Marcus and I had our issues in the beginning. Matter of fact, I thought I had lost him to the darkness."

"So, you do understand. Tell me about it. Oh, I don't mean to pry," Katie replied.

Cassie put her hand on Katie's shoulder. "I don't mind. Anything I can do to help Seth find happiness and finally be whole again, I'm on board." Cassie entwined her arm in Katie's. "Let's go for a walk."

An hour later and Katie had heard the entire history of how Cassie had first dreamt of Marcus, to their mating ceremony and not long ago, the birth of their daughter. From what she had been told, the baby was the first guardian born in a long time. As they made their way back to the crowd of people and she witnessed first-hand how Marcus and Cassie looked at each other, there was no doubt how much they loved one another. These people had begun to grow on her. They had been tasked to protect her and human kind, yet they lived much like the rest of the world. They loved and they mourned.

Katie set her shoulders and went in search of Aidyn to see about saving Seth. She would be damned if she would allow these people to suffer another loss. She spotted him a few yards away talking to Baal and she approached with a plan in mind.

"I want you to put me in the cell with Seth." She was done wasting time.

Aidyn gave her a surprised look.

Baal laughed. "See, I told you she was a firecracker."

"I'm not sure that is a wise choice," Aidyn replied.

She shoved her hands on her hips. "Fine, you got a better idea? I'm all ears, otherwise you leave me with him no matter how much he bitches."

"I think it's an excellent idea." A beautiful brunette stepped up beside Aidyn.

"Gwen, have you met Katie yet?" Aidyn asked.

"I've seen you in my visions, but I'm happy to finally meet you in person."

"Excuse me?" She accepted the woman's extended hand and was surprised at the strength in her grip. It wasn't something Katie expected from a woman who looked like she had just stepped off a model runway.

Gwen smiled. "I know everything is confusing. I have a gift of vision and often can see the future." She snorted. "Of course, it never shows itself when I really need it and often times what I do see can be iffy. I have seen you though and I know that you are the only one who can save Seth."

For a moment, she was at a loss for words. Every time she thought she had things figured out, something else popped up to surprise her. "Can you tell me anything else?" She tried to hide the hope in her voice. "Maybe how all this goes down?"

Gwen cast her gaze to Aidyn then back to her. "I'll not lie. I know that you will save Seth and he will assist in your transformation. I don't know if you survive. I can only see your body in flames." Sympathy filled her brown eyes. "I'm so sorry."

So was she. She knew there was a chance she wouldn't survive, but hearing this only slammed it home.

"Katie?"

"Huh?" Strong hands gripped her arm and she realized Aidyn was speaking to her.

"I have to trust that if you are to save Seth then you will survive.

If your mating is completed and you were to die, it would destroy him. Losing you makes no sense."

Gwen nodded. "What he says is true, I just wish I could give you a definite answer."

She cleared her throat. "I understand that once immortals are mated, the death of one of them can be detrimental to the other. But, is there a chance Seth would survive should I die?" She looked between the two, waiting. Finally, Aidyn spoke up.

"If you had completed the bond, and if as Gwen predicts it reverses the curse, then it is possible. Though in many cases the survivor chooses to join their deceased mate. It's why we lost so many during the last war." He rubbed his chin. "Though you can still bond but not mate. Meaning the mating ceremony will bind you together heart, body and soul. The chances of surviving after that is completed are slim to none."

Katie stood tall. "I think the first thing is to get my blood in him and see if he will come around. The two of you need to promise me to never tell him of your vision of me going up in flames." She sucked in a deep breath. "And if I don't make it, you have to promise to not let him die. My death can't be in vain."

"You have my word," Aidyn replied.

THE CELL DOOR opened and a woman walked through. Seth picked up his head to study her and recognition hit.

Katie.

The redhead turned to look behind her. "Lock the door and don't come back until later." The gate slammed shut and they were left staring at each other.

"Are you here to feed me?" he snarled. The need to have her gone pulsed through his veins. He would show her his darkest side if need be, even though he hated like hell that this would be the way she would last remember him.

She tipped her head and blue eyes flashed at him. "I'm here to save your sorry ass." Her gaze narrowed and she thrust her hands on her hips. "If you think you can fool me into leaving you, then you've got another think coming mister." She stepped closer. "How dare you! I need you to help me so I can set events in motion. If you want to drop out of the picture then you do it after you meet your obligations."

"You are as crazy as I am."

She raised her chin. "You bet your fucking ass I am. We make the perfect pair. Now, you gonna play by my rules?"

He let a slow smile curl upward and his fangs dropped. "You should fear me, because once I get my hands on you I will relish pinning you down while I take every last drop of your blood. Your body will be left here on the concrete floor to grow cold while I gain strength." He laughed. "Do you really wish to unleash my thirst on the world?"

The voices started chanting. *Kill her. Kill her.* One rose above the others and demanded silence then whispered, *Lure her in. You can finally have what you desire.*

Yes, yes he could and for once he had to agree. His hunger twisted his gut into a burning knot. He licked his lips. "Very well. Come closer and I will let you save my sorry ass."

She took a hesitant step and her fear slammed into him causing saliva to fill his mouth. He remained still, had to allow her to come to him then he could pounce. He would have to be quick because he was sure this was all a trick, but maybe he could use her to bargain his way out.

Their gazes never left each other and before he knew it she was within reach. He grabbed her arm, swung her around and jerked her to his chest. His cock stiffened when her tight ass brushed against him. He pushed her hair aside and exposed the silky flesh of her neck. He wanted to sink his fangs, instead he kissed the soft skin and she moaned, which caused him to harden further.

He suckled, taking care to bring the smaller vein closer to the surface all while the dark one screamed in his head to hurt her. He managed to hang onto the small thin scrap of sanity he had left and fight back. When he could stand it no longer, he pressed his fangs against her skin and let them slide into her vein. Sweet strawberries coated his tongue, then the back of his throat. His gut rumbled as the nectar reached it and his cock throbbed.

He'd never tasted anything so intoxicating in his entire existence. Even the voices sighed in relief at finally being fed. He wrapped his arms around her waist and held her firm to him. His mind hardly registered the moans that escaped her as her body experienced orgasm.

Her blood continued to flow, brought strength to weakened muscles. She struggled against his hold, but he pinned her in place not wanting to give up her taste. It was better than the addicts he had drank from and much more preferable to the blade he'd substituted in its place.

Realization smacked him, her heartbeat weakened and images of Vivian lying dead on the ground assaulted his memories, yet he still drank. Then something zinged through him and his body tingled. He lost his grip and Katie shoved herself away and turned to face him, blue eyes glared. Blood still trickled down her neck from the twin punctures and he wiped his hand across his mouth. Then dawning.

He'd tried to kill his mate.

CHAPTER NINETEEN

"WELL I'D LIKE to say that was fun but..." Oh, who the hell was she kidding? "Okay, I can't lie. It was until you tried to kill me." Katie reached up to touch her throat and wipe away the blood. The orgasm had been off the Richter scale and she was positive every immortal within twenty miles heard her. Not that she cared.

Seth stared at her with horror in his eyes then the mask changed to raw anger. "Are you stupid?"

"Well, love you too."

He snarled. His muscles bunched under the black tee he wore and the bindings that held him in place snapped. Katie took a step backward, never had she seen him look fiercer. She held up her hand.

"I'll zap your ass again if I have to."

"That's what that was?" He was to her in two steps and grabbed her by the waist before he flashed them from the cell.

Katie's head swam when they reappeared back in the main room upstairs. The chatter grew silent as several people looked at them, mouths gaping. Seth released her and marched to where Aidyn stood and got in his face.

"You fucking put my mate in harm's way," he spat.

Aidyn never flinched, only met his stare head on. "Can I assume it worked? Though I must admit I didn't expect her to release you this fast."

Katie cleared her throat. "Not me, he broke free."

That caused Aidyn's mouth to fall open. "Really? Her blood gave you the ability to free yourself from a bond that would leave the rest of us helpless?"

Seth flexed his fists at his side. Katie feared he'd do something stupid so she moved in next to him. Placed a hand on his arm and he appeared to relax, slightly. "Seth, don't do something you'll regret later. I was the one who insisted on this and there was nothing he or anyone here could do to stop me."

He jerked free of her. "You should have left it alone." He turned his fury back to Aidyn. "You should have taken my head and left me to finally be in peace." He flashed from the room, but his anger still clung to the air.

"Wow, what the hell just happened?" Katie asked.

"I'd say he was worse off than we thought. I knew he wanted to die, but I thought once you gave him your blood he would come around." Aidyn sighed. "I have to assume it worked, but to what extent I've no idea. Tell me exactly what happened down there." He motioned to a chair at the conference table.

Katie hesitated. "I should go after him."

Aidyn shook his head. "I need to know what happened first."

She took a seat and the others moved in to settle in their own. All of them held a look of concern. It was evident they worried for their comrade.

"Not much really. I offered my blood and he took it, but I did have to zap him. He wasn't going to let me go and I was growing weak. I don't think he had control over himself. Once I was free he seemed to come back to his senses, grabbed me and that's when we showed up here." She leaned back. "Oh, he snapped those restraints like they were rubber-bands."

Marcus rubbed his chin. "Interesting. I'm going to guess your goddess blood is more powerful than most."

Aidyn nodded. "Indeed. I doubt any of the rest of us could break those."

Katie crossed her legs and jiggled her foot. Her nerves were shot and time was running out. Heat crept through her blood and a migraine threatened. "What now?"

"We search for him," Aidyn replied. "Problem is, he has gone off grid again and I can't link to him."

She rubbed her temples. "Fucking great. When you locate him, I have a desire to kick his ass into next week. In the meantime, I need to lay down for a bit."

Gwen jumped up. "Let me take you to one of the guest rooms."

"Thanks."

She followed Gwen through the sterile corridor. "Tell me, is this how your vision went?"

The woman shook her head, her darks curls bounced. "No, but I didn't really see much. Only that you were the one to save him."

Katie sighed. "But not that he would save me."

Gwen opened a door and flipped on a light switch. A floor lamp in the corner lit to reveal a bed, couch, flat screen and a small table. It was by no means elegant, but it was clean and the bed called her name.

"I'm so sorry. I'm positive once he's had some time, he'll be back."

She threw on her best fake smile. "I'm sure you're right. I think a shower and a nap will do me some good."

"I'll leave you." Gwen pulled her into a hug. "Let me know if you need anything."

"Thanks again."

Gwen headed out and closed the door behind her. Katie decided she was too tired to shower and crawled into bed. Later, she told herself, she'd clean up. She curled up under the covers and didn't bother with removing her clothes. If she had to venture a guess, the blood loss was making her tired. She closed her eyes and tried to conjure visions of Seth. Wished his warmth were next to her so she could curl into him. It was crazy to want him so badly, especially when he seemed to fight his desire for her every step of the way. Maybe after a nap and shower she'd go searching for him if he hadn't come back yet.

SETH SAT with his elbows on the bar and listened to the two drunks behind him argue over who was cheating who at pool. His head pounded and since he didn't get headaches he knew it must be Katie's. Anger still radiated off him that they had interfered. He'd been ready to leave this world. Had enough of fighting with his own internal enemies every second of every day. Granted, his mind had been quiet since he'd drunk her blood and while it should make him happy it didn't.

He set his glass on the scratched up wooden bar. "Another." He wished he could drown his sorrows in alcohol, but unlike the humans surrounding him it wasn't possible. Now that the voices had vanished, the pain of Garin's death haunted him even more.

I would give up my sanity and my life if it would bring you back, my friend.

The bartender grabbed the bottle of whiskey and filled his glass. She didn't speak, but he could imagine his mood was evident. "Don't fuck with me" was written all over his face. When he'd entered through the front door of the tiny hole in the wall, people had rushed to get out of his way. He just needed to be alone and his brethren would never search a wooden shack of a bar in the remote hills of South Dakota. Only the bottom of the barrel came here and if someone was itching for a fight, Seth was in the mood to provide it. It was also a place where he and Garin had spent much time together. They never had to speak a word to understand how the other had felt.

"Thought you might be here."

"Son of a bitch." Seth turned to meet the golden gaze of Baal who'd sidled up next to him. "Demon, you're a damn pest."

Baal flashed a wicked smile. "I aim to please."

"Can I get you something?" The gal behind the bar stared at Baal like she wanted to lick him from head to toe. It was the typical reaction most Kothar men received.

"Sweet cheeks! You must be new here," Baal replied.

"I started last week."

"Well then, we'll have to get better acquainted, but in the meantime I'll have whatever's on tap."

"Coming right up." She moved off to grab a glass.

"Charming. If you want to fuck the bartender, you can move to the other end," Seth growled.

"You want her?"

He pinned the demon with a death glare. "Get serious. How did you find me anyway?"

Baal snorted. "I thought of the most remote place I'd go for a drink and here I am. Do you think you're the only one who has ever wanted to escape reality?" He looked up and thanked the bartender who set his mug of beer in front of him then took a long pull. "Question is. Why you here? You've got a woman back home and can I assume you're feeling better now?"

Was he? That seemed to be the big debatable question. "I just lost my best friend and I haven't a clue who I am anymore."

Baal sucked back half his beer. "I'm sorry about Garin, he was a good man. Tell me, have the voices left?"

Seth swirled the copper liquid in his glass, wishing he could drown in it. "They have."

"Then what's the fucking problem? I get you lost a friend, hell we all have in our long miserable lives."

He felt the demon's gaze burning a hole into him, but kept his eyes on the mirror behind the bar. His reflection stared back at him. "I don't know how to be normal anymore. I've lived for thousands of years and I was ready to leave."

"Even after meeting Katie?"

Seth sucked back his drink. "She would do any man proud, but I don't deserve a woman like her and gods knows she deserves better than me."

Baal tipped back his mug and drained it before setting it down and pointing a finger at the empty glasses. "Cupcake. Another round here." The girl smiled and grabbed clean glasses. Poured whiskey into one and a draft into the other then set them on the bar. Picked up the dirty ones and walked away.

"Seems to me that fate decided you were good enough for her so maybe you should stop fighting." Baal sipped his beer then wiped the foam from his mouth. "You love her?"

Seth stared into his glass. "I think so, but how can I be sure when I'm not even sure I'm sane?" When had he started falling for her? There was a spark of interest when he'd saved her that night on the docks. When he'd taken her in Egypt he'd lost another piece of his heart. Would he be able to give her all of it? Truth be told, it scared the shit out of him.

"I think what we need is to tie one on and then I need to fuck that bartender," Baal announced snapping Seth back to reality.

Seth simply shook his head. "You ever get tired of jumping from one bed to another? Oh, and in case you have forgotten, drunkenness is impossible for us."

Baal reached in the pocket of his black leather jacket. "To answer question one. No, I thought you knew by now I am a man whore. Two." He produced a small packet with a couple of tiny purple pills. "Our good friend the voodoo priestess has made a concoction that will allow us to enjoy alcohol the same as a human."

He raised a brow. "What will that woman come up with next?"

Baal waved a little purple pill in front of Seth. "Care to give it a try?"

Seth held out his hand. "Why not. I'm used to torturing myself. This could be fun." Hadn't he just wished to drown his sorrows? The demon was becoming a close friend so he held out his hand and let

Baal drop the pill in his palm. Seth swallowed it followed by a whiskey chaser. "How long does this last?"

"Three hours after you drink your last one." Baal flashed a wicked smile. "Let's close this place down."

LOWAN AND CHAVAL strode through the rock corridor, blood coated their clothing and dripped from their weapons, but the Dark Lord wore a smile. "Chaval, we may have been hit hard, but taking the head off that guardian made every second I have been trapped in Hell worth it. Tell me. Were you aware of what Raven was when you brought her to me?"

Chaval gave him a sideways glance. "A Satan worshipper."

"Ah, but she is much more than that. She's my ticket into the human realm." He stopped and turned to face his servant. "She is a virgin and chosen to serve me. Do you know what that means?"

Chaval tipped his head in thought. "I'm sorry, my lord. I'm afraid I don't."

"My good man, an offering of a virgin as a sacrifice to the gods brings great power. Already her blood courses through me and I can feel my body pulsing with so much power it's like I've been struck by lightning and the voltage is ready to be unleashed. When I take her virginity tonight, there will be nothing to stop me."

The demon showed no emotion. "This is a good thing then."

"Yes, it is and once we are in the human realm you will round up all of these devil worshippers and bring them to meet their new king."

"As you wish, my lord." Chaval bowed.

Lowan continued his trek back to his suite, anxious to bathe and take the virginity of the fair Raven. When he entered his room, she was there to greet him wearing only a red, silk robe. The fabric against her tan skin and black hair made a stark contrast. Her eyes were lined with heavy black liner and lips the color of ripe, red cherries.

She smiled. "My lord, I have your bath ready for you." She approached. "May I undress you and help you bathe?"

He ran his tongue over his fangs. "You may, but you will disrobe first so I can have the pleasure of looking upon your naked body."

"As you wish." She untied the belt and let the robe slip off her shoulders and pool on the floor.

Lowan pulled in a deep breath as she reached for his chest shield, unbuckled the leather bands and pulled it free. Next, she removed his shirt followed by his leather pants and when he was left standing naked, his erection jutting out it was her turn to inhale sharply. She took his hand and led him across the stone floor, down the stairs and into the bath.

"You do realize that tonight you will lose your virginity to me?" He sat on one of the built-in seats, the hot water a relief on his aching muscles. Even though he was a demigod, he had mostly fought by hand using his sword and dagger. Needed the feel of bone and flesh tearing under his physical power in order to sate his desire to destroy the guardians.

"Yes, my lord." She ran a bar of soap across his chest, followed by a cloth. Her touch gentle and he wondered if she realized when he took her he would be anything but.

CHAPTER TWENTY

KATIE WAS BURNING ALIVE. This had to be what Gwen meant by the vision she had of her on fire, because that was how she felt. The guardian swathed a cool, moist cloth across her forehead, but it heated up as quickly as it was placed there.

"Maybe I should send for some ice," Gwen said.

"I can't believe the bastard is going to leave me to die after I saved his sorry ass." Katie was grateful Gwen had excellent hearing since her voice came out as barely a whisper.

"I'm sure he'll be back any minute." Katie didn't think Gwen believed it any more than she did. He would have come back by now.

Aidyn entered the room. "Any changes?"

Gwen shook her head.

He sighed. "Then you have to take my blood and see if we can slow this."

"Fine," Katie croaked out.

Gwen got up from the edge of the bed and Aidyn took her place. He bit his wrist and placed it over her mouth. She drank, but he didn't taste like Seth. It wasn't bad, but not the same. As the blood coated her throat her skin cooled, but it still wasn't normal.

"I read the book. We need to get you to the temple."

"You know where it is?"

Aidyn gave a nod. She couldn't help notice how handsome he was. Chocolate eyes with collar-length, brown, wavy hair and like all the other men he was stacked with muscle. She didn't think there was an ugly duckling among them. Funny how he didn't stir the fire between her legs like Seth had. None of them did.

"I've seen the Phoenix god's temple. It sits off by itself. Do you feel well enough to go?"

She pushed herself to sitting. What choice did she have? She needed to go. Maybe they'd find some other answers that weren't in the book. "I'm ready whenever you are."

Aidyn helped her stand. Placed a strong arm around her waist and flashed them from the room. Moments later they stood inside a large, open portico that reminded her of the many photos she'd seen of Greek architecture. The floors and columns made of white marble with veins of red, orange and black running through. A bronze statue of the Phoenix, its beak stretched to the sky, wings spread wide perched majestically in the center of a fountain. Water bubbled around its taloned feet.

Katie walked to it and stared up at the beast, mesmerized by its beauty.

"This would be your father's home," Aidyn spoke softly.

She turned to look at him. "Have you ever been in here?"

"No. It always felt like sacred ground so I never dared approach." He grinned. "Though I've always been drawn to it and curious about its contents."

"Well, I guess this is as good a time as any to poke around," she replied and walked toward a wide opening that led inside. Once past the archway, she took two steps down into a sunken room covered in plush cream-colored carpet and throw pillows of various sizes. Their vibrant hues jumped out against the pale flooring. A mural covered one wall and depicted the Phoenix in its bird form transforming into a man then to fire only to start over again.

She shivered and rubbed her arms. "This place feels so desolate. I keep expecting someone to greet us yet no one does."

"I know the feeling. Let's keep looking."

Katie followed Aidyn across the room and down a wide corridor until they came upon what must have been the god's throne.

"It's beautiful," she exclaimed then rushed forward until she stood in front of it and reached out to touch it but hesitated.

"I'm sure it wouldn't hurt if you sat in it." Aidyn nudged her.

She shook her head. "Oh, that seems wrong." Though her heart ached to do so. Instead she fingered the large, gold-leaf Phoenix symbol that adorned the high back of the seat. Her father had sat here and it was the one thing she was positive he had touched. She fought the tears that filled her eyes. "I wish I could have known him."

A strong hand touched her shoulder. "Katie. Something tells me your father would be proud to have you sit here. After all, you are the first of his children to actually grace his palace."

She swallowed and turned. Placed her sweaty palms on the chair's arms and lowered herself until her behind hit the red velvet cushion. She closed her eyes. Love, like she'd never experienced wrapped around her and bathed her in its essence. She gasped as visions of a majestic bird with feathers of orange, red and blue soaring through the air filled her head. Fire blazed from the tips of its wings and tail, yet left the bird unscathed. Was it a vision of the father she never knew?

She opened her eyes and let the tears spill. "I cannot fail. Somehow, I have to find a way to make this work." Seth would come. He had to.

"I wish I could help you," Aidyn replied.

Katie stood. "You have already done so much for me. I could never ask you to tie yourself to me for all eternity." She stepped down and a wave of dizziness passed over her causing her to stumble. Aidyn caught her in his arms.

"You are becoming ill again."

She straightened herself. "I'll be fine. We should locate the altar."

He nodded. "Take my arm then."

She wrapped her hand around his bicep and they walked from the room. Headed down another corridor in search of the sacrificial altar. The place where the book had indicated she would have to make her transformation.

"Most altars are outside." Aidyn led her through another open archway and into a courtyard. Statues of Ra in black and gold marble lined the walk on either side. "I'd say we are in the correct area."

Katie looked up at the towering sculptures. "I feel like they are watching us." A shiver started at the nape of her neck and skittered down her spine.

Aidyn gave out a halfhearted laugh. "I have no doubt we are being watched." He pointed. "Over there. That's the altar."

Her gaze followed his direction and landed on a black marble slab that rose at least three feet into the air and was maybe ten feet long. It was adorned with a gold Phoenix emblem on the front and sat in the middle of a ring of red slate tiles. She quickly realized the thundering in her chest was her heart. For some reason she half expected if she were to look at the top of the altar, she would find bloodstains. Isn't that what the movies always showed?

The ground shook beneath their feet, followed by a loud rumble that lasted for several seconds and the sky grew black. Katie clutched Aidyn's arm to keep herself steady and stomp down her panic.

"What the hell's happening?" No sooner had she posed the question than everything quieted. The sky returned to a brilliant blue.

"Dear gods, it's started. That was Hell's gate opening." Aidyn met her with panic in his eyes. "Lowan has entered the human realm."

SETH PICKED himself up off the floor. The shaking had been so bad it had knocked him from his bed. He rubbed his eyes and cursed Baal for the pills Baal had given him last night. The bastard had forgotten to mention that along with the ability to get drunk came a hangover. He rubbed his temples and sent a thousand curses to the demon. "May every woman you attempt to bed, tell you to go fuck yourself." Clawing at the bed he pulled himself back up and plopped on the lumpy mattress. He ran his fingers through his hair. "Son of a bitch. Even my hair hurts." He questioned the sanity of every living human who put themselves through the drinking ritual on a weekly basis. "And they call me loco." He dropped his head into his hands, but then jerked up. Realization had taken a moment to sink in through the fog that surrounded his mind.

"Dear gods, Hell's gate." He opened his mind to his brethren and it was a jumbled mess of voices. It seemed everyone was trying to communicate at the same time and for a brief moment he found it comforting after having withdrawals from the ones he'd lived with for so long. To some silence was golden, but to him it would take another lifetime to get used to.

He shook his head and slammed the barrier back down so he could search for his link to Katie. Last night he might have wished himself gone from the world, but today he was still here and humanity needed him. Katie needed him. He was a warrior and duty called. In seconds he found the link to her and flashed from the boarding room. Spotted her in the arms of his king and he couldn't stop the snarl that formed on his lips as he strode toward them. Once he reached them, they pulled apart and he had to remind himself it was only a harmless gesture and he owed Aidyn everything.

Seth dropped to one knee and bowed his head. "My lord. Please accept my humble apology for my actions against you earlier." Deep down he knew Aidyn didn't give a shit, but respect meant everything to Seth and he refused to give up their customs. "I willingly accept your punishment."

"Look at me," Aidyn commanded.

Seth raised his head.

"You have been punished enough in your lifetime. I only want to know one thing."

"Yes, my lord?"

"Are you well?"

Seth nodded. It was just like Aidyn to worry for him and everything else be damned. "Other than what the mortals call a hangover, I'm happy to report the voices are gone."

A smile spread wide. "Stand up."

Seth pushed off on his right foot and rose. Aidyn pulled him into an embrace. "If you ever scare me like that again I will kick your ass from one end of this realm into the next." He released him. "So, you took the purple pill? I thought you knew Baal was trouble."

"I will keep the ass kicking in mind and I can only hope the demon feels a thousand times worse than me." He cleared his throat. "May I be alone with Katie?"

Aidyn winked. "It's about fucking time." He turned to Katie. "Don't take any of his shit and good luck. We will all be holding our breath." He flashed away and left Seth to deal with the wrath of a woman scorned.

She crossed her arms over her chest and glared. Yeah, he'd rather fight twenty demons than take on her fury.

"I'm sorry."

Her lips thinned before she pulled the bottom one through her teeth and hissed. "I should kick your ass."

"I have a better idea."

"And that would be?" Her glare never wavered.

"Give me a chance to make it right."

Her features softened. "Why did you leave anyway? I figured you left me for dead."

He closed in on her yet kept his hands at his side. He didn't want to push it. "I have lived a very long time with the voices. When they were suddenly gone, it was like I lost a part of myself. I still don't know who the hell I am anymore. I needed some time alone."

She drummed her fingers on her arm and exhaled. Loudly. "I guess it would be weird for you. Still, we worried. You could have at least let everyone know you were all right." For the first time she looked away and appeared uncomfortable. "So now what?"

He lifted the corner of his mouth. "I could toss you up on the altar and make you sacrifice your body to me."

She licked her lips. "And what makes you think I would want that?"

"Before, I could smell your arousal. Since having your blood, I can also feel it." He stepped closer. "And let's not forget, I own your body and you crave mine."

She moved back. "Be serious. Aidyn said Hell's gate opened. We need to do something."

It was his turn to sigh. "I need to start your transformation."

"Drink my blood until my heart stops." She laid her hand on the altar. "Here, so I can become whatever the hell I'm supposed to be and hopefully wake my father."

"Yes, but did you forget that sex is part of the mating? No matter what has happened, you are still mine and in order for me to begin your change I must pleasure you." This time he swept in and pinned her to the altar. His erection ground into her.

"B-but it will not bind us totally, correct?"

She didn't want to be tied to him. Could he blame her? Not really. His sanity was still debatable and who knew what he was capable of at any second of the day. Still, he couldn't help the small pang in his chest. He wanted to make her his. Instinct drove him to claim her completely and perhaps a piece of his heart did as well.

"No, without the ceremony we will not be completely bound together. Your soul will still be intact, sweet Kaitlyn." He couldn't help the sharp tone in his voice.

She pressed her palms against his chest and before he knew what hit him she gathered the fabric of his tee in her fists and pulled him closer. Her mouth found his and her tongue delved. Her desperation was evident in both her kiss and her musky scent. While he loved that she was sure enough to take control, he would not allow it. She'd know pleasure like none she'd ever experienced before and she would know it from him.

With a snarl he broke free of the kiss, grabbed the neckline of her shirt and ripped it from her body. "Too many clothes." Next came the bra, which ended up in tatters on the ground. Her breasts finally bare to him, he gripped her wrists and held them to her side as he dipped his head and ran his tongue across her nipple.

She moaned.

He swirled his tongue around the protrusion until it hardened into a tight peak then sucked it into his mouth.

She arched her back and pressed into him.

He let his fangs descend and lightly scraped them over her nipple.

She whimpered.

He pulled free and looked into her blue eyes. Her chest rose and fell with heavy breaths. "At this moment I own you. I will bend your body to my will and your orgasm will be mine to command." He dipped his head and suckled her other nipple before he broke free.

Her eyes darkened with desire. It was evident she wanted him to take charge. Katie was the type of woman who ran everything and for once Seth would give her the gift of totally letting go and handing over control.

He scraped his fangs up her neck until he reached her ear. He nipped the lobe. "Take off your pants," he whispered. He let go of her wrists and took one step back to give her room to obey him.

She didn't hesitate to reach for the button on her jeans and pull it free, lower the zipper and push the fabric past her hips along with her panties. In seconds she stood before him, naked and looking like the goddess she was. He was quick to forget all his other troubles.

CHAPTER TWENTY-ONE

SETH'S EYES raked over her and took in every inch of her nakedness. Katie should have been uncomfortable standing in a foreign place with a man she'd only known a short time. Yet every part of her yearned for him and it was all she could do to remain still. Besides, it wasn't like they hadn't had sex already. Mind-blowing sex to be exact.

She glanced at his erection. "Are you going to keep those clothes on?"

He grinned, showing a peek of fang and the thought of those points in her neck again heated her sex.

"If you want them off you need to come here and strip me."

She wasted no time and practically lunged at him. Grabbed the hem of his tee, pulled it free from his jeans and had it over his head in seconds.

"I would have ruined it like you did mine, but I'm afraid I would have embarrassed myself with my lack of strength."

He chuckled.

She traced lines down his chest until her fingers reached the top of his jeans. With a flick of her wrist she unbuckled the belt, worked the denim's rivet through the hole and pulled down the zipper. His erection strained to free itself so she quickly shoved his jeans to his ankles. She eyed the black biker boots.

"Um, I could use a little help."

Seth toed off each boot and kicked them aside and she was free to finish undressing him. Unlike before, when they'd been in a dimly lit tomb, she could see him more clearly. His body was perfection and rivaled that of any mythical god. Her gaze caught the tattoo on his left bicep. She ran her fingertips over the black ink. A winged Sphinx with an eye above it.

"It's beautiful."

"It was given to me on the day of my creation."

"Does it have a meaning then?" She became mesmerized by it.

"Yes. The Sphinx means guardian of the king and the eye of Ra is for his daughter, Vivian."

She tilted her head to study it further. "I met her."

He gripped her upper arms. "What do you mean? I killed her."

"She was the one who came to me when I was trapped. Gave me the ability to read the book and the power I had. She told me what happened. Well, not in words, but gave me the knowledge."

His grip loosened and he dropped his gaze to the ground as if ashamed of his actions that day. "She lives?"

"Not in the same sense as you or I, but she was real. Perhaps she moved on." She cupped his face and forced him to look at her. "You didn't kill her; not like you think. She wanted me to save you."

"So, I could save you." His back went rigid.

If she didn't do something quick, she was going to lose him again. His emotions bombarded her and he was in turmoil. She did the only thing she could think of and pulled him into a kiss. He resisted at first, but then his body relaxed and he parted his lips for her. She took advantage and plunged her tongue, sweeping and tasting his hot cinnamon essence. She gave his erection a tight squeeze before running her thumb over the head. How a man could be both soft as velvet and hard as steel always amazed her, but this man amazed her more than any other.

He moaned into her mouth before he broke free. "I'll be running this show." He placed large hands around her waist and lifted her until she was sitting on the altar. He pushed her thighs apart and kissed the inside of her calf. Licked his way up her leg, leaving a trail of fire in his wake. She trembled and heat flooded her core. She fisted his hair and tugged, trying to guide him to the sweet spot, but he refused.

"You tease," she said between heavy breaths.

He moved to the other calf and again kissed his way up until he was within inches of where she wanted his mouth. She sucked in a breath and held it. Waited for the fire he would stoke even further with his tongue. Instead he blew hot breath across her folds and she wanted to scream with despair.

"I warned you, your body is mine to command."

"You're evil."

He grinned. "Never forget that."

He glided his tongue along the edge of her folds. Taunted her with a slice of heaven, yet left her in Hell. She chewed her bottom lip. Wanted to beg him for release but refused.

"You'll bend to my will," he whispered.

"No."

"Then I will continue your torture." He ran his tongue so close to her clit she felt the heat of it. Her fingers dug deeper into his scalp and she hoped she drew blood. The bastard had her on the edge and he was going to make her beg.

"Tell me what you need and I will gladly give you what you desire."

She whimpered and dug her nails in his scalp until she could stand no more. "Please."

He stopped and looked up at her. His eyes had darkened to the color of sapphires. "Please what?"

You're an ass!

I know.

Damn it. "Please, I need release."

He smiled and swiped his tongue along her folds until he reached her throbbing nub. He sucked it in his mouth and swirled his tongue around it. Her grip in his hair tightened and every muscle screamed for mercy as her body tensed. Still she hung on the edge, waiting to fall.

He gazed up at her. *Come for me, Katie.*

Her orgasm started as a slow boil, and then erupted into a fiery pleasure that had her seeing spots and gasping for air. When it finally slowed and she was able to gain some sense of where she was, she noticed Seth grinning. *Bastard.* He'd been serious when he said he would control her pleasure. She couldn't be angry though. She felt too damn good.

Seth rose to his feet and hopped up on the altar next to her. His every move effortless as he swung his legs up and underneath his oh-so-fine ass until he sat back on his feet. In one heartbeat, he pulled her close and had her straddling his lap. He wasted no time in planting her over his cock and thrust deep.

She held his shoulders and let her body relax, adjusting to the stretch. Their gazes met.

"Are you all right?"

"Perfect," she whispered and she was. All their problems were forgotten and the moment was about them.

"Are you frightened?"

How to answer? "Yes, a little." Neither of them had any real idea what would happen once her heart stopped. Only a change would take place, but if one thought about it, death was a change itself and one she may never come back from.

He cupped her ass and gently lifted her then set her back down. The sensation caused her core to tighten around his thickness. She wanted faster.

"I am scared shitless, Katie. If I can't bring you back I'm not sure what I'll do."

She stared deep into his eyes. This was a side she had never seen and knew it must have taken immense courage for a man such as Seth to admit his fears. She leaned in until their foreheads touched.

"Careful, I might think you care."

He lifted her again, but this time he held her above him and thrust his hips until he was sliding in and out of her. Again, she hovered on the sweet edge of release.

"I do care, probably too much." His eyes darkened like a summer storm. "Come for me, Katie. I want to feel your pleasure running down my cock."

He increased his speed and she tossed her head back. Yelled to the sky as the wave of sheer bliss overtook her. When the pleasure began to subside, Seth leaned forward and sank his fangs into her neck. Heat rushed through her veins and straight to her sex, setting her on fire again. Orgasms came one after another until she had lost count. She barely remembered Seth's own release as she slipped into the darkness.

SETH DRANK until Katie's heart stopped. He held her to his chest, not wanting to let go. There were few emotions he had experienced in his ancient life. Fear had only happened when he'd drank from Vivian, but never again. Until now. It ran through his veins and mixed with another emotion. He loved her and there was not a doubt in his mind. He had fought a fierce battle and lost. She'd stolen his heart.

With the utmost care he untangled their bodies and laid her on the altar. He crossed her arms and laid them against her breasts. He smoothed her hair around her shoulders. She looked peaceful. He bit his wrist and held the open wound to her lips and let his life force run into her mouth. Had they been in his ancient home of Vandeldor, she would right now be submerged in the healing waters while her body went through the changes. However, the damn book dictated her heart be stopped and the change be made here. Would she come back as a guardian or a full-fledged goddess? He didn't care. He only wanted her to come back to him.

Seth leaned over and kissed her plump lips. Inhaled her strawberry scent for what he prayed wouldn't be the last time. He brushed his thumb across her cheek. "I love you, Katie O'Hara," he whispered. The words caused his pulse to race. It had taken him until the moment of her death to admit what his heart had known all along. As he took several steps back to give her room, he realized he'd taken the easy way out by declaring his feelings when she would never hear them.

Flames erupted at one end of the circle of tiles and quickly ran an invisible path all the way around until it came back to meet itself. The fire shot into the air and engulfed the altar. Seth fought the panic that rose and demanded he save his mate, but he realized the flames left her unharmed.

Several minutes passed which to Seth seemed like an eternity when suddenly Katie sat up. Her body shimmered and morphed into a Phoenix. The bird was breathtaking with its vibrant orange body. It looked at Seth. Did she know who he was? Before he could say anything, the bird took flight with the fire following a trail behind it. He was transfixed as he watched his mate soar until she was out of sight. He cupped his hand over his eyes, yet still couldn't see her. Pride poured through him that his mate had transformed into such a beautiful creature, but it was quickly followed by fear. It was evident she had transformed into a goddess which put him far beneath her station.

He grabbed his clothes and quickly dressed then began to pace, the predator in him begged to be set free. He wanted to rip something apart, limb-by-limb and itched to step into a fight. He tried to link with her, but was only met with silence. Either she was unable to communicate or chose to ignore him.

A growl started deep in his gut and rolled up to his throat at the thought of her possibly being in trouble. He closed his eyes and inhaled, searching for calm. She was fine. He would wait for her to come back and began to pace the courtyard, temple and the entire grounds. Hours passed and darkness fell on the Temple of the Gods. Stars lit the sky with their brilliance, yet he was unable to enjoy it. As time ticked by he grew more uncertain that she would return and more certain she avoided him. Still he waited, went back to the altar and sat on a bench across from it and stared. An old urge suddenly swept over him. He pulled the dagger from his boot. Caressed the wooden handle that felt like an old friend then gripped it. Twisted his wrist so the moonlight reflected off the blade.

"Old friend. Why do I have the desire to feel you biting into my flesh?" He brought the tip to his other palm and pressed, yet not hard enough for it to pierce his skin. Sweat beaded on his forehead. If he were any other immortal, he'd find his mate and claim her and to hell with what she desired. Yet he refused. The thought that she would really want him was laughable and her earlier fear of him binding them together had been evident. He was only a vessel in which to help her transformation. She was lost to him, but he tried to console himself in the fact that she lived. In this he was positive since he could still feel her. He would have known of her death, but his heart was still wounded. She hadn't even thought to come back and at least send him on his way. Instead he had been left here to worry and wonder.

He snarled at being made such a fool and slipped the dagger back into his boot before he flashed back to his room at the compound. Angry that the gods would play such a cruel trick on him as to give him a mate he couldn't have. Granted, she had saved his sorry ass, but to what purpose? He was stupid to think he would ever be allowed happiness. After a quick shower, he'd find the others and get briefed. It was time to focus on his duties otherwise he would drive himself back to insanity.

THE MOMENT LOWAN pierced her maidenhood, a burst of power

slipped down his spine. He'd fought to center his concentration on the task at hand. Raven was a special girl and he'd wanted her first time to be memorable. For some odd reason, her pleasure had been important to him when usually he only took and never gave.

He buttoned the black silk shirt he'd donned and tucked it into his slacks. "Once we are settled in the human realm, I will see to it that you have the proper clothing fitting your station."

She smiled. "Whatever pleases you, my lord."

He wrinkled a brow. "Does being my mistress not please you?"

She nodded. "Oh, very much."

"Then get dressed. I'm anxious to meet your people." He buttoned the slacks. "I've sent Chaval ahead to scout out a location for us to reside."

Raven dressed in jeans and a black bustier that showed off the creamy tops of her breasts. She dropped to the edge of the bed and pulled on a pair of knee-high, black leather boots and he made a mental note to have her wear those when he took her again later.

"You look good enough to eat, but I'm anxious to leave." He offered his arm and she accepted, then he held out his left hand, palm up and called forth the power he'd gained from feeding and fucking a virgin given willingly. A black mist formed in his palm then swirled and tightened until it became a sphere the size of an orange. Darkness grew larger and shifted from his hand to float in mid-air before it became big enough for him to walk through.

"Come along." He tugged Raven and they stepped through the portal and into the human realm. On the other side, Lowan sucked in a deep breath and reveled in the taste of his long-awaited freedom.

"I have waited for this my entire life." He scanned the room where they stood.

"Where are your people?" He flashed Raven an impatient gaze.

"They will be here after dark. Within a few hours."

"Good. We'll wait." He'd spent eternity waiting for this moment. He could spare a few more hours.

CHAPTER TWENTY-TWO

KATIE'S LASHES fluttered and when she opened her eyes, she was met with a pair the color of a spring storm and lined with heavy black liner. They bore into her and she gasped.

"Ah, you're finally awake." His deep voice rumbled.

A woman came into view. Emerald eyes and burnished copper hair accented the most beautiful face Katie had ever seen. "Hello and welcome."

Katie tried to sit up and found a pair of large, strong hands against her back, offering assistance. "Thank you." She looked around the room and realized she was in an oversized bed. Large archways across the room allowed light to stream in and a warm breeze drifted across her skin.

"Where am I?"

"In our temple. I am Qadira, the goddess of fire and creator of the Draki." The woman spoke in a soft voice and waved her hand toward the man. "This is my husband, Zarek. He is our king."

Katie's jaw dropped. Zarek was the creator of the guardians and from what she had surmised, ruler of all. "I... How did I end up here?"

"Let me help you. We shall move to the courtyard and have refreshments." Zarek extended his hand. She hesitated only briefly before placing her small one in his. She swung her legs over the edge of the bed and slipped to her feet. It was then she realized she wore a long gown the color of lemons. The material the softest of anything that had ever brushed her skin and she was thankful because the last thing she remembered was being naked as a jaybird.

The god folded her arm in his and walked her toward the arches. On the other side, several lounge chairs were scattered around a pool of deep blue sunken into the ground. Zarek led her to a long wooden table under a canopy out of the sun and pulled out a chair for her.

"Thank you." She plopped down on the soft cushion.

He took a seat to her right and Qadira to her left. Three women wearing white linen dresses that fell to their ankles, carried trays of fruits, meats and cheeses and set them down in the center of the table. Another came along and filled glasses with water and what looked to be red wine.

Zarek motioned to the food. "Eat. You need your strength."

Katie smiled and placed grapes, strawberries, ham and cheese on her plate. Her nerves were stretched to the breaking point. She had a shit-load of questions. "How long have I been here?"

"About a week." The goddess popped a grape in her mouth.

She rubbed her temples. "I don't remember much except for flying." She shook her head. "I must have been hallucinating."

"No. You shifted into the Phoenix and took flight," Zarek commented.

Qadira nodded in agreement. "Your bird is most beautiful."

She had no recollection. "How did I end up here?"

The god took a slow sip of wine, then wiped a linen across his lips. He was an extremely handsome, if not a somewhat frightening man. His face was framed by thick black hair that fell to his shoulders. His chest bare and she couldn't help notice every bulging muscle under his tanned skin. He wore a pair of low riding jeans, which she found odd. She had always pictured god in a white robe or something. Who knew?

"You fell from the sky and I caught you," he stated matter-of-fact.

Katie stiffened. "I see. Care to go into more detail?" Oh, she was so going to Hell.

His mouth twitched as he fought back an apparent laugh. "You're a saucy little thing. Reminds me of your father. He was forever pushing the limits and testing my temper."

She batted her lashes and he broke into a roar of laughter. The goddess next to her giggled and touched Katie's arm.

"I'm happy to have you with us. He needs someone to keep him on his toes and lord knows I try, but I could always use some backup."

Katie sipped her wine. "I'm glad to be your source of entertainment. However, I have a zillion questions. So, what say you?"

"You made the change, took off in flight and then lost consciousness. I sensed your distress and came to your aid."

"And I was out for a week?"

"Yes. Becoming a goddess took a lot out of you. Anything else?" He arched a black brow.

"So, you knew my father?"

His features softened. "Very well. He was a good man."

"So, I made the transformation. That should have set events in motion. Did it work? Has he been reborn?"

"I wish I knew, but unfortunately the only thing I've sensed was Hell's gate opening. Lowan is now in the human realm. The guardians have their work cut out for them."

Katie pressed back in her chair. "You're a god, why don't you stop him? This Lowan?"

He leaned forward, his brows slashed. "Your father was murdered in a war between the gods long before your world ever came to be. It is why he has taken so long to come back. I was the one who planted his DNA in the hopes that one day, one of his children would be strong enough to call him forth. It was because of his loss that we enacted a law that will not allow us to harm another god. We have tied our own hands for a very good reason."

"That sucks." Big time because she had a feeling now that Lowan was in the human realm, things were going to get really bad and fast.

He leaned into his seat. "Yes, it sucks a big one."

Realization hit and she smacked her forehead. "How stupid! Seth, where's Seth? He was with me when I changed."

"Gone," the goddess responded.

"Where to?" He didn't wait for her? Now she was being foolish. After all, she'd been gone for a week.

Zarek pressed his lips into a thin line. "Wife! Leave us, now."

Qadira lifted her chin then vanished and Katie's nerves stretched tight again. It was evident Zarek was not pleased with his wife. "She still holds a grudge against Seth for killing Vivian. It wasn't his fault. My daughter begged me to let her assist in his creation."

"But I saw her, she came to me so she can't really be dead. Can she?"

"She is dead to us. Lives on another plane of existence and most likely used any power she had left to come to you. I will not see my daughter until I leave this life and I plan to be here for a very long time."

Katie had a hard time wrapping her head around the fact he was able to let his daughter give up her life so easily.

Zarek's nostrils flared. "It was not a decision I made light of. The guardians were a necessity and Vivian knew it. I tried to talk her out of it, but in the end, it was what her heart wanted."

Well crap. She had to remember her mind was an open book and she slammed down the wall to keep it closed. Zarek laughed.

"You cannot hide anything from me." He leaned forward, his eyes narrowed and swirled into silver storms. "Like the fact that you really care for Seth, yet you refuse to admit it even to yourself."

She raised her chin. "Well I guess you don't really know all that much. I do care about Seth and have no problems admitting it." She cast her gaze at her plate. "I'm happy he seems to be cured."

He sipped his wine. "Yes, the one regret I have. Had I known his memories would be his curse I would never have given him that gift. The fact remains, you can admit all day long you care about his welfare, but tell me you haven't fallen in love with him."

Now it was her turn to laugh. "I hardly know him well enough for that. I still find it barbaric this mate thing. It's like arranged marriages." She was well aware she'd fallen in love with him, but it scared the hell out of her. What if he didn't reciprocate?

"Perhaps. Yet fate has a way of knowing what's best for us even when we don't. Search your feelings and make your choice before it's too late."

She glared at him. This sounded like one of the riddles Baal complained about. "What exactly does that mean?"

"It means you either accept your mate and live a happy life, or you deny him and live without love. For eternity."

Well, hell.

SETH SHOWERED and changed yet his mood hadn't improved. He sat on the edge of his bed and fondled the dagger in his hand. It had been Garin's favorite and Seth had found it in his room upon his return. As he stared at the shiny steel edge, he reflected on everything that had happened. Replayed his friend's death and it sat in his stomach like a ball of lead.

"I'm so sorry I wasn't there for you."

He'd not been able to attend Garin's service and say his goodbye. Hell, he still expected his friend to walk through the door at any minute, but Seth would eventually accept his friend's death.

"Why did you have to go and get yourself killed?" he ground out.

He'd lost many brethren in his long years of life and expected to see the death of many more. Didn't make it easy, only a part of life. Staring at the blade had him wanting to shove it in his chest and cut his heart out. Maybe it would stop the pain of losing his friend or better yet his mate.

He tried to shove Katie's image into the recess of his mind, but it was impossible. They should have been together planning their future. Instead, she'd become a goddess and he her servant. He fought instinct. Every fiber of his being wanted to go and search for her. Pull her close and never let her go. Her essence flowed through him and he knew she was alive and well, yet she hadn't come to him. He could make demands. After all, she belonged to him, but with the exception of the bedroom, Katie O'Hara wasn't the type of woman to be controlled. He grinned at the remembrance of how he took command of her body. Somehow though, that wasn't enough. He'd been around a long time. Been the protector of life and bore the stain of many deaths on his hands. Could he give up who and what he was for the love he held in his heart for his mate? It was too much to ask.

He rose from the bed and walked to the dresser where he wrapped the dagger in a cloth and tucked it in his drawer then exited the room. Aidyn had summoned him so he could be briefed and his duties assigned to him. From the rumors he'd heard, so far, the Phoenix god hadn't surfaced.

Strawberries.

He stopped dead in his tracks and watched as Katie materialized in front of him. He had thought it impossible she could become any more beautiful, but he was mistaken. Being a goddess apparently agreed with her. He fought to keep his fangs in place as he stared into her cobalt eyes.

"I see you've learned to flash." He masked his emotions.

"I have." She fidgeted with the hem of her shirt and he fisted his hands at his side to keep his feet planted.

"I'm glad to see you well. Did you learn anything of your father? I understand he still hasn't surfaced yet."

"I'm afraid I don't know anything." She let out a heavy breath. "Maybe it will take some time for him to awaken."

"Perhaps. I'm on my way to get my orders. Was there something you wanted?" The question was so cold she visibly shivered.

"What about us? Where does this leave you and I?"

"We followed the path fate led us down. You saved me and I in turn saved you." He shrugged. "Hopefully it will save humanity. Other than that? It was a good time, but you are not bound to me. You have your life as a goddess and I have mine." He would never admit he needed her. Besides, she'd previously made it clear she had no desire to bond to him and she was out of his reach now.

"I see. I thought I was your mate? Did I misunderstand what that meant?"

"I thought so too, but you are a goddess. How do you think it will work when I have to take orders from you? Bet you hadn't considered that." The look on her face said she hadn't.

"I thought Zarek was your leader," she whispered.

"He's everyone's leader, but I must also take directive from the others. I would always question your orders because I know more than you." Her body stiffened. He'd hit a sore spot.

"Are you saying you're smarter than me?"

"See, already you're riled like a territorial cat. I'm saying I've lived a helluva lot longer than you. Seen more than you and in the scheme of things you are now no more than a babe in a new world. I would question every command you issued." How could he tell her he could defeat armies of evil yet this was foreign territory to him? How was he supposed to say he felt unworthy of someone as good and pure as her?

"I see. Well then I guess there is nothing more to say." She vanished.

He gritted his teeth, fisted his right hand and swung. The wall in front of him cracked and his knuckles broke, but the pain in his hand hurt less than the one in his heart. He should just say to hell with it and take her, yet he couldn't bring himself to do it.

RAVEN ESCORTED Lowan to a secret chamber in the lower level of the building where they had arrived. He stared at the red pentagram painted on the floor. Candles were lit and placed in strategic places on the flooring and walls.

"Your throne, my lord." Raven took his hand and led him to a large black skull carved out of marble and polished to a high sheen.

He waved his hand to dismiss her then spun on his heel and planted himself on the black, velvet cushion. He ran his fingers along the cold stone. "Perfect."

"The others are beginning to arrive and are anxious to meet you, my lord." Raven bent at the hips and gave a bow as she backed away.

"Excellent." He crossed his legs and steepled his fingers, pressing them to his lips. Anxious to meet these humans and make them his minions.

People began to file into the room. Some dressed in black jeans and tees, others wore black robes. Lowan raised a brow at the hardware many had sticking from lips, brows, noses and ears. He had to wonder what purpose it served and made a mental note to ask Chaval about it later. Soon the room was full with men and women of varying ages. Raven came to stand next to him and a tall, husky, young kid called for everyone's silence. Raven leaned in to whisper in his ear.

"That's Ace. He's our local leader."

Lowan chuckled to himself. Ace was in for a surprise demotion, but then again, he might prove useful.

"Brothers and sisters. Tonight, our requests have finally been answered." Ace gestured to the throne. "Our king has arrived to lead us. Let us show him the respect he deserves." Ace dropped to his knees and everyone behind him followed suit. Except for one. A burly, grotesque man in the back with greasy hair and torn clothing remained standing.

Lowan narrowed his gaze to pinpoint on the one who dared disrespect him. "Who is this human that offends me?"

"That would be Jack, my lord," Raven whispered.

"Bring him to me," Lowan growled.

Two men in the back jumped to their feet, grabbed Jack by his arms and dragged him forward. Shoved him to the floor in front of Lowan.

"Why do you defy me?"

The human curled his lip to reveal missing teeth. "How do we know you are really who you say? You look like any normal man to me."

"Ah. So, it's proof you seek? Then I shall accommodate." Lowan rose and in two strides stepped off the pulpit, grabbed Jack around the neck and lifted him off the floor. "You will regret challenging me." His fangs extended and he bit into the fat flesh of the human and struck the artery. Blood squirted and splattered a few people nearby, but no one spoke out.

He drank until the man's heart stopped then dropped the body to the floor. Lowan held his palm in the air over Jack and the demigod's power ripped Jack's heart from his chest. Lowan squeezed it in his vice-like grip until it turned to dust. He then summoned his Wendigos.

"Remove this filth from my presence," he commanded.

"Yes, my lord." They bowed and proceeded to drag the body from the area, leaving a trail of blood in their wake.

Lowan scanned the room. All eyes were downcast and several people were visibly shaken. "Is there anyone else who wishes to question me?"

The only sounds that reached him were their rapid heartbeats. He turned and walked back up the stairs and took his seat. "You have witnessed only a fraction of what I am capable of. I am your god, and you will do my bidding or suffer severely." He leaned forward, his hands firmly on the small skulls that adorned either side of the throne. "The time has come for darkness to rule your world. Follow me and reap the rewards. Defy me and you will live to regret it."

KATIE FLASHED BACK to her father's palace. Fury dripped from every pore and it was all she could do to keep from going back and beating Seth to a pulp. Her mind kept wandering back to Zarek's words.

You either accept your mate and live a happy life, or you deny him and live without love. For eternity.

"Asshat." What did the statement mean really? Katie took it as more of a threat to force her into taking Seth as her husband, yet when she stopped for a moment...

She sighed. Her body craved him and she wanted nothing more than to chalk it up to the fact that he had a way of strumming her like a harp. He really had commanded her to one of the most intense orgasms ever. She touched the place on her neck where he had sunk his fangs and her heart skipped. Never had she felt more connected to someone. She'd also had a glimpse of Seth's memories and emotions. He had truly received a raw deal with the life handed to him.

"Katie?" A female's voice called out from the courtyard.

She flashed, liking the mode of travel and also needing the practice. Cassie stood by the fountain with a little girl in her arms. The guardian turned and smiled.

"There you are. I hope we're not intruding, but I wanted to see how you were and if I could help."

"Not at all. I'm actually thankful for the company." Katie stepped closer. "This must be your daughter." Katie had been told mother and daughter were sent to stay in the Temple of the Gods while the war waged. She'd seen first-hand how protective Marcus was of his wife and daughter, who was the first baby born in hundreds of years.

Cassie jiggled the little girl who laughed. "This is Ariana."

"She is beautiful." A small pang went through her heart. Would she ever have children? Was it even possible now that she was no longer human? She had to think it was since Zarek and his wife once had a daughter and Cassie stood before her with a child.

"Come sit." She led Cassie to a cozy seating area with several wicker chairs and a loveseat that sat under a trellis covered in jasmine. She adored the smell. Next, she snapped her fingers and a play area, complete with thick carpet, toys and a fence appeared next to them.

"Oh, thank you." Cassie placed Ariana inside the enclosure and the little girl went right for the pile of toys.

"I'm starting to get used to this power thing." Katie took a seat and flashed in refreshments. "The fact that I loathe doing housework makes it even more fun."

Cassie laughed. "Sounds like you're getting along then."

She smiled. "I can make do. It's so beautiful and peaceful here."

Cassie poured a glass of ice tea. "It is. However, it's also boring."

Katie leaned back into the velvet cushion. "Yes, I suppose it could be. I can travel to anyplace I wish though."

The guardian nodded. "Yes, but let's be truthful. It's not the same without him. Is it?"

Katie picked at invisible lint on her dress. "I don't know what you mean. I'm an independent woman and certainly don't need a man to make demands of me."

"How well I know." Cassie set her glass aside. "Look. I feel like since we were both human and dragged into this mess kicking and screaming, we are sisters of a sort. May I speak frankly?"

"Oh, gods please." She had to stop herself from begging. From the moment she had met Cassie she'd liked the woman and hoped they might become friends. Friendships were one thing Katie never really had. Oh, there were acquaintances, but no girlfriends to hang with and pour out one's soul to.

"Immortal men are overbearing," Cassie started.

Katie didn't stop herself from laughing. "To put it mildly."

"But there are ways around them. You have to be just as stubborn as they are and sometimes let them think they've won."

"I tried to talk to him and he was clear on where we stood." His iciness still stung like a sharp slap on the cheek.

Cassie rolled her eyes. "I know Seth pretty well. Marcus and I had our issues, but when he came up missing I helped search for him. It was a damn mess. Baal ended up being taken by the slave traders and to keep Seth from following, they sliced his gut open."

Katie cringed.

"Top it off with the dragons attacking us and Seth couldn't open a portal home. He was prepared to die in order to save me. I however, am a stubborn woman and refused to leave him so I slit my wrist and made him drink. To this day I think of him as a big brother. If I know Seth, he feels lost. Something tells me there is a problem with you being higher up the ladder so to speak."

"Ugh." Katie flipped her hand in the air as if she were dismissing something trivial. "He actually said he would question any command I issued."

"Well can you blame him?"

She let out an exasperated breath. "No, but he didn't even want to discuss it. I felt like I was being dismissed."

Cassie smiled. "Well a little bird told me that after you left him, he put a pretty nice sized crack in the wall and broke all of his knuckles. I'd be willing to bet he has it bad for you. If you care about him at all, you're going to have to make it work."

So, he rammed his fist into the wall? "I have to admit, he's gotten under my skin and now I'm not sure I want to live without him." She lifted her glass. "To our stubborn men."

"Cheers." Cassie touched her glass to Katie's and both women laughed.

BAAL HAD NEVER BEEN TURNED down before. Not once. Ever. He stared at the woman behind the bar who had so much as refused to even give him her name. He'd closed the place down a couple of nights ago with Seth, or had it been longer? He couldn't remember after taking a couple of those damn pills. Either way, he did remember craving a piece of the vision currently giving him the evil eye. Still did. He hadn't come across a female like her in a long time.

"Seriously, why are you working in this shit hole? You should be strutting your stuff in designer clothes and high heels." Black hair curled around her shoulders, blue, almond-shaped eyes were fringed with thick lashes, add to that high cheekbones and pouty lips and you had exotic perfection. Not to mention the curves he wanted to sink his fingers into while he fucked the hell out of her.

She laughed. "I suppose you're going to promise me a starring role in your next movie?"

He reached into his jacket pocket and pulled out a card. "Nope, but I need a hostess for my casino." He tossed the card on the bar. She rolled her eyes then threw her towel aside and picked up the card.

"Dragon's Cove?" She eyed him suspiciously. "I've heard of it." She snorted and tossed it back on the bar. "Right, and I suppose you're gonna tell me you own the place?"

He shrugged. "Okay, I won't tell you that, but I do."

"Please, I'm not that stupid. Why would someone who owned a highly successful Vegas club be here in —as you called it—this shit hole?"

"I came to help a friend who was down and out."

She reached for a dirty glass and ran it through the washer. "The dark-haired guy? He seemed like he'd seen better days."

"He has, but I think things will be improving for him soon. Now back to my offer. I was serious when I said I need someone. You think about it and if you'd like I'll fly you in for an interview and to talk terms."

She wiped her hands and picked up the card again. Stared at it while pulling her bottom lip through her teeth. He could almost see the smoke coming out her ears. "I don't get it. Vegas has to be full of people who qualify for the job. What do you want from me?"

No way in hell could he tell her what he really wanted was to strip her, toss her on top of the bar and taste every inch of her. He'd have to work his way up to that one. "You desire more than this, I can tell." No lie there. The ability to read a human's desire was bred into every demon. It's how the evil spread, some chose to use it for bad and others good. In this case his intentions were for a little of both. "Your beauty shouldn't be wasted here."

"I've always wanted to leave, but have never had the means to do so."

"Well, this is your chance." He tipped back the last swill of his beer and set the glass on the bar. "I have to leave and head back. You can Google me all night long and see that I'm who I say. Call that number and I will send a limo and my private jet to pick you up. You can have a room in the hotel. I promise, no strings attached." His charm and demon good looks would bewitch the pants right off her. He just needed the chance.

"I'll think about it." She tucked the card into her back pocket and suddenly he was jealous of the tiny piece of glossy paper.

He tipped his head. "Fair enough." Then headed for the door.

"Wait!"

He stopped dead in his tracks and held his breath. Had she changed her mind already? "Yes?" he asked and turned slowly.

"My name, it's Ranata."

"Beautiful name." He pulled open the door and stepped into the cool night air. Took a deep breath and scanned for any humans before he flashed.

CHAPTER TWENTY-FOUR

SETH SETTLED into the chair next to Daniel, prepared to pour over files and video in the hopes of figuring out where Lowan had landed. Things were quiet. Too quiet. He stared at the empty seat across the table. The last time he'd been to their New York home, Garin had taken up position there. He buried his emotions. There would be no room for those in this war. His goal? Kill Lowan.

"Dude. I can't believe the bastard actually found a way in. You guys figure out how he did it yet?" Daniel flipped through folders and shoved papers aside.

Seth turned to look at the young man. A Chosen, his family had worked for the guardians for generations and it was times like these their true worth shined through. Having humans planted worldwide was bound to turn up something. "No idea."

The kid cleared his throat. "I see you're talkative as ever."

He refused to allow himself to get close to anyone lest it be used against him later. "Show me what you have."

Daniel shoved a flash drive into the laptop. "These are sites that have been known to hide cult activity. You know, devil worshippers."

"I know what they are. Idiots haven't a clue what's in store for them. I've no doubt they will be who Lowan seeks first." Seth would be willing to bet his life on it.

The scent of strawberries permeated the air.

"There you are." Her silky voice softened his heart, but he steeled his features before spinning to look at her.

"Why are you here?"

"Who's that?" Daniel leaned in and whispered.

The redhead with sea blue eyes sauntered forward. Clad in black leather pants and a tight-fitting, white tee, she was a vision. "Hi, I'm Katie. Seth's mate." She slid Seth a sidelong glance.

Daniel's eyes widened. "Holy shit, dude. You didn't tell me you mated."

Seth curled his lip. "I haven't." He glared at Katie. "I hope you came with news about your father, otherwise you can take a hike."

Her hands flew to her hips and sat there as her gaze bore into him. "I have no news and you are plain rude."

Daniel fumbled with the folders, stuffing papers back inside. "Uh, maybe I should leave you two alone."

"Why? She was just leaving," Seth growled.

Katie moved in and took the chair on his other side. "Sorry. We need to talk."

"No, I need to work. Daniel and I were..." He turned to find the kid had left him high and dry. "Traitor," he whispered under his breath. He spun his seat to face her. Leaned back until the springs groaned under the stress and folded his arms across his chest. "Fine. Speak."

"I'm joining in the search for Lowan."

He dug his fingers into his biceps, but kept his expression veiled. "Why?"

"I signed the club over to my assistant so I need something to do." She chewed her bottom lip. Something he'd learned she did when nervous. He had to suppress a growl and keep his ass firmly seated, otherwise he was going to toss her over his shoulder and carry her to the nearest bedroom. If he even made it that far.

"Might I suggest you go shopping in Paris, or lie on the beach in the Mediterranean?"

She rolled her chair until their knees touched. Heat radiated off her and snaked across his skin. Gods the woman was tempting fate. "I've been fighting since I was a young girl. I can help you."

"I don't need your help and I sure as hell don't need you ordering me about."

She placed her hands on his thighs and leaned in. He tried not to notice the rise and fall of her cleavage as her breasts nearly spilled out of the V-neck tee. The woman was trying to seduce him. "I promise not to give commands."

He planted his boots and gave a shove, pushing his chair back a few feet. He needed distance. Another state wasn't even going to be enough. "Then work with one of the others. I'm sure Gwen would love some female company."

She leaned back on a sigh. "Okay. I'm not lying about wanting to help, but I also have an ulterior motive."

Finally, the truth was going to come out. He could hardly wait for it. "I'm all ears."

"I've never made friends easily. I don't trust and I've always carried this fear of something happening to those I care about so I simply don't care."

"I can relate." Gods knew his life had been spent wondering when it would end. Never wanting to get close for fear of hurting someone and when he had, well, Garin had lost his life because Seth had been too fucked up in the head to save him.

She brushed imaginary dust from her leather pants. "You and I have been through a lot in our short time together." She looked up and blue eyes met his. "I give a shit about you and I want to give us a shot."

He blinked. Not what he'd been expecting.

HAD SHE JUST BLOWN IT? He stared at her, his expression giving no clue to what he was thinking. She'd never opened herself up, but here she was waiting for him to break her heart. She swallowed down nerves. "I promise to let you give the orders. You were right, I don't know shit." *Say something!*

"What are you saying? Exactly."

Is he kidding? She tried not to fidget. Wasn't good at this stuff. Deep breath in and exhale. "I've never been a big believer in love at first sight, but you've done something to me. I find I don't want to be without you." She managed a smile. "Even though your ego is as big as a damn mountain."

The corner of his mouth twitched. "I'm still not certain I understand what you're trying to tell me."

She was going to kill him. "You stupid fuck. I'm trying to say I love you." His features softened and she swore she witnessed shock in his eyes. Had he really not been expecting her to confess? He was more wounded than she'd first thought. Sucking up the rest of her courage she rose from her chair and took the three steps to him. Knelt in front of him and took his hands in hers.

"Don't push me away. I know you hurt for your friend." She kissed his right hand. "Let me be your rock. For once you don't have to go it alone." She searched his eyes and witnessed turmoil. He struggled, now she had to give him an out. "I'm not asking you to love me back. Only to give us a chance."

He rose, scooped her up and flashed. When she opened her eyes, they were in a bedroom, she assumed still in the house. She didn't have time to study her environment before his mouth took hers. She parted her lips and his tongue slipped inside. He tasted of desperation. She ran her fingers through his hair and pulled.

He gripped her ass and rubbed her against his erection. Fire ignited deep inside her and brought a heightened sense of desire. Gods she needed him inside her now. He broke free and kissed down her neck, she tilted her head for better access. The thought of his fangs deep inside her had her on the edge of orgasm. When he'd kissed his way to her cleavage he stopped and looked at her. His eyes blazed with pure male lust.

She shivered.

"You are powerful now?" His voice had dropped low.

"Y-yes." She knew he inquired about her goddess powers, but less talk, more action. She fumbled with his belt.

He clasped her hands to her side. "Look at me." A hard command she dared not disobey so she lifted her head.

"We will get a few things straight. First, you will prove to me you can take care of yourself. If the fighting gets too intense, you will leave." She started to protest, but his face hardened. "Either you will agree or this ends now."

"Fine." She could relent, for now. "What else?"

There was that evil grin she'd witnessed before. "I will own you. Heart, body and soul and your pleasure will be mine to command."

Christ, he already did. "O-okay."

He released one wrist and ran his hand under her shirt. With a quick flick, he'd managed to unsnap her bra. Heated fingers reached around front and tweaked a nipple. Her knees went weak and she was grateful he still held onto her.

In seconds, he tore off her shirt and bra and flung them to some remote corner of the room. His mouth found her breast, his tongue swirled over the rosy protrusion and fangs scraped.

Dear gods, she couldn't take much more. "Seth..."

"Yeah baby?" He looked up from her breast.

"I need you."

"You're not ready yet."

Seriously? She was ready to spontaneously combust. He grasped the waistband of her leather pants and peeled them down her thighs until they were a puddle at her feet. She tried to kick them off, but when he slipped a finger along her thong and dipped it inside, her brain turned to mush. A second finger slid in next to the first and with a flick of his wrist, he twisted, stretching her.

She moaned.

His mouth found hers and swallowed her cries of pleasure and when she was on the brink, he pulled away. "Bastard."

He grinned and pushed her to the bed. When her back hit, he grabbed her pants and yanked them free.

KATIE LAY on the bed with only a thong and a pair of three-inch black heels. Seth restrained himself as he pulled his shirt over his head. His jaw so tense he thought his teeth would crack under the pressure. Next, he unhooked his belt and pushed his jeans to the floor. Toeing his boots off he managed to untangle himself before he took a nosedive. When she had said those three little words, he'd nearly come undone. Never had he expected her to fall in love with him. The fucked-up-in-the-head psychotic who still didn't know if he was coming or going. Yet, she wanted him. He worried for a moment she might change her mind, but he had to shove it aside.

He leaned on the bed and crawled up her body. Shoved three fingers in the waistband of her thong and ripped it free. "Now you're naked."

She giggled. "I still have on my shoes."

He curled his lips upward. "I know."

She flashed her own devil-may-care grin. "Kinky."

He touched the tip of his cock to her entrance and held it there. "I'm a dangerous man, Katie." She tried to impale herself on him, but he pinned her down.

"I like danger," she breathed.

He slid in a fraction of an inch. "My hunger is primal. I'll take you fast, hard and often."

She whimpered. "Dear gods, I hope so."

He lost his reserve and slid home. Seated himself deep in her heat. When he opened his eyes to look at her, he was taken aback. Love and desire swirled in her blue depths and he knew if he'd only drop his wall of defense he would feel her emotions. Dare he? He swallowed hard, tore down his barrier and let her in. He'd felt the emotions of his brethren, but this was so much different. So much more. He wanted to melt into it. She loved him. With his voices gone, for the first time he was able to truly experience the gift that had been blessed to him. His mate.

He grasped her hips and began to rock back and forth. In and out. Rubbing his thumb on her clit as he picked up the tempo.

"Come for me, baby."

In seconds, she fractured and screamed his name. Her orgasm coated him and her muscles squeezed. His own release had him tipping his head back and groaning. When he'd finally come back to earth he lay down next to her. Cupped her cheek.

"Maybe one day you can teach me how to be gentle."

She smiled sweetly. "Maybe, but I kinda like you rough and raw."

"Baby, swear to me if I tell you to go home you'll leave. No arguing, no questions."

Her brows furrowed. "I said I would. What's the matter?"

He wanted to speak what was on his mind, but the words stuck in the back of his throat. In a panic, he put his wall back up so she wouldn't feel his emotions. "If anything were to happen to you, Lowan will be the least of humanities worries." It was the only thing he could give her at the moment.

CHAPTER TWENTY-FIVE

"THIS IS LIKE OLD TIMES, my friend." Baal settled himself in for a long wait. He and Marcus were staking out a spot deep in the forest of the Black Hills. The place was remote and had all the indications of being a sacrificial ground used by devil worshipers. Baal had them shrouded in magic so they could get a close up view without being detected.

"Sorry, but you are not who I wanted to spend my evening with." Marcus ran a cloth over his dagger, polishing it to such a high sheen the moonlight reflected off it and nearly blinded Baal.

"Well, I can't say I blame you. Hell, I'd rather spend time with Cassie than your sorry ass."

Marcus flashed the blade under the demon's nose. "Careful, old friend. You know how I get about my mate."

Baal snorted. He knew first-hand and had seen the vampire's fangs on several occasions when Marcus had hissed out a warning to another male. He couldn't blame the man though. Marcus had been to hell and back and seen more heartache than any man should. Baal was glad the guardian had finally found happiness. It also had improved his mood immensely.

"What about you?"

Baal flashed a glance at the vampire. "Me what?"

"Do you wish for stability? A mate, children?"

The demon clutched his gut and tried not to laugh. "I thought you knew me better? I'm allergic to being with one woman." He shuddered. "I break out in hives at the thought."

Marcus laughed. "One of these days a female is going to chop your balls off."

"A few have tried. Unsuccessfully, I might add." Though he'd never admit it out loud, there had been a couple of close calls. Yeah, women didn't much care for sharing their men so he mostly stuck to the immortal variety. They could care less and were happy to share in a good time until their mate came along. He inhaled. "I smell humans."

"Ditto. I'd say the show is about to start," Marcus replied.

They didn't have long to wait before several people appeared in the clearing. All of them wore hooded, black robes. The one in front carried a tall staff with a skull on the top, it was evident he was the leader. Another shoved a young female, dressed in a white gown with a black sack over her head toward the front. Both warriors stiffened.

"I don't like the looks of this." Marcus pulled a second dagger from his boot.

"Neither do I. It looks like they plan a human sacrifice." Baal pulled his own blade free. "We can't simply rush in there or we'll break our cover."

The guardian pinned him with a lethal glare. "Then you'd best come up with a plan and fast. I cannot sit here and watch them kill her." He looked back at the gathering crowd, his lips in a thin line. "I, more than anyone, want to find Lowan, but not at the expense of a human life."

"It's very possible she volunteered."

"Don't give a fuck," Marcus snarled, his fangs extending.

"Okay, I'll go in if I have to, but let's see what they're up to first."

Twenty people gathered around the one who carried the staff and grew deadly silent. The girl was dragged to a makeshift altar while she tried to fight off her captors. Okay, so much for her volunteering.

"Brothers and sisters. Tonight, I am pleased to tell you that our god has finally answered our call," the leader spoke out. "He has sent us his very own grandson to guide us and show us the way."

There were whispers among the crowd. Some questioned the validity of his statement, but kept their tones hushed enough only Baal and Marcus heard them.

"Tonight, all of our brethren across the world will show their thanks by offering the blood of a human female. Let this moment mark the coming of the darkness."

The others began to chant in Latin as they tied the struggling girl down to the altar.

"Baal, now would be a good time for your plan." Marcus's voice was on the edge of panic.

The demon smiled. "Watch this." He flashed and reappeared at the foot of the altar. Baal shifted his form so he had thick, black skin and red eyes. Two horns protruded from the top of his head and the top of his shoulders. He enlarged his small fangs until they would make even a vampire cringe.

The crowd stepped back including the two who'd been heading toward the female, their fists wrapped around the daggers that were meant to bleed her.

"Release the female." Baal lowered his voice several octaves until it was a low rumble.

The gang dropped to their knees, including the one who had led the clan to the stone slab. He was the first to speak.

"M-my lord. Does the female not please you?"

"She will please me more alive." He sensed the woman's heart rate increase. Hell, he was scaring her as much as the assholes in front of him had.

"Of course, whatever you wish." The leader snapped his fingers at the two goons in front. "Untie her." They scrambled to do his bidding and pulled the female from the altar, dragging her to Baal.

"Now leave us so I may enjoy her at my leisure."

The people jumped to their feet and scurried away. Baal detected the sounds of car doors being slammed and engines revved as they squealed out of sight. Before he could react, the girl ripped off her hood, screamed at him and took off on a dead run. Shit, he had forgotten to shift back and now that she was untied, she had no trouble escaping into the darkness.

Marcus flashed next to him. "I'll fetch her and erase her memories."

"No. I'll get her, you wait here." Before he could move, demons attacked. Coming from all directions they had somehow managed to take the men by surprise.

Baal produced a sword, swung and made contact with one head then a second as he spun on the ball of his foot. Marcus, with a dagger in each hand, used a crisscross action that took out two more. Both men spun and wielded their weapons, but the demons didn't relent.

A scream pierced the night's sky.

"Shit, the girl," Baal yelled.

"Go, I'll be right behind you."

Baal flashed, found himself behind a tree. Two demons came out of the darkness straight at him. He summoned his magic and launched a fireball at each. It knocked them back, but they were only stunned. He tuned in his senses and picked up a struggle ahead. He flashed again. This time he'd hit pay dirt. The woman fought with a lone slasher. The creature looked the part of pure evil with its taloned fingertips, rows of razor teeth and horns lining its shoulders down to its wrists, but it was dumber than a box of rocks.

Baal whistled. "Hey, dumb shit." The beast turned to pin beady green eyes on him. "Yeah, I'm talking to you. Come get me, fucktard."

The demon lunged, but his seven-foot size made him slow. Baal produced his sword at the last second and decapitated the beast. The girl screamed and took off running again.

"Damn it, woman," he growled.

"We need to hurry and get out of here. There are more coming," Marcus yelled from behind him.

This time Baal took off running and followed the scent of fear. In seconds he was behind her. "Wait, I'm one of the good guys," he yelled. The girl was apparently too terrified to register what he'd said so he flashed in front of her. She ran right into him and he wrapped his arms around her slender, trembling frame.

"It's okay." He gripped her arms and pushed her back to get a look at her. Wild eyes looked up at him and he was certain the color drained from his face. "Ranata, how the hell...?"

Marcus came up behind him. "We need to get out of here, like yesterday."

Baal nodded and pulled Ranata into him and flashed.

KATIE STRETCHED. Her entire body hummed from the mind-blowing sex, but there was one thing that bothered her. Seth had not said those three little words. Why it ate at her she didn't know, but his statement about anything happening to her had indicated he felt something. He'd dropped his guard, but the second she tried to reach for him he slammed the wall back into place and kept it there. He was a complicated man. A warrior who was fierce, strong and unafraid. There was also a side to him that was vulnerable and if she didn't know better, scared. That was the side she needed to reach, but his past haunted him. Vivian had given Katie a glimpse of how her death had affected him. Even though the goddess had sacrificed herself to give him life, the incident had traumatized him and imprinted itself on his memory at a time when he was nothing more than a newborn. She imagined it was why he waited until the last possible moment to feed.

"So, what now?"

He pulled away and sat on the edge of the bed, his back to her as he reached for his jeans. She missed his warmth.

"What do you mean?" The tension in his voice was evident.

She summoned her courage for the next question. "What about us? Do you think we will ever complete the bonding?"

His back grew rigid. This was definitely a touchy subject. "You know Vandeldor is off limits."

Yeah, she knew that and it was the one place that held the sacred room where the guardians performed all their ceremonies. "What if I told you that Zarek has moved the Throne room and it's now located in the Temple of the Gods?"

His head snapped around and the look on his face said it all, but before he could answer, his phone chirped. Saved by someone's poor timing.

Seth grabbed his phone and read the text. "Shit. We have to go. Now." He stood and pulled on his jeans while she dressed.

"What's going on?"

"I don't know. Aidyn ordered me to grab Daniel and head to the compound immediately."

They finished dressing in silence. Seth flung open the door and strode to the end of the hallway where he hurled open that door. Power rolled off him and hung thick in the air. "Pack only what you need and be quick about it. You have exactly sixty seconds."

Katie slid in next to him. "What are you not telling me?"

He gave her a sideways glance. "It can't be good. We've never evacuated the Chosen before."

"Oh shit." She ran into the room. "What can I help you with?"

Daniel kept shoving clothes into his bag. "The laptop and files over there on the desk."

"Got it." Katie ran over and scooped up the files shoving them into a bag next to the desk then grabbed the laptop.

"Kaitlyn, leave. Now," Seth commanded.

She didn't dare question him or hesitate, but threw the bag over her shoulder and flashed.

SETH WENT into warrior mode the minute the text arrived. His senses told him demons were already on the move and headed toward the house. "Times up, Daniel." He grabbed the kid's arm and flashed them back to the compound.

Chaos greeted them as both humans and immortals raced up and down the corridors. Gwen ran up to greet them.

"Demons are everywhere. You're needed in the conference room. Daniel, follow the others and someone will get you settled in."

"Have you seen Katie?" He tried to reach her, but she must have closed herself off. He fisted his palms as worry burned through his veins.

"She's in with the others already." Gwen's reply soothed him, but he was anxious to see her with his own eyes. The woman was going to drive him to the brink of madness and here he was stupid enough to think he had his sanity back.

With purpose in his stride he headed for the conference room and came up beside Katie. Everyone stood, their eyes transfixed on the wall of monitors. All were tuned to various news stations around the world. What he saw made his blood run cold.

Demons claimed the streets and the public ran screaming. No longer were the spawn of Hell hiding, but had come out into the wide open. Major cities such as Chicago, New York, Los Angeles, Paris, Hong Kong. The list went on and not a country had been spared.

"Holy fuck," someone whispered.

"How the hell are we supposed to stop this?" another asked.

Warm fingers wrapped around his arm and he looked to see that Katie had latched onto him. When she finally broke her gaze away from the news and looked at him, she had tears running down her cheeks. He wanted to pull her close, take her away from all this, but there was no running. Instead he put his arm around her and pulled her to his side.

"There are so many and how many more of them are out there that we don't see?" Her eyes glazed with fear. "And where the hell is my father? Did I miss a step? Is there something else I need to do in order to wake him?"

He kissed the top of her head. "Don't worry, baby. We'll figure this out."

Aidyn began shutting the monitors off. "I've seen enough, we need to put our heads together and come up with something." Everyone moved toward the table in the center of the room. All the guardians from across the globe were in attendance. Caleb and Lileta sat in for the Draki and he caught Baal out of the corner of his eye as the demon slipped into the room late and took a seat. Aidyn stood at the head of the table looking haggard.

"I don't even need to spell out what a fucking mess this is. It's obvious the gate has opened. Panic is running rampant with the humans and you can't blame them." He rubbed his jaw. "I'm open to suggestions because I'll be frank. We are way out-fucking-numbered."

Murmurs circled around the table until finally Caleb stood. "Well, we know that my people could take out the demons, but we have to fight hand-to-hand. There is no way we can be seen by the mortals, it's far too dangerous and they are not ready to learn about us." The shifter laid a hand on his mate's shoulder. "However, you have my people's full support. We'll do what we can in the air in remote areas and fight like men on the ground where we can't."

Aidyn nodded. "Thanks."

Baal stood. "I don't have to tell you that my people will stand by you. We'll weave magic any place you need it, but there is only so much ground we can cover."

The guardian king simply blinked and nodded. Katie rose out of her seat and wrung her hands together.

"Um, I know I'm the newcomer here, but I want to help." She drew in a deep breath. "I'll go back and see if I can figure out why the Phoenix hasn't awakened. In the meantime, I've gained a lot of knowledge. I know something that will help protect people, but the logistics..." She shook her head. "I'm not very familiar with what the knowledge I carry means."

All eyes were on her. Aidyn leaned forward, placed his palms on the table. "Tell us what you know."

"The Cave of Knowledge holds sacred water. If any of the gods' servants drink from it they can then leave a blood cross on a building to protect its occupants."

All heads turned back to Aidyn who still leaned over the table, his eyes narrowed. "Gods' servants would be either guardians or the gods' warriors of death. So, if I understand you, I can drink from the water then bleed myself and trace a cross on, say this building?"

"Yes, no demon can cross." She looked directly at Baal. "That includes your people too. As long as the occupants remain inside they will be safe."

Aidyn plopped in his chair. "So, that still leaves us with disposing of the demons that are here now. Finding Lowan, because taking him out is the only way to stop this shit. Not to mention getting to the caves which are heavily guarded by Lowan's henchmen and the biggest? In order to place those safeguards, we need to expose ourselves to the human race. Need someone in their midst to be our liaison."

"Why the hell can't Zarek take care of this?" someone asked.

"Because that's why he has us?" Gabriel answered from across the room where he leaned against the wall. He pushed himself away and walked toward the head of the table. As he passed, he bumped Seth's chair then leaned down, placing his lips within inches of Seth's ear.

"You haven't bonded with your mate yet. I'll be sure to check in on her after your death. She's one hellcat in bed, but I'm sure you know that already."

Seth growled and knocked the angel to the floor, his hands around the angel's throat. "I'll rip those wings right off your back and shove them up your ass until you're spitting out feathers."

"Enough!" Aidyn commanded.

Several hands grabbed Seth and yanked him off. His lip bled where he'd sank a fang into it, but he didn't give a shit. All he could see was red. He grabbed Katie by the arm.

"I need to speak to you. Alone." He flashed them from the room and into the corridor.

CHAPTER TWENTY-SIX

"WHAT'S GOING on with you and that angel?" Katie asked, a mixture of concern and agitation in her voice.

He glared at her. "Funny, I was about to ask you the same question." Seth could scarcely believe the words had passed his lips.

"I've only seen him when he was in my father's front yard. The time you were watching me. Who is he anyway and what did he say to you?"

He rolled his fingers into his palms and squeezed. "He was telling me what a good time in bed you were."

Her jaw dropped open for a brief moment before it snapped shut and she regained her composure. "You believed him?" It was her turn to fist her hands and he half expected a ball of fire to be launched at his head.

"You didn't answer the question." *And I am an ass for even thinking she would sleep with him.* His gut told him Gabriel was fucking with him to get even, but his messed-up mind? Well it questioned everything.

He watched as her jaw tightened. "You think I hop from bed to bed?"

"You were in the business of selling sex." Oh, did he just say that? Yes, it was his voice he heard and the pain in her eyes had him wanting to cut open his chest and rip out his heart so he could hand it to her. He doubted it would hurt any worse than what he'd just done to her.

"And to think I wasted my time on you." She vanished and he was left standing alone with his thoughts, which were not good. He knew he was being a dick and he sucked at this relationship stuff. Gods help him, how was he supposed to tell Katie he was still scared to death he'd end her life. He would have succeeded too if she had not had her own power to push him away the first time he fed from her.

He squeezed his eyes shut and wished himself anyplace but where he was. Taking in a deep breath, he opened them again and headed back to the meeting. He was here and had a duty. Katie needed time to cool off before he tried to talk to her again. Back in his seat everyone eyed him and he knew they were all wondering where his mate had gone. Gabriel sat in the corner with a smirk Seth itched to wipe off the angel's face. He would too, as soon as this nightmare was over. He planned to finally have it out with the dark warrior.

"It is decided, Gabriel and I will approach the Pope and beg the Vatican's assistance. I think we can all agree that in a time when demons are running the streets, people will be looking to their faith. Perhaps they can help bring together the world's leaders," Aidyn said.

"We are still so few, how are we going to fight off Lowan and his henchmen?" Lucan asked.

Aidyn's shoulders slumped. "I have no choice but to ask for volunteers. We can train the military on how to kill demons, but they will still not be strong enough to fight magic. We also need to keep them from doing something stupid like dropping bombs or worse."

Everyone knew what he meant. Gods help humanity if someone hit the panic button and launched a nuclear warhead. They were fighting more than just a war against evil. There would be a war with the very humans they were sworn to protect. Some would refuse to believe they were the good guys. Seth hated to admit it, but Gabriel and his brethren fit the image mortals had of their angels. The guardians were more apt to be labeled the same as the demons. Evil bloodsuckers that should be eradicated. It was one of the biggest reasons they had always stayed hidden and used the Chosen to aid them. Hiding in the shadows was no longer an option. The volunteers Aidyn spoke of? The king was the only one among them who could transform a human who wasn't a mate into a guardian. It was a check and balance system, otherwise some of his brethren would transform humans without regard to their welfare. Being converted without a mate also proved dangerous. Blood lust took over a human in the first couple of days and like a child they needed to be taught how to feed and use the power given to them.

Seth rubbed his temples. This was going to be one helluva clusterfuck, but it was what they had been created for. It was what they lived and breathed for.

Aidyn rose. "Gabriel, you will appear to the Pope first and explain the situation. Once you're done I need you to report back to me. The rest of you will take major cities and for now try and stay hidden while you take out as many demons as possible. Capture and use any means available to you to try and locate Lowan. We need to get our hands on the water back in the caves."

"I'll go," Lucan replied. "I should be able to slip in and out undetected."

Aidyn nodded. "Good. Your gift should prove useful on this mission."

Lucan nodded and wasted no time in flashing from the room.

"Then it's done. We know what we have to do for now. As soon as I have any more information I will summon you." Aidyn dismissed everyone.

Seth started for the door. He needed to go to his quarters and gather supplies and prepare for his next assignment.

A hand grabbed his shoulder. "Wait up, I'll walk with you." Marcus gave him the 'we need to talk' look.

"Don't bother to tell me I'm an idiot, I'm well aware," Seth growled.

Marcus snorted. "Am I that obvious?"

He cast a sideways glance. "Yes. I've seen your 'lecture face' many times."

"Lecture?"

"Yes, the one you get when you're about to ream someone's ass."

"Huh, I didn't know I got a face." Marcus sounded genuinely surprised, but they'd all seen it. Marcus was Aidyn's second in command and he had chewed a lot of backsides over the years. Seth held a great deal of respect for the man. He was honest, fair and would never ask his men to do something he wouldn't do himself. Often times Marcus was harder on himself and had been the one tasked with taking Seth out of commission if it had come down to it. Seth was happy Marcus had never had to do it. The man had suffered enough to last a thousand lifetimes. Killing his mate and father in the same day thanks to a demon war should have been more than any immortal could be expected to handle.

Gods, he hoped like hell they didn't suffer the losses they did when they had fought Drayos, Lowan's father.

"I have been worried about the same thing." Marcus could always read Seth even with his barriers intact. "If Lowan is capable of throwing a curse at us..."

Seth held up his hand. "Don't go there."

"Fine, then I'll move on to the subject of mates. Are you fucking crazy?"

Seth cringed. "How many heard?"

"I'm pretty sure everyone in the compound." Marcus chuckled. "I was ready to start taking bets on if you'd come back in one piece."

"I must admit I'm surprised myself." Seth pushed open the door to the room he used while staying at the compound. "I accused her of sleeping with another man, but do you really think you have any room to offer advice? After all, you made Cassie think you used her and was still in love with your dead mate."

"It was to save her life and she bonded with me, didn't she?"

"Point taken." He plopped in a chair. "I don't know if she will forgive me and more important, keep forgiving me. We both know I will stick my foot in my mouth again and again." He tipped his head to rest on the back of the chair and closed his eyes. "The jealous rage I felt at the thought of her with another man, it…"

"It will happen again." Marcus interrupted. "Get used to it, learn how to control it better and most of all be prepared to spend a lot of time on your knees begging for forgiveness."

Seth lifted his head. "That doesn't help."

"Sorry, but as Cassie points out all the time, we are stubborn, overbearing jackasses. But we love them with all we have. You do love her, right?"

"More than anything. I crave her touch, her smell and the look of contentment on her face, but I don't deserve her."

"No, you don't, but don't question it, just accept. You've lived so long being messed up you've forgotten what normal is, what it's like to really live. You have a second chance, don't lose it. Be open and tell her how you feel and for gods' sake bond with her."

He knew everything Marcus said was right and he wanted Katie and he wanted to make her his. "A bonding ceremony will have to wait, this isn't the time."

Marcus held up a hand. "You'll do me no good with your head up your ass. Patch things up with her."

"You're right. I'll give her some time to cool off first."

"Good luck." Then he was gone and Seth was left with his thoughts, which on its own seemed ironic. He hadn't had his thoughts to himself in centuries. He would follow the advice of his brethren. Find his mate and grovel, then he would ask her to be his for eternity and gods help them both.

KATIE PACED the marble floor of what was now her home in the

Temple of the Gods. Fury at Gabriel caused sparks to fly from her fingertips. The angel was an ass. *Why did he say those things?* It didn't matter, she'd deal with the angel later. There was anger and hurt that Seth would even question her on the issue, but the person she was really mad at was herself. She still had feelings for him and was well aware that he struggled with the changes he'd gone through. Instead of talking it over, they both blew up. From great mind-blowing sex to accusing each other of who knew what else, she had to wonder if they ever stood a chance, or would their relationship always be so rocky.

She stopped in her tracks. There was no sense in eating up the floor when there were things to do. She'd give Seth some time and hopefully he would come around. In the meantime, she headed to where she kept the book and her dagger hidden. There had to be something she'd missed. A reason why her father, the Phoenix god hadn't awakened yet.

Procuring the book from under her mattress, she plopped on the bed and opened it. The first couple of pages talked about her and how she had to save the guardian. She read every word carefully, made sure she missed nothing. As far as she could tell she had saved him. His voices were gone and Marcus had reported Seth's stain, the blackness that was the curse of Drayos on his soul, had started to shrink.

Next was the bit about her own transformation. Again, she was careful to read each word. She had done what it said, allowed her mate to drain her so she could be reborn. She closed the book and put it back in hiding. "I have to be missing something." She was going to confront Zarek. Tried to flash to him and nothing happened.

"What the hell?"

She tried again and found herself locked in the same spot. Was he blocking her somehow? She decided to try one of the other gods she'd met, but nothing was working. "Okay, don't panic." She held out her hands and tried to conjure fire, but all she got was smoke and a headache began to pound in her temples. Dread coursed through her as she came to the realization her power had slipped away and all the ailments she'd experienced previously had returned. Katie opened her mind and searched for a connection to anyone. God or guardian, but there was only silence. Her stomach burned with hunger, but the thought of food made her want to retch. As her limbs grew weaker, she managed to make it back to bed and lie down and that's when the sweat began to trickle down the back of her neck.

Deep in her soul she knew she was dying. The fact itself didn't frighten her, but being alone did. She'd finally met people who she felt a connection to and now she would leave them. Perhaps this was her fate after all. Maybe the only way her father would be reborn was upon her real death, yet she didn't want to leave Seth. Fought to hold on, but black spots danced in front of her and she slowly closed her eyes.

CHAPTER TWENTY-SEVEN

SETH FINISHED LOADING himself down with weapons then flashed to Chicago. As much as he hated the city, he found himself wanting to help Katie's people. He walked into the Fire and Ice with the hope he might find her there protecting her employees. Granted she'd signed the rights to the club away, but he knew she cared a great deal for the people who had once worked for her.

He didn't sense any humans or a goddess, but there were demons that most likely searched for the dagger. Producing his sword, he slipped through the dark bar and toward the back of the building. The sound of wood being splintered reached his ears as he parked himself outside her office. He pushed the door open enough to peer through and spotted three demons. They were so focused on tearing the place apart they didn't sense his presence. He was about to flash in behind them when he sensed someone approaching.

"You need to come with me."

He turned to face the sweet feminine voice. "Why are you here?"

Qadira frowned. "Your mate is in dire straits."

He stiffened. "What do you mean, and keep your voice down."

She snorted. "Oh, never mind them." She raised her hand and

power zipped by him raising the hair on the back of his neck. The door blew open and the three demons, who were headed toward them dropped to the floor. Seth ran into the room, but they had already begun to turn to ash by the time he reached them. He strode back to the goddess.

"Why in the hell don't you simply smite them all and save your people?" He was hard pressed to contain his temper and had to remind himself he spoke to the love of Zarek's life.

Her emerald gaze narrowed. "You know we have rules."

He sighed then remembered she had said something about Katie. "Why did you do this? I thought you despised me?"

The goddess touched his arm. "I have my reasons." The she flashed them. He stumbled at the sight of Katie lying in bed. Flames encircled her entire body.

"What the hell?" He stepped closer, but the heat from the fire scorched his skin. His mate however, seemed unaffected by the flames.

"I came here to apologize to her."

He spun to face Qadira, his jaw clenched. "What did you do to her?" He'd kill her if she had harmed Katie in any way and to hell with the consequences.

"I was behind Gabriel's behavior. I held you responsible for my daughter's death and wanted revenge." She cast her gaze to the bed. "I realize my error. Vivian would never have wanted this. She sacrificed so that you could live. When I got here I found her like this."

He turned back to look at Katie. The fire had grown brighter. "I'll deal with you later, now how do I help her?" He tried to keep his growing panic at bay. It would do neither of them any good.

"She is in a dire state and can't control her power. The Phoenix is trying to consume her. If you don't feed her she'll die."

Seth took a desperate step closer. The heat caused sweat to bead on his forehead. "Are you sure my blood will save her?" He wasn't afraid of burning. Hell, he'd burn himself alive to save her. He just wanted to be positive of the treatment.

"I am the goddess of fire and recognize her symptoms. If you hurry you can still help her. Wait much longer and she will be beyond hope."

Qadira hadn't even finished before he pushed closer. Heat seared him and he was amazed how the entire room hadn't gone up in flames. He had to assume it was some kind of magic. This was the home of the Phoenix.

He bit his wrist, stuck his arm in the fire and placed his bleeding appendage to her lips. As his flesh began to burn it sent waves of needle-sharp pain to every nerve ending and caused him to grit his teeth. There was a time not long ago that he lived for such pain, but Katie had saved him. He would gladly set his entire body on fire if it would bring her back.

"The fire is cooling," Qadira whispered from behind him.

He hadn't noticed. Had been so intent on feeding his mate, but the fire had indeed grown smaller and was almost gone. He pulled his wrist free from her mouth, his charred skin began to mend.

"Will she be okay now?"

"I believe so, but it may be some time before she awakens. I'll leave you, but if you have need of me you only have to call out." Qadira touched his shoulder. "And I am sorry for the trouble I've caused. I'll rein in Gabriel." She flashed before he could reply.

Seth smoothed his palm over Katie's hair. The fire now completely gone and her skin returned to a normal temperature. He lay down beside her and pulled her into his arms. There was nothing that would remove him from her side. Not even the end of the world.

KATIE RAN her fingers over something hard. The last thing she remembered was being faint and hot then going to lie on her bed. She nestled into the comfort that surrounded her like a warm blanket. Arousal heated her apex and she ground into a firmness that pressed into her. Someone called her name, but it sounded like they were miles away, their voice so faint. She chose to ignore it.

"Baby, you keep grinding into me like that and I'll have to rip your clothes off."

She forced her lids open and found herself gazing into a pair of dark blue eyes that swirled with desire. Her fingers were splayed over his tight abs. She shot backwards and off the other side of the bed to land hard on the floor.

"Ouch, shit." She peered over the top of the mattress. "What are you doing?"

Seth lay on his side propped up on one elbow. "I was rather enjoying your soft curves."

She crawled back up and perched herself on the edge of the bed. "What happened?"

"Qadira came to me and said you were in trouble. I gave you my blood and you seem to have recovered." The corner of his mouth lifted and she wanted to kiss the grin off his face, but remembered she was still pissed at him.

"I guess I owe you thanks, but is this how it's going to be? I have to have your blood in order to survive?" She rose and crossed the room, arms folded over her chest she stepped out onto the veranda. The cool air helped put out the fire that burned between her legs. She stared up at the stars, sensing his presence beside her.

"Is having my blood distasteful to you?"

She turned to glare at him. "You accused me of sleeping with that angel. I find everything about you distasteful." If only it were true then she wouldn't have to hate herself for wanting him right now.

"Qadira came to you to apologize. It seems she was behind Gabriel's little game. She was seeking vengeance for Vivian's death and that was when she found you."

"And she came to you?"

"She did, but I was prepared to come to you anyway. I wanted to give you time to cool off."

Well, at least she had an explanation as to why the angel had said those things, but that didn't excuse the goddess. She would have to swallow her anger, however, because she might be new at this immortal stuff, but it didn't take an Einstein to know Zarek would kill any who hurt his wife. "I guess I should thank her as well then, but why did you want to see me?"

"Can we sit?" Seth glanced over at the wicker furniture. She nodded and moved to plant herself in one of the chairs. Seth took the seat across from her.

"I'm sorry for how I acted, I never meant to hurt you."

His apology was a start, but she needed more. "Then why did you?" She wasn't about to let him off the hook. He was going to have to work for her forgiveness and even then, she wasn't sure she'd give it.

He laced his fingers together and leaned forward, resting his elbows on his knees. "I have fought the darkness and my own mind for a very long time. Kept anyone close to me at arm's length." He stared at his hands. "I killed one goddess already and would have done the same to you in that cell had it not been for your power."

She gave a nod. "But you didn't hurt me. Your words stung more than anything else." She swallowed her emotions. Wanted to forgive him and understood the turmoil he'd been living. Yet she was still unsure of where this left them. She couldn't live her life always being a slave to his blood and his body. Her heart couldn't take it.

His eyes met hers. "And for that I'm truly sorry. I hope you can forgive me."

"I suppose I can forgive you." She couldn't stand the pain in his eyes. Wanted to jump into his arms, but refrained.

"I have had to dominate my own mind and become an emotionless man. Today the voices are quiet and now I have to learn who I am all over again." He stood, shoved the small table that was between them out of the way then dropped to one knee in front of her and took her hand in his.

"I will continue to make mistakes. I'll be overbearing, demanding and stubborn, but I'll love you with every fiber of my being. I want to spend eternity with you, Kaitlyn O'Hara."

He opened himself to her, allowed her to feel how vulnerable he really was. Yet he also showered her with his love and it wrapped around her like a comfortable blanket.

"What are you saying?" She had to be sure.

"If you'll have me, I want to complete our bond. I've no idea what will happen when we do so, but I don't care." He swallowed. "I will even obey your commands, but know this." His fangs dropped. "I will always own your body, and I will strum it like a fine instrument so take care when issuing those orders."

She couldn't stop the shiver that started at the base of her spine then skittered upward, or the heat that went straight to her core. A wicked thought crossed her mind. "I will put you to the test right now. I command you to satisfy my desire."

He arched a black brow. "Now?"

She licked the corner of her mouth and let her fangs drop. "Now."

He flashed her a crooked grin as he grabbed the hem of her gown and ripped the fabric up the middle to expose her naked body underneath. He planted a kiss on her stomach, then swirled his tongue around her belly button and kissed his way to her inner thigh. His hair brushed her clit and caused the bundle of nerves to tighten.

So close all she could think of was his hot tongue laving through her folds and bringing her a much-needed release. Instead, he cupped her breasts, rolled her nipples between his fingers then sank his fangs into her thigh. Every nerve fired simultaneously and she arched her back, tipped her head and rode a tsunami of sheer bliss. Never would she have thought a simple act would have given her body such monumental pleasure.

When she'd finally regained some composure, she looked down to see Seth grinning ear to ear. "Who owns your pleasure?"

Oh, he was a wicked man, but there was no denying it. "You do." She was breathless.

He thrust two fingers deep into her center and twisted. "And I always will."

She was powerless to argue as he brought her to the brink of another orgasm. Her muscles tightened and she dangled on the fringe of ecstasy, but he left her to hover in a limbo of hell. He pulled free. Tore off his jeans and another desire engulfed her. Before he could react, she dropped to her knees, fisted his cock and flicked her tongue across the velvet tip.

He hissed.

She moved her gaze upward to witness parted lips and fangs that had grown thicker than she'd remembered. "Now I own your pleasure." She sucked him into her mouth.

He slid his fingers into her hair. "Damn if you don't, baby."

Katie moved in a slow rhythm. Swallowed him, then pulled free and swirled her tongue across the tip then down the thick vein. She let her fangs scrape gently against his flesh and realized the canines were as sensitive as the rest of her body. Who knew?

On a growl Seth pulled her to her feet. "I need inside you." He cupped her ass and lifted until he was able to slide his cock inside her. She wrapped her legs around his waist and in a frenzied motion he rocked his hips while he lifted her and brought her back down on his shaft.

She nuzzled his neck. Licked the vein that pulsed beneath her tongue then on impulse pierced his skin. The sensation was unexplainable and she worried if she had done it correctly since it was the first time she'd actually fed this way. Chocolate essence trickled down her throat and the friction between her thighs intensified. Pressure built and she headed toward orgasm.

Seth dug his nails into her backside. "Can't hold out." He roared with his release and Katie followed with him as they both soared beyond the heavens and back again.

She retracted her fangs and licked the twin puncture marks. "I think I like having fangs," she whispered in his ear.

"I definitely like you having them." He flashed them back to her room and they both tumbled on the bed. "You can sink them into me anytime, baby."

"That's good, because I was planning on doing just that." Katie rolled to her side to gaze at him. "Are you sure you want to bond?"

He traced his thumb across her cheek. "If you'll have me, but you have to promise to tell me when I mess up and I promise to make it right."

She rubbed her foot along his calf and loved the hardness of him. "I can do that. We'll take one day at a time."

He smiled. "I like that. When would you like to get married?"

"How does now work for you?" She didn't see any reason to wait.

CHAPTER TWENTY-EIGHT

BAAL RUSHED through the compound in search of Ranata. The need to make sure she was unharmed slammed into him like a freight train. He hated that innocents were already caught up in their war and he hoped she could tell him how she'd almost become a human sacrifice. He spotted Marcus leaving Seth's room.

"Where did they take the girl we rescued?"

Marcus halted. "She should be with the Chosen on the lower level."

That was somewhat of a relief. At least she was with other humans. "Who will be guarding the compound when we all leave?"

"Aidyn has arranged for several Draki to stay behind."

Baal rubbed his chin. "Good choice. I need to speak with the girl, I'll catch up to you later." He flashed to the lower level of the compound. People were parked at various tables in the large room and tapped furiously on the keys of their laptops. Some stared at the wall of monitors and whispered into headsets. Baal knew these were the worker bees and would keep their fingers on the pulse of what was going on. They had families though who must be stationed in another area and most likely that's where he'd find Ranata.

He scanned the room and spotted Daniel seated alone at a table. Baal sidled up beside him. "Where are the other humans?"

Daniel looked up from his computer. "They are spread out all over this wing. Who you looking for?"

"The one who doesn't belong here."

"Ah. The dark-haired girl who looks like she's about to freak out any minute?"

"Precisely."

"I believe they put her down the hall in a private room."

"Great, I'll find her." Baal spun on his heel and headed out of the room and into the corridor. He took in a deep breath. Being a demon came in handy, he could smell fear better than any other immortal and there was a strong scent coming from several doors down.

He snarled and moved toward the smell until he found himself standing outside a heavy door. She was on the other side, there was no doubt about it. None of the other humans in the compound would be this afraid. They were used to dealing with the supernatural. He had to remind himself he was on the good side of the fight and rein in his instinct to prey on people's fears. He was a demon after all.

He rapped on the door. "Ranata?" Silence greeted him. It appeared she wasn't going to answer, not that he could blame her. With a sigh he jiggled the handle. Locked.

Damn it. He was going to have to use his magic to open the door and probably terrify her further. "I'm coming in so you best make sure you're decent." With a quick burst of power, the lock released and he pushed open the door.

Ranata greeted him with a scowl from the chair across the room. "Have you come to release me?" Her tone was anything but pleased.

"What? No thanks for saving you?"

Fear radiated off her and turned her aura an orange-yellow encased in black yet she lifted her chin, pulled her shoulders back and tried to put on a brave front. "Thanks. Now can I leave?"

She was a strange girl, which fascinated him even more. "It's not safe out there, which brings me to the question of how you ended up with those people?"

"Are you my father now?"

He usually had an even temper. Was even what they called easy going, but this chick was pushing his buttons, which pissed him off even more. "No, I'm not. I am however the one who saved your ass. Do you not realize what they were about to do to you?"

She shivered. Pulled her knees to her chest and wrapped her arms around herself. "I do and I'm sorry." Tears welled up in her blue eyes. "I thought I could find my sister, but instead I only got myself into trouble." A single drop slid down her cheek. "I'm afraid for her. What if those people sacrificed her? I need to find out and I can't do it in here."

Well now, didn't he feel like a shithead? "I'm sorry about your sister. Come with me, I need to show you something."

She stood and walked toward him. He held out his hand and she hesitated for a moment then accepted it and he led her out the door. Steered her along the same corridor he'd just come down and back to the hub of activity. He pointed to the bank of monitors on the wall. "Have you seen the world news?"

She approached with caution and slipped into a vacant chair. Her eyes glued to the TV's as the media continued to show the masses trying to exit the city in any fashion they could. Traffic had stopped and people abandoned their cars and took to running on foot. Humans were being trampled by their own or attacked by demons. Some were dragged off screaming while others were being tortured in front of the cameras.

Baal fought to control his anger lest he frighten her more. His heart went out to all the innocents and he itched to jump into the thick of things and start slicing through evil. "It's not safe out there."

She looked up at him with terror-filled eyes and he wanted to scoop her up. Tell her everything would be fine, but he didn't have a crystal ball and he wasn't even sure the gods knew what the outcome would be. Her lip trembled. "My sister, she can't be dead. I'd know."

She glanced around the room as if finally noticing her surroundings. "Where am I and who are all these people?"

He sighed. "It's a rather long story and one that will have to wait for another day. Just know that you are in one of the safest places right now. As for your sister..." He couldn't believe what he was about to say. "I'll try and find her for you."

LOWAN'S MINIONS along with Chaval had stormed the White House where the so-called leaders of the United States resided. The president had managed to escape, but the others had their heads removed and placed on display on the front lawn. He opened the gates and allowed the camera crews in to film what was left of the house's residents. His demons had free reign in the major cities of the world and had been encouraged to put on a show. He wanted the world in a panic. Wanted them to see what destiny lay before them should they choose to disobey him. Soon he would step forward and offer to save them all.

He laughed as he watched the television news. Humans scurried to flee the cities like frightened rats in a maze. A few had locked themselves in their churches and other places of worship in the hope that their god would save them. Little did they realize their gods had forsaken them. Their hands tied by their own foolish laws, laws that he himself would never obey. He dared, no hoped that one of them would be so brazen as to show themselves.

"My lord, are you pleased with the outcome of things?" Raven had come up behind him and began to massage his shoulders. He reached up and cupped her hand.

"I couldn't have asked for more. Have you decided which of the bedrooms we will occupy?" He'd been so pleased with his new mistress he had given her the task of setting up house for them. It was a small thing and it made her happy.

"Yes. I hope you like it." She maneuvered around in front of him and slid into his lap.

"Does it please you?"

She gave him a wide smile. "Very much."

"Good. In a few days, things will calm and you can go out and shop for new clothes. You just let me know where you'd like to go and I'll have Chaval find you an escort."

Her eyes lit up. "Oh, thank you."

Lowan found he enjoyed Raven's company. She made no demands of him and obeyed his every whim so he wanted to spoil her. He'd spent many years without a female while trapped in his hellish prison. When it had become too much, he'd taken demon lovers but quickly grew tired and disposed of them. Human females were rare in his realm and the ones that did show up had their own grand visions of ruling.

He turned back to the broadcast. "Tell me, Raven. Does all of this frighten you?"

"No, my lord. Should I be frightened?"

"Not as long as you obey me and take care I never grow tired of you." He focused his gaze back to her. "Disappoint me and I will snap you like a twig and not think twice about it. I don't love, Raven. I find the emotion a waste of time." He'd given his love to one woman. His mother and she had been a failure. Never again would he be so stupid.

KATIE LEFT the comfort of the bed and already ached to crawl back in and snuggle into Seth's warmth. "We should dress and I'll take us to where the Throne room is."

His eyes swirled with desire as he watched her cross the room. "I like you naked. We could always perform the ceremony in the nude."

"Um, no. Don't get me wrong, I could look at you naked all day long, but what if we end up with company?" She was pretty sure if any of the other females were to see his glorious body, her Phoenix would come unglued and that wouldn't be a pretty sight.

He snarled. "Point taken. Any male who lays eyes on you unclothed will have to die by my hand." He rose. "Be right back." He flashed out of the room, Katie assumed to find his clothes.

She tapped her finger on her chin. "What to wear?" Flashed to the walk-in closet and flipped through the gowns that lined one side. She chose a strapless black chiffon with a sheer gold lace overlay on the bodice that allowed the color underneath to show through. A thin gold belt settled at the waist. She eyed the gold and black heels. "Perfect."

Katie slipped into the dress then pulled on the shoes and buckled the gold strap across her ankle. She turned her attention to the jewelry hutch in the corner of the room. The thing was the size of a wardrobe.

"I have to see what's in there." She glided over and pulled open the door. The glare from diamonds, rubies, emeralds and nearly every stone known to man hurt her eyes. But it was a pair of gold bands that caught her attention. She lifted the cuffs from their velvet-covered perch and placed one on each wrist then nodded in satisfaction.

Since she didn't have time to fuss, she used a little magic to sweep her hair up into a mass of curls that cascaded from the crown of her head downward. She moved in front of the mirror to examine her work.

"Stunning." The deep voice behind her purred.

She whirled to face Seth. "Do you like it?"

"You are a vision of perfection."

"Thanks." She scrunched her nose. "Why the hell are you wearing that?" He had put back on his jeans and tee. That simply wouldn't do, not when she'd dressed up.

"Don't worry. I'll be wearing our traditional garb. Just take me to the site and I'll change."

"Thank gods. Okay, let's go." She touched his arm then hesitated. "Are you sure?"

He cupped her cheek. "I love you and I'll be damned if I'll let you go again. My stubbornness has already cost us time together. Let's go before someone calls me back."

She nodded then flashed them to the location where Zarek had placed the Throne room. Inside she was slightly taken by surprise by the vastness. Red carpet blanketed the floor and marble columns lined both sides of the room. A large golden throne adorned the end of the room with twin onyx statues of a Horus guard on either side.

"It looks just as I remember. Wait here and I'll change." Seth stepped into a side room before Katie could even answer.

She ran her hand along the smooth surface of the marble pillar next to her and stared out the window. The sun shone in a clear blue sky with only a smattering of white clouds. She wondered if the weather in the Temple of the Gods was always so perfect. She heard the door open and spun to see what Seth was wearing.

Her mouth watered as her gaze roamed from his deep blue eyes then down along his half naked flesh. She worried if they'd make it through the ceremony. "Wow. I was not expecting that. You look like an Egyptian god." He wore a black linen shendyt that featured a gold medallion of the sun fastened to the front. His bronze muscular chest was bare except for the emerald green feathers dipped in gold that formed a collar around his neck and the gold band on each bicep. Perfect blue eyes lined with Kohl stared at her.

"Careful, I see a spot of drool on the corner of your mouth." He chuckled.

"That's because you look good enough to lick."

He laughed again and offered his arm. "Shall we?"

She touched his bicep just below the gold band. "Yes, and I must say, seeing you laugh does my heart good."

"It's all because of you that I am finally able to enjoy my life."

CHAPTER TWENTY-NINE

HE DOUBTED she had any real idea how much she had changed his life. He still didn't feel he deserved her, but as he escorted her down the red carpet toward the throne, he was happy as hell she belonged to him.

As they passed the third window, bursts of light dotted the room and took shape. Argathos and Qadira, along with several of the other gods and goddesses appeared before them. Aidyn flashed in and stood beside the throne.

Katie looked at Aidyn. "I thought you were fighting?"

"I summoned him." Zarek spoke and all dropped to one knee. He motioned for them to stand. "We cannot have a mating without the guardians' leader."

Aidyn smiled. "I would not wish to miss this. The others send their love, but had to stay behind." He moved to Seth and pulled him close. "I have waited a long time for this day my friend, but you have waited a lifetime." He released Seth then stepped in front of Katie and kissed her cheek. "You are the perfect match and I know you will keep him on his toes."

The guardian king waved the couple to step over the eye of Ra embedded into the marble floor in the center of the room. Seth took Katie's hand and guided her into position next to him and both faced the dais.

Aidyn moved back to his throne. "Kneel before your gods and king," he commanded.

Seth and Katie knelt and bowed their heads, hands still joined. Aidyn took his seat and Zarek stepped in front of them.

"Seth, my son. The day I picked up the darkness and cupped it in my hand began your creation. Vivian was the light that balanced you. Each of my guardians carries a piece of you and her. She loved you and would be very proud of the warrior you have become. You have suffered alone for far too long so I am happy to bestow upon you a mate, but not simply any mate. One who is a goddess in her own right, one befitting an ancient such as yourself. Do you accept her as your own and promise to protect her?"

"Yes, my lord." He raised his head to look over at Katie. "Until my last breath."

"Then proceed." Zarek flashed back to his position next to Aidyn and Ranis appeared.

"I am Ranis, god of darkness. I bring you the king's dagger."

Seth accepted the blade that was only used for the mating ceremony and clutched its gold handle. He turned Katie's hand, palm upward. "You can still back out."

She smiled and shook her head. "Not a chance in hell. You're stuck with me."

He made a quick slice across her palm then repeated the process on his own. He placed his hand over hers. "With every drop of blood, I bind myself to thee for all eternity. I place your life and happiness above my own. I freely give my heart, my soul and my undying love. I willingly sacrifice my own life to protect you and our children. Should your soul leave this world, I will follow you into the next life."

Something inside him stirred and he realized it was part of her soul. He felt her as if they were one and it took his breath away. He had known what the ritual entailed, but never imagined it would be like this. He handed the dagger back to Ranis and cupped Katie's cheek with his free hand.

"I know we have had a rocky start, but I give you all that I am. You complete me, Kaitlyn Ruiz." He liked how her name rolled off his tongue.

Zarek moved in front of them and placed his hand on Katie's head. "Kaitlyn, daughter of the Phoenix."

She hissed as the mark was placed on her right shoulder blade. A replica of Seth's tattoo to show they were mated. Her Sphinx however, was being watched over by a flying Phoenix rather than the eye of Ra.

"You are a goddess, therefore you must take care when interfering in the matters of the guardians. There are repercussions not even I can foresee. The safety of your mate should always come first, but be wise and know that you cannot slay another god to save him. Our laws bind you and breaking them could mean your death. You will pledge your loyalty and protection to their king, just as you do to myself. Do you agree to this?" Zarek asked.

She chewed her bottom lip and Seth knew it was going to be difficult to give up something she'd grown to love. She would no longer be allowed to fight the demons.

I will find those that killed your father and seek retribution for you.

Her eyes met his and they were filled with gratitude. "I will pledge my loyalty to their king and to you."

"Then go to him and give him your vow." Zarek stepped back.

Katie rose and walked to the throne where she bent to one knee at Aidyn's feet. Bit her wrist and offered him her blood. He took her hand and drank from her for several seconds before he released her then stood, pulling her to her feet. "Welcome to the family. I'm sorry that this ceremony had to be overshadowed by the current events. The others really wanted to be here."

"We both understand," Seth replied.

"Good, and I'm afraid I have to cut my visit short. Lucan has the water and I must appear on public broadcast tomorrow." Aidyn smacked Seth on the shoulder. "You stay here with your mate for as long as you need. At this point one more body isn't going to make much difference."

"Thank you. So, the people will know the truth about us?" Seth asked.

Aidyn nodded. "Let's hope they don't damn us along with them." He flashed away, and the gods followed behind him. Katie and Seth were left alone in the vast, open room.

"I heard. So tomorrow the world will know that guardian angels are real." Katie smiled.

He couldn't help snarling. "Tomorrow they will know that vampires who feed from them exist. I've lived long enough to know this will not end well."

KATIE KNEW HE WAS RIGHT. Humanity had proved time and time again that many of them couldn't adjust to change. "You should go."

He gave her a funny look. "What? You kicking me out already?"

She slid her arms around his neck and gazed up at him. "No. I simply mean that you're a warrior and I know how much fighting means to you. You're needed so you should go and help."

He pulled her close, his arms around her waist. "And what will you be doing?"

"I plan to visit a certain god and do some snooping. Something tells me there is more that I can learn. Maybe something to help us." She rested her head on his chest and listened to the sound of his heartbeat. "I need to find out why my father hasn't risen yet."

He kissed the top of her head. "I would like to go and see what's going on. Are you sure though? I mean, aren't we what you call newlyweds?"

She leaned back and planted a kiss on his lips. "Yes, but we'll meet up later. I guess there are some things we should discuss too like where we will live?"

"I don't care, as long as it makes you happy. Gods knows you deserve it after all you've been through." He kissed her. "I'll go now, but keep communication open so I know you're safe."

She smiled. "I will." He vanished and she suddenly felt cold without him.

Don't fret, baby. I'll always be with you no matter how far apart we are.

A surge of love swept over her and at that moment she realized just how lucky she was. *I love you too.* Then she flashed to where Argathos would be.

The god lounged on a brown leather sofa watching a sixty-inch flat screen in only a pair of faded jeans. His brow quirked up and he stared at her.

"I expected you sooner." He pointed to the other end of the couch as he sat up.

"Really? I didn't know you were expecting me at all, but then again I understand you are the god of vision." She plopped down on the supple leather.

"That I am and you seek answers." He flashed white fangs.

"Well since you know why I'm here then you can save both of us some time by not making me ask the questions."

He shrugged. "I suppose. You want to know who we are and where we came from."

She sat back and crossed her legs. Suddenly realized she was still in her gown, but whatever. "I'm dying to hear the story."

He sighed. "You made a beautiful bride today."

She studied him and realized he seemed sad. "Why do I sense these ceremonies don't make you happy?"

"Oh, I'm happy for all involved." He looked away and stared across the room at nothing. "I had a wife once and I'm reminded of how lonely I am."

"What happened to her?"

"She was killed."

Katie sucked in a breath. "I'm so sorry. It was the war, wasn't it?" She chewed her bottom lip. "I've been given all these memories, but I can't make sense of everything."

He rose and walked to the archway that led outside. Spread his arms to press his palms against the wall and stretched. Even mated, Katie appreciated every muscle that flexed along his spine.

"Yes, it was the war. A fight for all of our lives. We once lived in a different solar system. Our home was called Vandeldor."

"Oh. Then that's why the guardians' realm holds that name?"

He looked over his shoulder at her. "Yes." He sighed and turned, headed back to a chair opposite where she sat. "There were two classes of people. Those like us who held great power and those who were weaker and had either little or no power. They were considered commoners and many were enslaved to those more powerful. Most of us treated the commoners with kindness and they wanted for nothing. We didn't agree with differentiating between us and them." He tapped his finger on the arm of the chair.

"The war started over a marriage to a slave. I fell in love with Brianna and made her my wife. There were those who thought she was beneath my station and slit her throat while I was away."

Katie brought her hand to her mouth. "Oh, dear. Didn't you see what would happen?"

He curled his lip. "Love is blind no matter who you are." He stared at the floor. "Our people were separated, brethren fought brethren. Zarek and your father were the most powerful among those on my side, yet we lost your father. In the end, our home was destroyed and the only survivors are the gods you see here today." He looked back at her, his eyes cold as death. "We vowed when we came here that the life we created would be given free will. It is also why we have the rule to never raise arms against each other again lest an entire race should cease to exist because of someone's arrogance. It was also why Zarek created the guardians. Everything must be balanced. You can't have good without evil and we knew the scum of the universe would eventually end up here. They will always be where we reside."

Her mind was numb. "Wow. I...umm."

He held up his hand. "There is a lot to soak up. Let this sink in for now."

She rubbed her temples. "I feel overwhelmed. I thought it was bad enough there were demons, but to find out there are beings who can shift into dragons and a bird of fire and—Oh, why does everyone have fangs and drink blood?"

He chuckled. "Blood is the essence of life and holds great power. It's also what we were all created with...fangs, that is."

She stood and smoothed her dress. "I can't thank you enough, but one more thing."

"No, there are some things even I can't see. I have no idea the outcome of this battle, but it was what your mate and his brethren were created for. I am confident they will prevail."

At least that made her feel somewhat better, but there was one question that hadn't been addressed. "Why has my father not risen? Did I miss a step?" Argathos stared at her until she wanted to fidget, but she refrained.

"Your father has already begun to stir, but it will take him some time to fully awaken. Even then he will not be able to reveal himself."

"What? Why? I mean he will at least send the demons back to Hell once he's awake. Right?" Otherwise what was the point of everything they'd been through?

"Not until another close to him makes the ultimate sacrifice. Only then will he be fully reborn and possess all of his power."

"Oh, for the love of..." She fisted her hands at her side and watched his brows rise. "I don't suppose you can reveal who and when?"

He rubbed the dark stubble on his face. "I can't say who and even I don't know when or if the sacrifice will be made."

"Well, this is just great. What happens to him if the sacrifice never happens?"

"He will never regain his full power." He leaned forward, his brows slashed downward. "I will tell you this much. Keep his dagger hidden well. It was that very blade that killed him and I don't need to tell you what will happen should it fall into the wrong hands. Again."

She shivered. None of them would be safe from a blade that could end an immortal's life.

CHAPTER THIRTY

KATIE HAD FLASHED BACK to her father's palace. Changed into a pair of jeans and a yellow tee before she searched for a better hiding place for the dagger. After chatting with the god of vision, she'd decided the best thing to do was never carry the blade again. Hopefully it would stay safe in hiding until her father returned to reclaim it himself.

Next on her list was to go back to the human realm and snoop around. There was nothing said she couldn't try and figure out who her father was and move things along. She was a goddess after all. It should all be easy stuff. First, she wanted to visit her other father's grave so she flashed directly to the cemetery. It was already dark and everything was quiet. She'd checked in with Seth and discovered the meetings with the Pope had gone better than expected. Next, the Pope would hold a public broadcast and introduce Aidyn and Gabriel. She gritted her teeth, still wanted to kick the angel's ass and just might after this mess was all over.

She crossed the path to the gravesite and stopped in front of his headstone. The dirt was still fresh, but the flowers had faded so she flashed them away and brought in a colorful bouquet of Tulips to place in the vase.

"Poppa, I sure do miss you, but I hope you're with mom now." She wasn't going to cry, instead took in a deep breath. "I married the angel, I know that will make you very happy. I'm also a full-fledged goddess now." She let out a laugh. "Not that I know any more than I did before, but I'm safe finally."

"I wouldn't be so certain of that."

Katie spun, ready to defend herself and faced the deep voice that spoke from the darkness. What met her gaze was a man taller than any of the guardians she'd met. He moved out of the shadows and stepped under one of the lamps that dotted the cemetery. He was most certainly not human. His black eyes a clear indicator of that.

"Who are you?"

His lips curled into a sinister smile. "Why goddess, let me introduce myself. My name is Lowan and you have something of value to me."

SETH SLIPPED through the darkness and rounded the back of the next townhouse. At the rate he was going it would take him until morning to mark every home on the street he'd been assigned. Lucan had made it back with the water from the caves and it was decided they would wait until nightfall and try to mark as many homes and churches as possible without being seen. Of course, nothing was mentioned about what people would think should they leave their homes in the daylight and find a bloody cross on their front door. Aidyn had said it didn't matter where the cross was placed so Seth had tried to put his in an inconspicuous location. At any rate, he doubted many people would be leaving their homes with all the activity going on. Tomorrow, Aidyn would broadcast to the world they were here to save them, but it was going to take a helluva lot more than his blood and that of his brethren's wiped across some aluminum siding to stop the madness.

"How's it going?" Lucan's voice flowed out of the darkness before he appeared next to Seth.

"This is never going to work. What we need is a fucking miracle," Seth snarled.

"I agree. There are not enough of us and well, the last time I looked in the mirror I certainly didn't fit the image of the humans' vision of an angel."

Seth snorted. "You're more likely to sprout horns than wings. This is going to go down in a real bad way. I can feel it in my bones."

"What I want to know is where are all Lowan's henchmen? I haven't seen a single demon all night."

Lucan was correct, neither had Seth and it had him worried. "Where do you suppose they are?" After all, they were on the edge of Chicago and the city had been filled with them earlier.

Lucan rubbed his chin. "Wish I knew. We need to remain on high alert. Something is going down and soon. I better move on."

Seth nodded and watched the dark one disappear into the night. He needed to touch base with Katie, even though she was a goddess she was still not at full strength.

Hey, baby.

She didn't answer.

Katie, now is not the time to ignore me.

I'm not.

Are you okay? Where are you?

I'm fine. Just...umm a bit busy.

You don't sound fine. I'm coming to you.

No!

Seth ignored her and flashed to her location. What greeted him made his blood run cold. Lowan had his arm around her waist and a blade to her neck.

"Well, vampire, I knew you'd come. Now we can get this party started."

"Let her go," Seth demanded.

Lowan glared and let his fangs drop. "You are not in a position to make demands." He ran his tongue along Katie's neck and Seth had to keep his feet planted firm to the ground while he gritted his teeth.

Can't you zap him with your power?

She twisted her wrist and something flashed in the light. *It seems since I mated you I've become allergic to silver.*

Son of a bitch! Woman, I swear to the gods…

What? How was I supposed to know? She pinned him with a death glare. He had to admire her. Even with a blade stuck to her neck she was still a firecracker.

"What makes you think you can harm my mate and live?" Seth sent out a message to all his brethren. No way was he foolish enough to jeopardize her safety. He received back the answer he expected, they were on their way. Now he needed to form a plan.

"You know she is a goddess and a simple dagger will not kill her." He feared the reply that would come, but needed confirmation.

"You foolish man. Your friend Lucan would have died by this blade had it not been for the interference of your guardian healer."

Seth scanned the area. He detected demons, but couldn't see them. If he had to venture a guess there were at least fifty if not more scattered about the graves. So, this is why it had been so quiet. "Take me. I'll come with you if you set her free."

Lowan laughed. "I want the dagger of Embara. Bring it to me and I might consider letting her go. Cross me and I'll bend her mind until it turns to gel. One way or another I'll get what I desire." He grabbed a handful of hair and jerked her head back and kissed her cheek. "Maybe I'll show her what a real man is capable of."

Would you kill this bastard already!

Believe me I'd love to, but it's not that simple. Not when he has a knife to your throat. Between the silver that weakens you and the poisonous blade, I refuse to take chances.

"You know it's against the rules to kill a goddess," Katie ground out.

"Do I look like a man who follows rules?" Lowan scoffed.

"Lowan, you know I'm an ancient. Imagine how much power my blood could give you." Seth prayed Lowan would make the exchange and tried to keep his emotions cooled when the Dark Lord's expression changed.

"You are indeed very old. Minions!" Two Wendigos appeared.

"Yes, my lord?"

Lowan shoved Katie at the demon closest to him. "Watch her and bring me the vampire."

The other Wendigo was at Seth's side in two steps and grabbed him by the arm. Seth jerked free. "I can walk on my own." He moved toward Lowan.

Seth, no. He noted the panic on Katie's beautiful face, but he refused to speak. He had a mission and it was to save her.

Aidyn, you better fucking hurry. If you have to take me out to get to Lowan then so be it. Just be sure Katie is taken care of.

You're not going to die, Aidyn shot back.

He stopped in front of Lowan and spread his arms wide. "Disarm me."

The Wendigo that had followed Seth patted him down. Dislodged the blade from his boot and the one sheathed at his hip then shoved him at Lowan.

"He is disarmed, my lord."

Lowan sent out a jolt of power that froze Seth in place. The Dark Lord then circled like a cobra ready to strike. Lowan flashed his fangs, then grabbed Seth by the hair and snapped Seth's head back. Lowan's fangs sank deep into Seth's flesh. Katie screamed as Seth's knees buckled and pain shot through his entire body.

Fire burned him right to his bones as his lifeblood was drained. Lowan greedily drank and Seth felt his heart slow. Through the ringing in his ears he heard Aidyn yell. At least he could relax in the knowledge that his brethren were here and they'd save Katie.

KATIE SWALLOWED her panic as she watched in horror while Lowan drank from her mate. With their connection she felt his pain and knew his heart slowed. He was immortal, but what happened if Lowan drained him? Certainly, that could kill him.

I'm a damn goddess. I should be able to help him. Yet she hardly had enough strength to fight the demon that held her. She couldn't even help herself.

A sudden flash of light lit up the night's dark sky and before she could even comprehend what was happening, a bolt of lightning zinged through the air. It shot into Lowan's back causing the Dark Lord to screech before it exited straight into Seth's chest and out the other side. There was a flurry of movement and somehow, she was knocked to the ground, but her focus remained on Seth who lay several feet away. She tried to crawl toward him, dug her nails into the cool dirt, but every movement was like lifting dead weight. A Wendigo's head rolled past her and smoke burned her lungs. With no care to what was going on around her, she continued to pull herself forward.

Someone grabbed her by the waist and flashed her from the battle.

"Let go of me!"

"Shhh. Everything will be fine," Gwen whispered in her ear. "As soon as we have a Kothar or Draki in the room they can remove your silver. Luckily, it doesn't appear to have any Kothar magic weaved into it or we'd be in deeper shit."

Katie settled into a chair and it was then she noticed they were back at the guardians' command center. "Where's Seth?"

Lileta flashed into the room and ran for Katie. She placed her hand on the silver and the band fell to the floor. "He is right behind us."

Aidyn appeared with Seth tossed over his shoulder and was quickly followed by Marcus and Lucan. The men shoved all the contents on the conference table to the floor and Aidyn laid Seth across the wooden surface. With the silver gone, Katie was already beginning to regain her strength.

"His heart stopped," she yelled. Had felt its last beat back at the cemetery. She approached and ran her knuckles across his still warm cheek. A tear slid down her own.

"Don't worry, I've got him," Marcus spoke across from her. She lifted her head to meet his gaze and he smiled at her. "He's gonna be hungry though so be prepared."

She watched as Marcus closed his eyes and laid his palms on Seth's chest. Golden light encased her mate and became a bright pinpoint near his heart and suddenly she felt the stir of the first beat. His lids snapped open and Marcus took two steps back.

"Son of a bitch that hurt," Seth whispered.

"Take him to your home and feed him. He'll be back to his normal pain-in-the-ass self in no time," Marcus said.

Katie let out a sigh of relief. "Thank you." She touched Seth to flash them away, then stopped. "What about Lowan? Did you kill him?"

Aidyn shook his head. "He vanished. He's stronger than we thought. I'm afraid this nightmare has only begun."

She gave a nod then vanished with Seth and went straight to her bed. Without hesitation she bit her wrist and pressed it to his mouth. He latched on and drank for several minutes. His color returned to normal and he finally released her.

"Your blood is super charged." He sat up and propped several pillows behind his back.

"I'm not sure if I should kiss you or smack you upside the head for scaring the hell out of me." She was going to kiss him.

He raised a brow. "It seems to me I had to come to your rescue."

"Oh, shut up." She leaned forward and brushed her lips across his, but when she would have pulled back he grabbed her by the arms and crushed her to him.

His tongue speared her mouth and tasted every inch of her and she couldn't help but melt into him. When he finally released her, he studied her for a moment. His eyes searched for something.

"Baby, I may have fought this relationship in the beginning, but I'm so glad you didn't give up on me. I can't imagine my life without your sassy mouth."

She grinned. "My mouth can be sassy in more ways than one."

It was his turn to smile. "I know."

She tipped her head. "Would you mind if we stayed here? At least until my father awakens?" She felt grounded in this palace and also hoped being in her father's home might bring him back faster. She had so many questions to ask him.

"We will live wherever you're happy. Besides, I feel more comfortable having you here. I know it's safe." He kissed the tip of her nose.

"Yeah, about that. I'm sorry. I didn't mean to scare you. I only wanted to..." He pressed his finger to her lips.

"See your father, I know. There is no way either of us could know that silver would have that effect on you." He kissed her. "But promise me you'll be careful and try to stay here until Lowan is dead. Now that he knows about you he'll come after you again."

She folded her bottom lip through her teeth. "I feel guilty for having two fathers so I needed to visit Poppa."

"Don't fret. The man who raised you loved you like his own. I could see it at the hospital and the one who's DNA you carry...well, I've no doubt he'd love you just as much if given the chance. They would both be proud to call you daughter."

"Thank you for understanding." She sighed. "You know though I can't simply sit here. Besides, it had to have been a fluke that Lowan found me." She swirled invisible circles on his chest with her fingertip.

"No fluke. I don't doubt being a demigod he was able to sense you."

"Shit. I hadn't thought about that." She'd die of boredom if she had to sit here and do nothing. It wasn't her style.

He pulled a lock of her hair through his fingers. "There will be other things you can do to help. First, you can start with taking those clothes off."

"Well, now you might be pushing things. After all, you did just die." Saying the word made her cringe as she realized how close she had come to losing him. "I love you. It seems crazy to feel like this in such a short time, but I do."

"I love you too, baby. Now, I'm in charge in the bedroom. Remember?"

Her heart rate increased. "Yes."

"And since it appears that's where we are. Strip."

She jumped up and shed her clothes in record time, and with a flick of her finger and a little magic she had him naked as well. "I like having powers."

He flashed a grin that revealed extended fangs as he leaned forward, wrapped his arms around her waist and flipped her to her back. In a flash, he was between her parted thighs and buried deep inside her.

"I couldn't wait. I need to feel all of you," he growled.

"You're not going to hear me complain." She gasped as he moved inside her.

"Good." He scraped his fangs along her neck right before he pierced her skin. Their connection deepened and their souls touched. Had someone told Katie a few months ago she'd become a goddess and the mate of a vampire she would have had them hauled off in a straight-jacket. However, today she couldn't be happier that the gods had deemed a crazy vampire and a sassy redhead should fall in love. The future of the world may be uncertain, but together they could conquer anything.

CHAPTER THIRTY-ONE

AIDYN STOOD outside the compound and watched the sun rise. The wounds on his chest and back still stung, but he breathed through the pain. There were worse things yet to come in life, one of which was saving humanity. He knew it would be difficult for people to accept what they were let alone their assistance and right now he and his brethren weren't much help.

He sensed a presence behind him. Inhaled the scent of jasmine and closed his eyes.

"You didn't waste any time coming here."

"Did you really expect I would?" The voice behind him held way too much anger.

"No, not really. I fully expected your arrival."

"Is that why you're out here? Were you waiting for me?"

He smiled. "Yes and no. I enjoy the sunrise." The air stirred behind him and the presence moved closer.

"What happened to your back?"

He still refused to turn around. Wasn't ready yet to look upon her face. "I disobeyed the gods."

"You?" The voice softened. "The almighty king of the guardians disobeyed? Has the world come to an end already that you—" The voice grew shaky. "Would dare?"

He turned and watched her blue eyes widen as she stared at the same nasty wounds on his chest. Wounds that would scar him for life, because when a god sought retribution they made sure to leave evidence. "What's the matter? Does the sight of my scars disgust you?"

She quickly regained her composure and smiled, her eyes glowing with amusement. "No. On the contrary, I find them pleasing and the thought of what they must have done to you brings me great joy."

He stepped closer, fisted his hands to keep from touching her. He swore an oath that he would never claim her. She hated him. Instead he dropped to his knees in front of her.

"I bear these wounds for you."

She took a step back, astonishment crossed her face then she schooled her features. "Did you think by doing so I would spare your life?"

"No. I fully expect you to take it, just not today."

She produced her sword. Her lips pursed in anger, the emotion radiated across his skin. "You think to test me?" The tears that stung her eyes did not go unnoticed by him. He ached to kiss them away.

"You say you disobeyed the gods, yet when I begged you to spare my father you had no qualms in killing him." Her lower lip trembled. "I am no longer the young girl I was that day."

"No, you're not. You have grown into a beautiful woman." The morning sun danced off her raven hair and he had to dig deeper for his resolve.

"Your compliments will not spare you."

"Then do it. I grow impatient. I'm kneeling before you, Leria. If you have the strength to kill your mate today then here I am."

Her mouth dropped open.

"What? Surely, you've sensed it by now. I knew the day you knelt before me and begged for your father's life." Actually, he knew the day she was born, but saw no point in telling her now.

She swallowed. "Do you think that will sway me?"

"No, I do not. I fully expect you to carry out the deed. What are you waiting for?" He stretched his neck, pushed back his shoulders and cupped his hands behind his back. His gaze never left hers. He wanted to see her beauty up until his last breath. "Do you grant a dying man his last wish?"

"Why should I? You didn't even let me see him before you took his life." She looked toward the sun that was mid-way in the sky then back at him. "What would be your last wish? If you were to receive one, that is."

"To kiss you."

She licked her lips, her pulse increased along with her breathing. She stepped back. "I can't grant you that, but I will give you this day only because humanity needs you. Just be aware, I will kill you one day." In a swirl of magic, she shifted and flew off.

"I'm counting on it."

ABOUT THE AUTHOR

Award winning and bestselling author Valerie Twombly grew up watching Dark Shadows over her mother's shoulder, and from there her love of the fanged creatures blossomed. Today, Valerie has decided to take her darker, sensual side and put it to paper. When she is not busy creating a world full of steamy, hot men and strong, seductive women, she juggles her time between a full-time job, hubby and her German shepherd dog, in Northern IL. Valerie is a member of Romance Writers of America and Fantasy, Futuristic and Paranormal Romance Writers.

Sign up for Valerie's newsletter and be the first to hear about new releases, receive special excerpts and exclusive contests. http://valerietwombly.com/newsletter-sign/

Follow Valerie
www.valerietwombly.com

Taken By Storm Book 2

Jinn's Seductions Series

Spanish Nights

Sultry Nights

Beyond The Mist Series

Passion Awakened (Beyond The Mist)

9 781732 630697